Love + Prayers

10-2-14

BOOK TWO IN THE GLIMMER SERIES

# GLIMMER'S NEW BEGINNINGS

## THE TRAINING YEARS

YOVETTE B. BROOKS

WestBow Press books may be ordered through booksellers or by contacting:

WestBow Press
A Division of Thomas Nelson & Zondervan
1663 Liberty Drive
Bloomington, IN 47403
www.westbowpress.com
1 (866) 928-1240



ISBN: 978-1-4908-4877-8 (sc)
ISBN: 978-1-4908-4876-1 (hc)
ISBN: 978-1-4908-4878-5 (e)

Library of Congress Control Number: 2014914940

Printed in the United States of America.

WestBow Press rev. date: 9/2/2014

# CONTENTS

"Lindsey, wake up." Matthias was shaking Lindsey. She opened her eyes only to close them again it became so bright. A man appeared like lightning at the end of their bed, his clothes were white like freshly fallen snow.

"Don't be afraid, for you are blessed above all mankind."

The Messenger was the most beautiful man Lindsey had ever seen, with his long flowing blond hair and his eyes of turquoise.

"Your twins turn five today, and today their training must start for they have been chosen for a great task."

"Training for what, what kind of task?" Matthias asked before Lindsey could.

"All will be answered in time." He looked directly at Matthias, "They must know it by heart from cover to cover."

Lindsey wondered what they needed to know from cover to cover? She looked at Matthias sitting there beside her on the bed.

"How much time do I have to accomplish this?" Matthias asked.

"Nine years," He turned and looked at Lindsey. "You shall bear another son; you shall name him David for he will be great among all men. In nine years time your twins will discover many things about themselves as you once did."

Lindsey's heart almost stopped. Could he talking about…

"The power they receive will be far greater than either of you ever had."

## CHAPTER 1

# A NEW BEGINNING

9 years later...

"I had another dream last night, Mom. So what does a red aura mean?"

Mom looked up from her book. "Are you sure it was red?" she asked as she closed it.

"Yeah, is it a sign of evil or something?"

Mom had managed to get up and wobble her way across the living room and to the bar where I sat eating breakfast. Being eight months pregnant she was now wobbling instead of walking, and her aura... well, I guess being pregnant, and happy made her brighter than most. Her pink aura with a spot of blue where David was, was now so bright, I almost needed sunglasses to look at her.

"Do you think it's about time we told them, Matthias?" Mom was now talking to Dad, who had came out of the kitchen to help Mom sit down on the edge of a bar stool to my left. I was still amazed at how Dad's blue aura and Mom's pink one turned purple when they stood close together.

Kyle, my twin brother, was sitting on my right; he smiled and looked at me.

"*What do you think they have to tell us?*" He casually asked in my head so Mom and Dad couldn't hear him.

"Can you hear him?" Dad asked me.

I turned to look at Dad, startled. Could Dad hear Kyle? "What?" I asked.

"Do you hear your brother's thoughts and does he hears yours? Do you have to be touching?"

How did Dad know? "Yes and No." I answered slowly. I wasn't sure if that was the right answer.

Dad smiled. "I thought so; I could see it in his eyes, then in yours."

Kyle looked as surprised as I did.

Mom was starring at Dad. "It looks like you were right, there is more going on than we know."

"Yes, it's time Lindsey," Dad told her.

Time for what, I wondered.

Dad helped Mom back down from the bar stool. "We better find you a comfy spot. This may take a while."

Mom smiled. "The couch will do."

Take a while? What was going on? Kyle and I got up and followed Mom and Dad back to the living room and piled on the couch with Mom. Dad stood in front of us. He paced back and forth for a minute.

"Where to begin?" he finally said.

"Just start in the forest." Mom told him.

Dad took a deep breath. "Alright then, from the beginning. Well, I guess I should start with Daniel and me camping in the woods after a failed hunting trip."

"You and Uncle Daniel used to hunt?" Kyle asked, all excited. Dad gave Kyle *the look* and Kyle shut up.

"Back then, you hunted or you didn't eat." He pulled the ottoman over and sat in front of us. "As I was saying, we had been out on a hunting trip and were returning to the village." Dad put his hand up to stop Kyle's question before he could ask. "Yes, I meant to say village. Back in those days, we lived in villages. There were very few towns, and they wanted nothing to do with Indians, well except for a few missionaries like my Dad. He was a preacher from what's now Tennessee who had come out West to help educate the so called savages in the area. Anyway to continue, Daniel and I were just a few days travel from the village and were camped by a stream." Dad closed his eyes; I guess he was probably playing it over in his mind so he could remember it correctly. He laid his hand on Mom's leg. I glanced at Mom she too had her eyes closed. She reached over and placed a hand on both mine and Kyle's arm as Dad continued with his story. "I remember Daniel and I talking about it being so strange not to have seen any deer…"

My mind started to swirl in Dad's words. I closed my eyes when the room started to spin and grabbed Moms arm to steady myself. The black of my mind suddenly was taken over by a bright shining light. The light took on shapes and colors until it finally came into focus. I found myself looking at two men crouched at a fire. Their blue auras were so vibrant. It was Dad and Uncle Daniel. I could see what Dad was telling me! I could see and hear it all: the woods, and the water running over the rocks in the stream nearby. I could smell the smoke from the fire. How could I see it? What was happening? It was like I had been pulled into his very thoughts. I looked at Dad and Uncle Daniel. They barely had anything on. Whoa, what were they wearing? It looked like…like… it was breechcloths, oh, my, gosh. They looked like the Indians we had seen in old pictures on the reservations out west.

"What do you think has happened?" Dad was saying to Uncle Daniel.

"It is strange; I have never been out and not come across even one set of tracks." Uncle Daniel replied.

Dad suddenly came to his feet. "What is that?"

Uncle Daniel stood too. I strained to listen for what had he heard. A faint noise was now coming from the woods. It got louder and louder and sort of sounded like someone crying out from being scared, but it was continual. The cry got louder, and as the sound got closer, it didn't sound just like one person's cry, but thousands of people crying out. It was a frightening sound, and it was coming from the woods straight in front of us. As I searched the woods with my eyes in this dream-like world/vision, a small red glow became visible. The glow got brighter and larger as the sound got louder. Then, a large, hooded figure stepped out and onto the bank of the stream. It sort of looked like a man, yet it looked very different at the same time. Fear gripped me as the creature grabbed for Dad and then Uncle Daniel. I wasn't sure what it was doing to them. Maybe it was eating them or drinking their blood, I really couldn't tell. The only thing I could really see was that they were turning green…no brown. They were dying at the hands of this red glowing monster. The creature suddenly looked towards the woods where it had came from. It dropped Dad and Uncle Daniel, and then fled into the woods just as a very bright silvery white light appeared. It lit up the night like it was mid-day. It was so bright you couldn't look directly at it. I squinted, but all that I could make out was a hand outstretched towards Dad and Uncle Daniel. The two of them rose into the air as if by magic. They hung about ten feet off the ground. The brown aura of death that held them had started to change into a red glow like the creatures that had attacked them. A voice like a raging storm came from the light. "CHOOSE", it said. Dad hung there only a few seconds before he turned a silvery white, similar, but not as bright as, the light of the thing that was holding him. Uncle Daniel's aura did the same, changing from brown to red then to silver. They both were slowly lowered to the ground, but they did not stand; they both fell to their knees, then down on their faces, as if worshiping the light. "GO" came another thunderous command. They both disappeared and the vision faded. I opened my eyes. Dad still had his eyes closed. He took a deep breath and opened them. I looked at Mom and she smiled at me.

"You ok, Kara?" she asked me.

I wasn't really sure. I looked at Dad and his bright blue aura, confused.

"How old are you?" Kyle asked Dad before I could answer Mom's question.

"One hundred and eighty six." I looked at Dad, and was still confused. Could this be real, or was I dreaming.

"It's alright, Kara." Mom patted my arm. "I was a little freaked out the first time your Dad showed me that, too." I looked at Mom then back to Dad. Again I noticed his aura; it was blue like always, not silver like in the dream or vision or whatever it was. So why…what…how?

"*Ask him.*" Kyle interrupted my thoughts.

"If that was real, then why are you no longer sliver?" I asked him.

Dad smiled at me. "Simple" he said, "I am not an Angelic anymore." He looked towards Mom.

"Angelic! That silver light was an angel?" Kyle blurted out, "How cool!"

"Yes, and the red one" Mom looked at me, "was a demon."

My mind swirled. Angels…demons…what was going on? I grabbed the arm of the couch; I felt like I was going to pass out.

"Where did you go when you vanished?" Kyle was now up on his knees on the other side of Mom.

"We were sent to Africa. We had become healers. Well, I was the healer and Daniel was like my guide."

"Healer, what do you mean by healer?" Kyle asked

"I think the word healer tells you what it is, Kyle." Dad looked at him.

"You know what I mean Dad, what did you heal people from?" Kyle probed.

"Well let's see, I have healed blindness, leprosy, lameness, and just sickness in general; everything from hearing loss to cancer. You name it and I have probably healed someone from it."

I listened as Dad talked, but I was still stuck on the fact that he wasn't silver anymore, why he wasn't an angel anymore? "Dad, why are you not …" I couldn't believe I was going to even say it, "an angel anymore?" I looked at him.

"That's where I come in," Mom said, "I am the reason." She smiled at Dad and he smiled back at her. They were looking at each other with that lovie dovie look. Aw yuck, that look always grossed me out.

"She had cancer, and I was sent to heal her," Dad told us.

"Or so we thought." Mom grinned. Mom laid her hand on Dad's arm and Dad placed his hand on both Kyle and me. Great, the room started spinning; here we go again…

When light came into focus again, I could see a large room that was a lab of some kind. Granddad and Mom were sitting on a couch talking to Dr. Jenkins. I hadn't seen him in at least a year, but I was sure it was him. He and his wife Mary usually come in the restaurant once a year for a cancer convention held in town.

"Well, to be honest," he was saying, "I am not so sure myself. Let me clarify a little: since it is in your nodes, we can't do anything to it, but since it's not attacking your organs, we really don't need to. And we really don't need to worry about anything until it does. And then at that point, we will have to just see what it does. I'm really sort of baffled as to why it's not attacking. It is...well... it's like its hibernating or something." He went on about not doing anything and to just live life, but you could tell Mom was still quite confused about the whole thing.

So, Mom had been diagnosed with cancer, but for some reason, the cancer wasn't killing her. The next thing she showed us was her in some kind of office; it looked like it was at school. She was looking at Dad. I gathered by her wild expression, that it was the first time she had seen a silver aura, and I knew how she felt. The next thing I saw was them being stuck on some book report together. It was sort of strange seeing them in high school, but you could see the attraction between them every time they got close. It was really sort of sickening watching them flirt and then kissing in a meadow. Yuck. I guess the only cool part was learning that Mom had the power to lift them off the ground.

The last part of the vision was the most interesting. It was the camping trip after Mom and Dad graduated. They were laying in the meadow as Granddad went to clean up in the nearby stream. Mom sat up when she heard the sound, I would recognize it anywhere. It's a sound you don't forget easily. She immediately sent Dad to check on Granddad just seconds before the demon attacked. Uncle Daniel came out of nowhere and got between them. Dad reappeared and jumped in to help Uncle Daniel, but neither one was a match for the demon. But Mom, wow, she was great. She used her new found power to snatch them out of the demon's clutches and hold them at the other end of the meadow, away from the demon so he couldn't hurt them again. The demon grabbed Mom, and when he did, she began to shake violently. A large black cloud emerged from her body and engulfed the demon.

Then Mom fell to the ground and didn't move. Her aura was orange, so I knew she wasn't far from death. The demon tried to escape, but couldn't. The whole meadow then lit up and the angel appeared. Dad and Uncle Daniel were now at Mom's side. Dad stretched out over Mom, hovering just above her. Her color was fading fast; she was dying. Uncle Daniel now had his hands on both of them. I was sure they were trying to heal her, but it wasn't working.

"CHOOSE" came from angel in what sounded like a clap of thunder. Almost instantly, Mom changed to bright pink. Dad and Uncle Daniel turned blue. The demon vanished, along with the cloud that held the demon, and then the scene faded away. I opened my eyes. Mom's eyes were already open, and she was smiling at Dad. I could see a tear shimmering on her cheek.

"Wow!" Kyle said. "That was too cool." Dad laughed. "So how old are you, Mom?" Kyle asked.

I couldn't believe it. Out of all they just showed us, Kyle was thinking about ages, not the fact that Dad had been an angel and Mom had…well Mom had this amazing power. I looked at Dad then Mom as though they were suddenly strangers. Who were these people?

"Not as old as your Dad." she smiled. "The three of us lost all of our power that day, except for my ability to see auras."

"That is until you guys turned 13, last year." Dad smiled.

"That's right, it was on their birthday." Mom patted Dad on the arm. "You were restless in your sleep and I reached over to soothe you and was drug right into your dreams."

Dad took Mom by the hand. "We both knew things were getting ready to change."

"So, do you have all your power back? Can you heal again?" Kyle was so easily excited.

I looked at Mom and Dad. Their color was the same as always, purple, since they were close to each other.

"No," Dad said, "the only thing I seem to be able to do ..." he touched Kyle and my arm "*is this.*" He finished the sentence in our heads.

"What about you guys?" Mom interrupted "What else can you guys do?"

"Nothing like you guys can. I just see Kara's dreams, or dream with her, or something like that."

Dad smiled "Do you talk to her in the dreams, or are you just a bystander and watch?"

"I just watch." Kyle answered him.

What did all this mean; my head was starting to spin again. I knew being twins that we had a strong connection to each other, but now that I thought about it, it had been just over a year ago that all the other things started happening; the dream sharing and the thought sharing. Why could we do this? How could we do this? The man in red came into my thoughts. Was I now dreaming about a demon? Was it because of Dad and the fact the he was an angel once? Could it be because of Mom killing one and now they are after me? I suddenly noticed it was silent. I looked up to find Kyle looking at me. Dad was holding onto Kyle and Mom.

"I wish I knew the answer to those questions," Dad answered my thought, "but I don't."

We all sit there in silence just looking at each other for a few minutes. I figured it was about time to wake up because it had to all be a dream.

"I have to pee." Mom said, braeking the silence. Dad pulled her up off the couch and she waddled off to the bathroom. Dad went back to the kitchen and I got up and went to my room.

I flopped down on the bed. *Lean not on your own understanding* kept coming into my head. Why this verse? I wanted to understand! I wanted to do more than understand; I wanted to know why! This was insane. It had to be a dream, it just had to be. Wake up Kara! I told myself over and over.

"*You're not dreaming!*" Came from inside my head. "*This is most definitely not a dream.*" It was Kyle, who was still in the living room.

"*How do you know?*" I asked him

"*Because we don't talk during your dreams.*" He was right. I never saw him or talked to him in any of my dreams. But if it wasn't a dream, then what was going on? *Lean not on your own understanding.* There it was again.

"*Kyle*"

"*It's not me,*" he answered, "*but I hear it too.*"

It suddenly hit me. Dad had made us learn it word for word. It wasn't just another book; it was for real!

## CHAPTER 2

# ORDINARY LIFE

I stood looking in the mirror. I was sure glad summer was coming so I could wear shorts; my jeans were getting too short again. I was already 5'10". How much taller was I going to get? Dad was 6'3". I sure hoped I didn't get as tall as him, but I was glad to be taller than Mom. She was about 5'4. I ran my fingers through my new hair cut. It was shorter than it had been in years and barely touched my neck. It was layered and curved in nicely at the bottom. It parted on the side and my bangs were almost as long as the rest but they hung gently to the side. I pulled the little picture out of my pocket that I had taken with me to show Jill, my hairdresser, what I wanted my hair to look like. It was really silly that I wanted my hair to look like my avatar on my favorite online game. Although my avatar had dark brown hair and mine was jet black, like Dads, I still liked the style. Jill had laughed when I showed her the picture. I looked back in the mirror and liked the way I looked. One good thing about Dad being an Indian was our skin color, I always looked like I had a tan, even in the winter. I didn't even have to spend hours in the tanning bed like my friends did. I wasn't near as dark as Dad or Kyle, but I liked my natural tan. It showed great when I wore white, as I did on this day. My white T-shirt looked great.

"Oh stop it, I can't take it anymore." Kyle came into my room and pushed me away from the mirror. Kyle ran his hands through his wild, sandy brown mess he liked to call a hair style. "How do you like my hair?"

"You never even brush it."

Kyle smiled. "That is the whole beauty of it. You just get up and go."

I walked back and stood beside him.

"And look at my tan, never going away." he teased.

"Alright." I shoved him. He got back up and stood on his tip-toes to look me in the eyes. "How's the weather down there?" We both busted out in laughter. I was a good four inches taller than Kyle. The only thing that we did have alike was our green eyes.

"So," Kyle said as he walked over and flopped on my bed, "I still say March the 30th!" We had a bet going on as to when our little brother, David, was going to be born.

"Nope, going to be May the 2nd." It was the third week in March and Mom didn't seem to be showing any signs of getting ready to deliver. She was still doing alot her normal stuff, the paper work for the restaurant, and she was even still going to her yoga class every Thursday night. I was always amazed at how flexible she was for nine months pregnant. Flexibility, she had, but stability, not so much. She didn't do any of the standing poses anymore. Well, I guess she had given up some stuff. She had also stopped teaching a fitness class when she was six months pregnant, but she still walked every day.

"I bet he has Dad's eyes and is as white as Mom." Kyle laughed. It did make sense: we were both dark like Dad and had Mom's eyes.

"He is going to look funny with ebony eyes and really light skin." Kyle laughed again.

"He is going to be adorable." I told him. My cell phone buzzed and vibrated across my night stand. Dad's picture was on the front. "Dad" I told Kyle, and then answered the phone. "Hey Dad, what's up?"

"Can you work from five to nine tonight? Heather called in sick."

I took a deep breath. "Sure, Dad no problem."

"Thanks, babe, I knew I could count on you. Got to go. Love you, Sweetie."

I closed my phone and sat it back down.

"Somebody's got to work." Kyle smarted off.

I smiled. "Yeah, well, someone is going to see their Uncle this summer in England and someone else will be stuck here working in her spot because they don't have enough money to go themselves." Kyle's little smirk dropped fast.

"Anyone for lunch?" Mom yelled from the kitchen.

Kyle sprinted out the door. Most the time you couldn't get him to budge, but mention food and he was the first one to move.

I loved living above the restaurant and I loved that we had a dumbwaiter even more. Just call down to the kitchen and Dad would send up whatever we wanted. Ah, the perks of your Dad being a chef.

Kyle had his sandwich half eaten by the time I walked into the kitchen. Mom with her rosy pink glow was trying to sit on one of the bar stools, but was having difficulty with her belly throwing her off balance.

"You think I would just learn not to even try to sit here." She finally gave up and went to the couch.

"How you feeling, Mom?" I asked her as I grabbed my plate and sat down in the chair beside her.

"Like a balloon about to pop." Kyle looked up and smiled. "But I have felt like that for months." she continued. "Hopefully I don't have much longer." Mom rubbed her belly. "Ok, I'll eat. Little guy thinks he's starving." She looked up at Kyle. "Guess he's going to be like his brother when it comes to food." Mom and I both laughed. Kyle just smiled as he shoved the last bite of sandwich in his mouth.

"Dad called earlier and I have to work tonight five till close."

"Someone sick?" Mom asked.

"Heather." I told her.

"That poor girl, she's always sick." Mom said.

"Mom, she is not always sick you know. She just wants to go out with her friends so she calls in."

Mom smiled. "Yeah, I know, but I try to give her the benefit of the doubt."

"Hey Mom, do you care if I go to the mall with Rhett this afternoon?" Kyle asked.

"I need to go myself, so I can give you guys a ride there, but you have to find your own way home. Will that be okay?"

"That would be great." Kyle pulled out his cell phone as he walked down the hall towards his room. I liked Kyle's friend Rhett. He had great hair; it was always styled and neat. I wished he would teach Kyle some neatness.

"Not a chance." Kyle yelled from the other room. Mom looked up at me.

"Just wishing some of Rhett's neatness would rub off on Kyle."

Mom laughed. "Amen to that."

Kyle and Rhett were making plans on the phone, but of course I heard everything.

*"Hey Rhett, Mom said she needed to go to the mall so she would give us a ride." Kyle told him.*

*"I'm still not sure if Kelly is going, April said she wasn't feeling well this morning, but I'll see if she will call her again and see."* April was Rhett's sister and Kelly was April's best friend and the girl Kyle liked. I'm not real sure why though. She was pretty but had nothing going on upstairs.

*"Man, I hope she is not bad sick."*

"Kara, Kara!" Mom was shaking my leg.

"What?"

"Stop eavesdropping on your brother."

"But Mom, he has been in my head all morning. This is just payback."

Mom laughed.

"So, what are they planning?"

"Well, Kyle only wanted to go to the mall because Kelly was going with April. But it seems that Kelly is not feeling well and may not go."

Kyle came bouncing back into the living room. "She is too going; April sent me a text while Rhett and I were talking."

"What do you see in Kelly?" I asked him.

"Are you blind? She is gorgeous?"

"Looks aren't everything." Mom threw in her parental two cents.

Kyle looked at Mom. "When you're a teenager, looks are everything."

I had to laugh. "If looks are everything, then why would she want to be seen with you?"

Mom laughed. "She has you there."

Kyle took a deep breath. "You just don't understand. I am totally cool," he said as he ran his hand through the mess of hair on his head.

"If you say so."

Kyle turned to look back at Mom "Can we go about two o'clock? Rhett has to clean up his room before he can go."

"Maybe you should do that, too." Mom smiled at him.

"But I know where everything is now, and if I moved it …"

"Yeah, yeah, Lord forbid you get organized."

Kyle smiled.

"I at least want all the dirty clothes put in the laundry room. Okay?"

"No problem, Mom. I'll go do it now." He darted down the hall.

"If he ever moves out, I think I will just gut the room and start from scratch. There is no way I could ever get it clean." Mom shook her head.

Five o'clock came way too soon, and being a Saturday, I knew it was going to be a long and busy night. My first table of the night was a nightmare. The lady was not happy; no matter what I got her, she always wanted something else. I should have known she was going to be difficult by her orange glow. On my third trip to the kitchen to change her order, Dad intervened.

"Kyle called," Dad said as he took the order ticket from my hand, "said you were on the brink of a meltdown."

I smiled. Thank the Lord I was a twin with special abilities.

"I'll handle this." He smiled.

"Thanks Dad" I gave him a quick kiss on his check.

"Thank your brother," he told me.

It took just a second to do that. I could find Kyle no matter where he was or how far away he was from me. I just had to think about him and it was like tuning in a radio station; he would become loud and clear in my head. *How in the world does she live on so little food?* he was thinking and must have been watching someone eat. He was in a great mood; I could feel it, so I knew it had to be Kelly he was watching.

"*Thanks bro."* I interrupted his thoughts.

*"No problem, what are brothers for."*

I just had to smile. *"Do you really want me to answer that?"*

*"Ah, go back to work."*

I laughed and went back to waiting tables.

Most of my tables were great. Blues and pinks everywhere, a few purples mixed in. I still thought it was quite strange how "meant for each other" made a purple aura. Why wasn't it red for love? But as I had recently found out, red was about the furtherest thing from love as it could be; it was pure evil. Demons wore a red aura. Demons! It gave me chills just to think that one day I could actually run into a demon. Just thinking about it made me glance around the room at all the aura colors. Whew, no reds.

"Mr. Jenkins, so nice to see you." Doc Jenkins was sitting at one of my tables. Come to think about it, it was about time for the cancer convention. He booked our third floor convention room for meals every year. He was quite blue but looked worried.

He looked up at me. "Would you do me a favor and check on Mary? She went to the Ladies' room."

"Sure, no problem. Is something wrong?" I asked.

"She got to feeling bad when we came in."

"I'll go right now." I turned and headed back to the restrooms. "Mrs. Jenkins?" I said as I entered the Ladies' room. I could hear her throwing up on one of the stalls. I stood outside her door until she came out.

"Kara." She smiled.

"Are you alright?" I asked her. To my surprise, she was bright pink. I figured on an orange glow since she was sick. But one good look at her told me the reason for her sickness.

"I don't know what's wrong with me. I was just fine till we walked in and then the smell of all the food made me so sick," she said. I had to smile. Her and Dr. Jenkins would be great parents.

"Why don't you and the Doc go up to the house? Then you won't have to smell all the other food. Just have Mom call down what you want."

"Oh we couldn't impose on your mom like that," she told me.

"No imposition, Mom would be thrilled to see you. Come on." I took her by the arm and led her back out into the hall. "Go up the back elevator." I pointed down the hall to the elevators at the end. "26453 is the code for the elevator. I'll go get the Doc for you."

She smiled. "Thanks Kara."

I pulled my cell phone from my pocket and texted a quick note to Mom warning her of her impending company. I also added that Mary was pregnant and evidently they didn't know it yet. It was great to share Mom's ability to see people's auras, but why she couldn't tell pregnancies and I could was one more thing I didn't really understand.

I picked up a pitcher of water and refilled glasses as I passed by tables on my way back to Doc. Jenkins. He was sitting there still looking quite worried.

"She's fine. I sent her up to see Mom." Relief seem to wash over him. "Go on up and join her. I'll send whatever you want up."

"Thanks so much Kara." He got up and headed for the main entrance.

"Doc," I stopped him, "use the elevator by the restrooms. It's quicker than going back out."

"26453 is the combination."

"Thanks again." He smiled.

"Miss, I am ready to place my order." The man at my table behind me said, quite stern and agitated.

"I'm sorry you had to wait, sir. There was a lady not feeling well that I had to see about. Please let me take ten percent off your bill tonight since you had to wait." The man's aggravation seemed to melt away.

"I hope nothing serious."

"No, sir. She's expecting."

"That's wonderful. Now I will have the…"

I had to take ten percent off three other tables' bills, but they all left happy, or at least the tip they left said they were. Dad found me on one of my five minute breaks to ask about the ten percent discount I had given the four tables. He wasn't mad, but just wanted to know the reason. He was always good like that. He never seemed to get mad over anything. Aggravated yes, but not mad. Now knowing all he had seen and been through over the years, I guess I sort of understood why. Man, my life was complicated in a simple kind of way.

By nine I was beat. I was never more glad to see my last tables empty out. I was even happier not to be on the cleanup crew that night. It had been an exceptionally busy night. I guess being the only authentic Indian restaurant had its advantages. Well, I didn't know if authentic could be used since Dad took the recipes and added his own bit of flare to them.

Rabbit, deer, bison and quail were the big ticket items here at The Village. But it seemed people liked the alternatives to regular beef and chicken. Yep, our Village was doing well. I smiled as I trudged up the stairs. Mom always fussed if we took the elevator; sometimes living on the fifth floor really sucked.

"*Come on, you can make it.*" Kyle was suddenly in my head urging me on. "*Rhett is here.*"

Great, I had just worked a full shift and felt like crap; probably looked like it too.

"*He won't care.*"

I was dead on my feet when I hit the fifth floor door. I took a deep breath and went into the hallway. Rhett opened the door to the house before I got my hand on the handle.

"Have a rough one?"

I smiled. He was so cute with his dark brown eyes and brown hair.

"I've had worse shifts, but man, this one seemed to just go on and on." I walk into the living room to find Doc Jenkins and Mary still visiting with Mom.

"There she is, the savior of our dinner." Doc Jenkins announced.

I smiled and laughed as I walked pass them towards my bedroom with Rhett right behind me.

"So what did you and Kyle do at the mall today?" I asked him.

"April and Kelly were there so 'me and Kyle' really didn't do anything"

"Like you didn't know that would happen."

"I thought you were coming."

I turned and smiled at him. "Sorry he didn't tell you that I had to work."

"That's okay. Next time I'll ask." He smiled back at me.

"Did you ask her?" Kyle came out of his room.

"Ask me what?"

Rhett gave Kyle a look. "I was just getting to it."

"Okay," Kyle said and went back in his room.

I stopped at my bedroom door and turned to face Rhett.

"Uh… well, do you want to go to the movies tomorrow afternoon? Kyle and Kelly are going, and your Mom said it was fine."

I smiled at Rhett. How could I ever say no to him? "Sounds great." I looked him squarely in the eyes. Hmm, they had a little green in them. I had never noticed that before. Man, I could get lost in those eyes.

"*What if I just kissed her right here,*" came into my head.

"*Is Kelly here?*" I asked Kyle in response to his question.

"*No,*" he answered.

"*Then who do you want to kiss?*"

Rhett was standing there smiling. "Mom will take us; we will pick you guys up at two. The movie starts at 2:45."

*"Kiss? What are you talking about?"*

"So what are we going to see," I asked Rhett as I talked with Kyle in my head.

"*Didn't you just say what if I kissed her right here?*"

"That new movie with Sandra Bullock. I can't think of the title. Hey, Kyle, what is the name of that movie again?"

"*No, I didn't say anything about kissing anybody.*"

"I don't know; Kelly picked it." Kyle stepped back out in the hall.

"*Then who did? I…*" I looked at Rhett.

Kyle laughed.

"What?" Rhett turned to look at Kyle?

"Oh, nothing."

Did I actually hear Rhett's thoughts? I had never heard anyone else's. I smiled; I could hear other people thoughts. This was great! Then it hit me: oh crap, Rhett wants to kiss me.

Kyle was now laughing hysterically.

"Okay, what is so funny?" Rhett asked as he looked at me, then Kyle, then me again.

"You okay?" Rhett asked me. "Your face is red."

"Yeah, I'm fine. I'll see you tomorrow, Rhett. I'm really beat. I think I need to take a long, hot shower and call it a night." I turned and went into my room and shut the door. I stood there with my back to the door.

"What was that all about?" Rhett asked Kyle as they went into Kyle's room.

"Why didn't you tell me you liked Kara that much?" Kyle asked Rhett.

"What?" Rhett asked.

"*What are you doing Kyle? He dosen't know I heard him."*

*"Don't worry."*

"I saw the way you were looking at her." Kyle told him.

"Okay, so I like her a little. What's the big deal?"

"A little! It looked like scene from one of those old movies where the guy grabs the girl and kisses her"

"*Kyle!"*

*"Oh, shut up, and listen Kara."*

"You're crazy." Rhett told him.

"I know what I saw, man. And I am not the one crazy, you are. You should have told me you had a thing for Kara."

"I didn't know if you would be okay with me liking your sister," Rhett finally answered.

Kyle laughed. "Why would you say that? I think it's great! I know you."

*"Now tune out, so we can talk about you in private."*

*"What? Are you crazy? I want to know what he thinks. I can't hear him anymore."*

I really couldn't. I was thinking of Rhett, but nothing was coming in.

"Do you think she likes me?" I heard Rhett ask.

"Well..." I heard Kyle say

*"You better not."*

*"Then get out of my head and let us have some privacy."*

*"Alright, alright I'm gone."*

I didn't want to, but I had to, or no telling what Kyle might tell him. I grabbed my pajamas and IPod and headed to the bathroom. I really did like him. This was going to be harder that I thought. I had to get my mind occupied to keep from focusing on Kyle and Rhett. I hit shuffle and got in the shower. When I climbed in bed later, I left my ear buds in to keep my mind occupied.

## CHAPTER 3

# THE STRANGEST DAY

Where was I? I looked around for something familiar. It was dark and the street lights weren't very bright. There was a large lake or river not far from me, but I was in a vacant lot of some kind. I could hear all the city sounds and see the shapes of buildings and other street lights all around me, but the place wasn't familiar to me. I heard a garage door lift. Over to my left was what looked like an old factory of some kind. The loading dock door was opening. Five guys emerged, and they all looked really rough. I tried to run into the shadow to hide, but I couldn't move. Great! I was going to be seen. The five walked towards me. As they got closer, I could see one of them had a tattoo of a tiger on his forearm. He also had some of the biggest gauges I think I had ever seen in his ears. The guy next to him had a large gnarly looking scar on his upper arm. They stopped about five feet from me. I was terrified.

"What do you want?" The one with the tiger tattoo asked me. I started to answer, but before I could, another voice came from behind me. I suddenly found myself looking from beside the guys and now there were two sets of men standing there. The other group had been behind me.

"I need to know if you are responsible for the killings over on Elm." The guy in the front was talking. This group didn't look any better than the other. They were all covered in tattoos and wore red bandanas.

"No, I told you no more killings."

"I told you," one of the guys to the right of him said.

"Do you know who did it?" the other guy asked.

"No, that's why I called you here. Would you keep your eyes and ears open and let me know if you hear or see anything? We have had peace for five years. I want it to stay that way."

"I agree. The only thing I have heard is the guys talking about us getting blamed for this."

"Yeah, some of my guys have been saying it was you. I will make sure that those rumors are put to rest." As the two men talked, a small light from the corner of my eye caught my attention. It was a soft red glow. It was in the darkest shadow, and I could not make out a figure. My attention was brought back to the meeting when a gun shot rang out.

"Filthy traitor!" one of the men yelled. I saw the glimmer of a knife. Two men lay dead on the ground. Another shot rang out, then another. Soon, all ten men were dead. A noise brought my attention back the red glow. It was…no…was that a laugh or a chuckle? I wasn't sure, but the glow disappeared. I looked back towards the men on the ground. What had happened? Had the demon done this? He must have because they were talking peace. I woke with a shutter when Kyle burst into my room.

"Wow, that was just freaky!"

"You're telling me." I lifted my covers, and Kyle climbed in the bed beside me.

"What do you think it means?"

"I don't know" I told him. "The last time you saw the red glow…"

"He wasn't near people; he was in the woods," I said finishing his sentence.

"But do you remember the glow of the city in the distance."

"Yeah, when he came out on the bluff, you could see it."

"Do you really think he's a demon?" Kyle asked.

My light suddenly flicked on.

"You two okay?" Dad was standing at the door. Mom came waddling up behind him. Dad came in and sat on the end of the bed.

"Yeah, Dad. What's wrong?"

"Your Mom woke me said she could feel something was wrong."

I looked at Mom, who looked quite white.

"Kara was dreaming about a demon again," Kyle told Dad.

"What did you dream?" Dad asked as he laid his hand on my arm.

The dream came flooding back instantly. My eyes opened and Dad was still sitting there on the bed. Mom had now joined him. I glanced over at the clock on my nightstand, and it read 5:30 a.m. I was sure glad it was early morning because there was no way I was going back to sleep now.

"I need to think," Dad said, and he got up and left my room.

Mom looked at me, then at Kyle. We all knew Dad was heading to the kitchen.

I didn't want to think about the demon anymore, so I changed the subject. "Mom?"

"Yeah, sweetie?"

"I think I heard Rhett yesterday. I mean, I think I heard one of his thoughts."

"Really?"

I smiled at the thought of kissing Rhett. It was quite nice now that the panic had subsided. "I'm not real sure it was him, but he was the only one around besides Kyle."

"And I didn't say I wanted to kiss her," Kyle added with a goofy smile.

"Ouch."

I punched him in the ribs. *"I wasn't going to tell her that, you idiot."*

Mom laughed. "I'm not thrilled about the thought of Rhett kissing you, but that is how I found out I had power." Mom smiled.

"Okay, Mom, I don't want to see that picture of you and Dad kissing in my head again. No. no… ah." It was there before I could keep it out.

"Kara." Kyle turned his head, he had seen it too. Mom just laughed and went back to the door.

"Well, you might as well get up. It smells like your Dad is doing some serious thinking." Dad always cooked when he needed to think.

"Great!" Kyle threw off my covers. "I'm starved."

Mom and Kyle left me still lying in the bed. I thought of Rhett and what I was thinking yesterday when I heard him. Oh yeah, his beautiful eyes all brown with just a small tinge of green in them. I closed my eyes as they appeared before me. I knew I could probably get lost in those eyes.

I found myself looking at Rhett. He was riding a glowing sliver horse. Someone was behind him, but their head was turned the other way and I could not see who it was. Rhett pulled a sword and held it up just as a large red dragon came swooping down from the sky. "You cannot have her!" he yelled at the beast.

"Kara…Kara." Kyle was shaking me. "Come on, Dad fixed a huge breakfast."

I smiled as I threw back the cover. Dreaming of Rhett I liked. "I'm coming."

I followed Kyle into the kitchen. He wasn't joking. There was enough food for twenty people, and Dad was still cooking. Mom was sitting at the table eating.

"Come on, you two. Better eat before we make the trip to the shelter."

We always took any left over's from the restaurant to one of the homeless shelters in the city. Today it looked as if they were going to get some breakfast as well as supper leftovers.

Dad had cooked two kinds of omelets, three kinds of muffins, cheddar biscuits, white gravy, hash browns, some kind of soufflé, and was still going strong. Wow, he was really into some heavy duty thinking.

I grabbed a plate, a blueberry muffin and some hash browns, and then sat down at the table beside Mom. Kyle was heading back for seconds before I even had my muffin half way eaten.

"This isn't working," Dad suddenly announced as he shut off the stove and sat his spatula down. "I need to dome some hiking." He looked up at us. "Anyone want to come?" Mom looked at him with her "Are you crazy look?" Dad laughed. "Anyone but Mom want to come hiking with me," he revised his statement.

"I want to." Kyle raised his hand.

"I'll help Mom." I didn't want to leave her to deliver all this food by herself, not in her condition, even though I loved hiking.

"We are leaving in fifteen minutes," Dad announced, and then headed back toward his and Mom's bedroom.

"I only need two," Kyle said, then shoved another bit in his mouth.

"Go get ready, then you can finish," Mom told him.

"Alright." He grabbed a muffin and left the table.

Mom looked at all the food then at me. "Looks like we've got our work cut out for us."

"We will have it all delivered before ten."

"I hope you're right. I invited Terry and Mary over for lunch today and need to get things cleaned up."

I glanced around at the house. There wasn't a mess in sight except in the kitchen, but if I knew Dad, he had called Michelle and she was on her way to clean up.

It was a good thing Michelle was flexible and always needed the money because Dad called her to come clean all the time, and at all hours day or night. He didn't use always do that, but since her husband died and she needed the money, he would call her in to clean up even at the smallest of messes. At least now she was back living with her parents, and they could watch her son, Jeremiah, while she worked.

"I'm going to go get dressed," I told Mom as I got up from the table and sat my plate in the sink.

"Me, too," she said.

I opened my closet. What to wear? I pulled out a pair of jeans and put them on. Man, I really needed new jeans. I rolled the bottoms of them up three times and put on flip flops. I grabbed a blue shirt and put it on, then looked in the mirror. Oh, well, at least my hair was cute. I came back into the living room as the door bell rang. "I got it!" I yelled. I opened the door to find Michelle standing there.

"Your Dad called," she said as she came through the door. "Oh, my. Did he do all this this morning?" She looked at the kitchen.

"Yep." I told her.

"Okay, what did you or your brother do that had him so worked up?" she asked.

Mom laughed from behind me. "You know him well."

"You about ready to have that baby?" she smiled at Mom.

"I sure hope so," Mom answered. "I feel like a whale."

"Well, you don't look like a whale; you look beautiful." Dad said as he came in the kitchen and kissed Mom on the cheek. Mom smiled up at him.

"I'll be back by eleven and have lunch ready before the Jenkins get here."

"Oh good. You remembered." She gave him a kiss back. "You guys have fun," she said as Kyle came in and grabbed two more muffins and a bottle of water.

"Ready when you are, Dad."

After they left, I headed down to the restaurant to get some take-out containers for us to put all the food in. Michelle helped us get it all packed up and loaded in the SUV. I grabbed what was left over from the restaurant and off we went.

"So, who needs this today?" Mom asked as I pulled the small white pouch out from under the seat.

Mom had a system. In the pouch was a bunch of small pieces of paper and on each piece of paper was the name of a shelter. Mom would reach in and draw one out and that's where the food went. This way she said she wasn't the one choosing. "Ah," she said as she looked at the paper she had drawn out. "Looks like St. Michael's receives the blessing today."

St. Michael's was on the lower South side of town, so it would take us a good thirty minutes or so get there, depending on the traffic.

"So," Mom said, "what do you think about Rhett wanting to kiss you?"

Oh great, I was going to get a speech on boys. "Well, I don't know. I think he's cute and all, but I don't know about kissing him."

Mom laughed at me. "Come on, be honest with me."

"I didn't say I didn't want to kiss him. I just said I didn't know about it' I've never kissed a guy before."

"Well, I am not going to lecture you on the subject. You know what's expected of you and what's wrong and right, so all I'm going to say is: trust what you know, not necessarily what you feel."

That was a lecture all in itself.

"Okay Mom, don't worry. I am not going to do anything stupid."

"He is cute *and* neat." I had to laugh. I thought the same thing. "Not at all like your brother."

"I know, it's crazy. How in the world did those two end up best friends?" We both laughed.

"So, what are you guys going to see this afternoon?" Mom asked.

"Some movie with Sandra Bullock in it."

"I like her; she was in The Proposal."

Mom loved movies. She didn't get to go see the theater very often, but Dad keep us supplied with all the latest ones so she could watch them at home.

We arrived at St Michael's church just after seven. The shelter was in the basement and housed thirty homeless men and women every night. It wasn't a big shelter, but it helped all that it could. Father John was glad to see us when we walked in the door.

"God is so good," was the first thing out of his mouth. "Brenda, our cook, called this morning and is sick, and Helen is visiting her sister in Georgia."

Mom smiled as she handed him some containers. "Nothing is ever by chance."

He smiled. He knew how Mom's system worked. "Amen."

"Not only do we have supper leftovers, but Matthias was in a cooking mood this morning, so you have breakfast as well."

Father John raised his hands in the air. "Praise the Lord!"

He turned to face some of the people sitting in the fellowship hall. "Mike, Jay, go help them unload!" Two guys got up and followed me out to the Explorer.

"Your Dad has the best leftovers," one of the guys said as he pulled several containers out. I smiled at him and he smiled back. His smile was sad. He only had about three teeth leftin his whole mouth, and they were black.

"The very best in town," the other man piped in. He had his top front teeth but that was it.

We had it all taken in with two trips. Mom and Father John were in the kitchen opening and heating all the breakfast food. I separated the supper leftovers and put them in the 'fridge, then helped Mom and Father John serve breakfast.

I always like St. Michael's. They hosted several families. The Corneal's came to my mind; they were a family that had been here once. They had twin girls. I guess that's why I remembered them so well, that and the fact that Mom gave them our car. Mr. Corneal had lost his job in Maine. He and his wife had sold everything trying to survive. Then he got a job in Missouri, but while traveling across country, they had been hit by a drunk driver. His wife had been killed and it had left him with twins and no car. Needless to say, they didn't have the money for another one and soon they found themselves at St. Michael's shelter. Mom handed Mr. Corneal her car keys as soon as she heard his story and told him to go before the job was gone. Mom had such a big heart.

After breakfast was served, Mom and I headed back to the house. It was going on 10:30 when we got home. Michelle had cleaned and was gone. Mom always insisted we shower after leaving any shelter. Too many things you could come home with, she always said. After my shower, I stood in my towel looking in my closet.

"*You guys home yet?*" Kyle broke onto my thoughts of what to wear.

"*Yes, you on your way?*" I asked back. It was going on eleven.

*"No, Dad is sitting on his rock in the meadow. He has been sitting there for an hour, not moving."*

*"Go touch him. Maybe you can see what in his head."*

*"Are you crazy?"*

I had to laugh a little. I wouldn't have done it, either. I could almost see Dad sitting there on his rock. I could see the meadow, so beautiful. And suddenly, I was aware of the vision Mom had shown us of the demon in the meadow. Now I understood why that spoy was so special to him. We had gone there almost every week when I was small. We didn't go as often now, but Dad went when he really needed to get out of town and think.

I closed my eyes and pictured Dad on his rock, but as I did, a man appeared in front of Dad. He was in a shinny white robe and had eyes of turquoise and long blond hair. He looked up and smiled in my direction, then went back to talking with Dad.

Dad's aura of bright blue grabbed my attention. It seemed to be pulsing with silver. I was suddenly back looking in my closet. *"Kyle, is anyone else with Dad?"*

"*No, just me and Dad. Why?*"

*"I just got the strangest vision of a man talking with him."*

*"Hey, he's moving. He lives!"*

"Kyle," I could hear Dad through Kyle's mind. "We need to get home. Tell Kara to let your Mom know we are going to be a little late."

*"I heard him."* I told Kyle.

I pulled out a pair of jeans and a white button up shirt and got dressed. I then went to the restroom and put on a thin layer of makeup. I usually didn't wear any, but today I thought I might use just a little. I think putting on just a little was harder than putting on lots. I put it on and removed it three times before I finally got it the way I liked it.

Mom was sitting at the table looking at a cook book when I came into the kitchen. She looked up and smiled at me. "Looks good. For not wearing it often, you do a good job blending when you do."

"Thanks. Oh, by the way, I talked to Kyle earlier and they are on their way home, but they are going to be late."

Mom was a good cook, but she hadn't cooked much in two months. Her feet swelled if she stood too long. And right now, they were pretty swollen from serving at the shelter.

"Yes, I know. Your Dad called. He said he called Jake in to do some cooking for him so I wouldn't have to." She smiled.

By eleven thirty, Mom was getting antsy. Jake hadn't brought any food.

"Ok, this is ridiculous. He knows we're having company." Mom said as we and I got busy setting the table.

The dumbwaiter motor suddenly kicked on, to Mom's relief, and lunch was ready. The doorbell rang as Mom sat the last plate of food on the table.

"Are we too early?" Mary said when I opened the door.

"No, just in time," Mom called from the living room.

"*We are still forty-five minutes away,*" Kyle told me. I'm sure he was listening for the Jenkins to arrive.

"The guys had to run an errand and are running late, but they said to go on and eat," Mom told us.

"We don't care to wait," Mary said.

"They are still about 45 minutes out." I told Mom.

"No, there is no sense in letting the food get cold." Mom smiled and ushered everyone to the table.

"Well," Mary said, "your suspicions were right. I'm pregnant!"

"Congratulations!" Mom told them. "So, what do you want, boy or girl?"

"Well, we haven't given it much thought, but I would say either would be fine," Doc Jenkins answered.

"Oh yes," Mary added, "either will be just fine." She said. Her pink glow was just beaming.

Lunch dragged by with baby talk and parental advice. I thought I would die if I had to sit through anymore of it. About 12:45, Dad and Kyle came in and joined us at the table. Of course the congratulations started again all over again, and all the advice and now, Dad's take on it all.

"Kara, what do you think: boy or girl? You know she has never been wrong." Dad had now pulled me into the conversation.

"They may not want to know, Dad."

Mary looked at me. "You haven't ever been wrong… not even once?" she asked.

"Nope. I just have a sense about these things." What an understatement, I thought.

The Doc and Mary looked at each other. "Well, do you want to know?" he asked her.

"I think I would."

"Alright, what do you think, Kara?"

I got up walked and over to Mary.

"Stand up, please." Mary pushed away from the table, stood, and turned and faced me. She was completely pink except for one small blue spot on her belly. "Boy," I said, then went back to my seat. Mary looked down at her belly and smiled then sat back down.

"Never ever been wrong?" Doc asked.

"Nope, never." I glanced at the clock on the wall. It was 1:45.

"Mom, can we be excused? Rhett and his Mom will be here to pick us up at 2:00." Kyle asked.

Oh thank the Lord, I had heard enough baby talk to last me a life time.

*"I agree."* Kyle added in my head.

"Of course. You guys have a good time." she told us.

I pushed away from the table and went to the bathroom to check my hair. Kyle walked in behind me.

"Rhett's here," Dad called from the other room.

"Do I look okay?" I asked Kyle. "Never mind." I looked at him, he laughed.

I rode in the middle, between Rhett and his Mom. Kyle rode in the back with Kelly. Mrs. Williams dropped us off at the doors and told us she we would be waiting when the movie was over. Rhett and Kyle bought the tickets while Kelly and I used the restroom.

"I didn't know you and Rhett were going out," Kelly said as we washed our hands.

"We're not," I smiled at her. "Not yet, anyway." She smiled and we both laughed.

We meet back up with the guys at the snack bar. They both had a large drink and popcorn for us to share with them. The theater was pretty full and we had to set close to the front. Not my favorite place, but it was okay.

As the lights dimmed and the movie started, Rhett slid his hand into mine. I was immediately sucked into his thoughts.

"*Well, she's not pulling away. Not yet, anyway.*" I glanced over at him. His eyes were glued to the screen. "*She smells so good tonight; I wonder if I should tell her that. Her hand is so soft.*"

I wanted to pull my hand away from his. As much I wanted to hear his thoughts. I didn't want to hear them, either.

"*She is so beautiful. She has a body...*" I pulled my hand out of his. I didn't want hear anymore. I wanted to get up and run. My head started to spin.

"*Calm down, Kara.*" Kyle's voice came into my head. "*He is just a guy who thinks you're hot. You should be flattered, not terrified.*" I cut my eyes over toward Kyle. He was looking at the screen and holding Kelly's hand. I took a deep breath. Had I overreacted? Should I put my hand back in his? Was it better to know what he thought, or better not to?

"*Give him a chance.*"

I reached over and got the drink from the cup holder as if that's why I had taken my hand from his. I took a drink and put it back, then slid my hand back in his.

"*Just getting a drink .Calm down, Rhett. You just over reacted. She wasn't repulsed at you, just thirsty*".

I smiled. He was as nervous as I was.

I looked up at the screen. I didn't even know what was going on, I had been so weirded out.

"*I wonder if she would cared if I called her later. I have to be the luckiest guy alive. Brad is going to be so jealous when I tell him she came to the movies with me...and held my hand!*"

Brad? Why would Brad be jealous?

*"My gosh, Kara, are you that stupid? Brad has had a crush on you since the very first time we went to Youth group."*

*"Really? I didn't know that."* Well, the things you learn from reading other people's mind.

Kelly's arm was on the arm rest next to mine, but we weren't touching. I moved it just a little so our arms touched. I wanted to see if I could hear her, too.

*"Well, looks like Rhett is getting his wish. Now, if only I could get mine."* Kelly's voice was as clear as if she was talking to me out loud.

*"Kara, if I asked, would you go out with me?"* Rhett was saying, and I moved my arm off Kelly is to listen to Rhett.

*"No, no, I can't just say it like that. Why does this have to be so hard?"* Rhett was going over things in his head.

*"Go back to Kelly,"* Kyle interrupted, *"I want to know what she's thinking."*

Crap, this was a nightmare. I couldn't hear Rhett for Kyle butting in. *"Shut up, Kyle, I'll listen to Kelly in a minute."* I had no more than said it when Kyle's Coke fell out of the cup holder and into his lap. Kyle jumped up out of the seat. He looked at me.

*"Crap, do I do that?"*

"*Thanks,"* Kyle glared at me and left the theater.

"What happened?" Rhett whispered.

"Kyle spilled their Coke," I whispered back.

*"No, I didn't; you knocked it in my lap."* Kyle was mad.

*"Kyle..."*

I felt bad now. I didn't mean to, actually, I wasn't really sure I did it. Kyle came back in the theater and he and Kelly moved over a couple of seats, since his was now wet. Could I really move things? *"Kyle I'm sorry."* He never answered. I glanced his way, but he didn't look back. Great! Now Kyle was mad at me. I was so ready for the movie to be over so we could go home.

"Is something wrong," Rhett whispered. I was suddenly aware of his thoughts again. *"Something's definitely wrong."*

I smiled at him. "No just feeling sorry for Kyle having to sit there soaked in Coke." I whispered back.

*"Kyle I really am sorry."* No answer still. I looked toward the screen. I still didn't know what was going on, but I better at least watch some of it. My mind kept trying into wander off as I watched the screen. Come on, movie, end, I caught myself thinking.

*"Don't be thinking like that, or the projector might tear up."* I glanced over and Kyle smiled at me. I smiled back. If I had knocked his Coke out of the cup holder, then he was right, I better not be thinking of the movie being cut short.

Mrs. Williams was waiting when we walked out of the theater. "Was the movie good?" she asked as we got in the car.

"It was really good, Mom. You and Dad need to go see it." Rhett told her.

"It was good," Kelly chimed in. "My Mom will love it."

"What I saw was good, but I our Coke spilled all over me, as you can see, and I missed some of it." Kyle told Rhett's mom.

"I was hoping you spilled something and didn't pee on yourself," Mrs. Williams said.

We all busted into laughter. The ride home was a lot better than the movie, I thought. Rhett got out and walked me up to the door of the stairs.

"Thanks for the movie," I told him.

He was looking at me so intense. *"Do I kiss her or just shake her hand?"* was going through his head.

The thought of him kissing me was quite scary, even though I sort of liked the idea, too. This was torture, just standing here. I leaned up and kissed him on the cheek. "'Night," I said then turned and bolted through the door.

Kyle was standing there, laughing. I paused and listened to see if I could see what Rhett thought. *"Heaven. I've died and gone heaven."*

Kyle laughed even harder then.

"Shut up." I punched him in the gut and ran up the stairs. He caught me by the third floor and raced on up the stairs in front of me. He grabbed the fifth door fire door and tried to open it, and I focused all I could on the door and tried to hold it shut. I smiled as I caught up to find him pulling with no success to open it.

"Let me," I said as I opened it with ease.

"No fair, you were holding it shut." We got to the door just as Dad opened it.

"Alright, you two." Dad had heard us coming up the stairs. "Come in and have a seat."

Mom was sitting on the couch and Kyle and I flopped down on either side of her.

"I had a visit from a Messenger earlier," Dad looked at me, "the guy in white." "He didn't tell me everything. He never does. But things are going to change drastically for you in the next two years." Dad looked at me and Kyle.

"What's going to happen?" I asked Dad.

"I don't know. I was only told to prepare you for some things that are getting ready to happen."

"What kind of things?" I asked.

"I wish I knew. You have mental ability now, but it's now time to get some physical training."

Mom had been quiet up until this point. "What kind of physical training? You mean like fighting?" she asked.

Before Dad could answer, there was a knock at the door and Uncle Daniel came in.

"Uncle Daniel!" I ran to give him a hug.

"Hey, Sweet Pea." He hugged me back.

"How about me?" Granddad stepped around Uncle Daniel.

"Granddad!" We hadn't seen them in over a year.

Mom was struggling to get up off the couch. Granddad helped her up and then hugged her.

"How you feeling Lindz?" he asked her.

"I'm good."

"How about me, do I get one of those hugs?" Uncle Daniel asked Mom

"You bet." Mom turned to hug him. "Wow," Mom put her hand on her stomach. "David knows you're here. I think he's doing flips." I looked at Mom's stomach and could actually see it moving.

"Calm down, little one." Uncle Daniel put his hand on Mom's belly.

When we all got seated, Uncle Daniel started talking. "Have you been visited by the Messenger, too?" he asked Dad.

"Yes, we were just discussing that. So, what were you told?"

"Well, we are to receive our power back for a short time."

Uncle Daniel had no more got the words from his mouth when his glow turned bright silver. Dad's also changed, but so did Kyle's and Granddad's. They were not as bright, but they were still sliver. From Mom's reaction, she also saw the change.

"You're silver again," Mom told Dad. "But so are Kyle and Dad." Mom was now looking at Granddad. "Dad, are you okay?" she asked.

"Daniel has been trying to explain to me this all day, but I am truly lost. At the same time, it does explain a lot of things, too."

Mom smiled at him. "Sorry I didn't tell you before, Dad."

"That's okay, Lindz."

"Angels," Granddad said. "It's the darndest thing."

"What, Dad?" Mom asked.

"Your grandmother Clara use to talk about seeing angels. Said she had been healed from polio by one when she was just a girl."

Dad looked up at Granddad. "Clara Newport?" he asked.

Mom almost looked faint. "You healed my grandmother?"

Dad laughed. "Evidently I did. Didn't know she knew what I was, though."

Oh, this was crazy. My Dad had healed my great grandmother from polio. What's next?

"She saw auras like Lindz," Granddad told me.

Mom looked utterly shocked.

"Why didn't you and Mom tell me?"

This was just getting better and better. Again I had to wonder, who were these people?

"We all thought your grandmother was a little crazy. And when you started talking about them too. And well..."

"Well what? Did you thing I was crazy, too?" Mom was sounding upset enough that Dad got up and went and set down by her.

"No, Lindz, we thought it was just Clara's influence on you. You know she lived with us until she died." Dad put his arm around Mom as Granddad continued. "But after she died, you keep right on talking about them, so your Mom and I decided to talk to you about it. But she got sick before we got the chance. Then after she died, you never said another word about them, and, well... honestly, I forgot. Until now."

Mom shook her head. "I can't believe this. All this time I thought I was the only one." She looked up at Dad and he just patted her on the shoulder.

The plot thickens. I had to wonder what would be next.

"Matt and I will finish the house in England this week and be back next week. In the meantime, you two need to help Kara and Kyle with their skills. Michael will be here in two weeks." Uncle Daniel said now that there was a few seconds of silence.

"Who is Michael?" Kyle asked.

"You know who he is. He is always referred to as one of the Chief Princes."

Kyle's face turned white. "You mean Michael the Archangel, the angel of protection?" Kyle gasped.

"Who else would it be?" I said sarcastically.

Dad laughed. "Take a deep breath Kyle, before you pass out."

"You're going to be meeting several angels over the next two years." Uncle Daniel added. "Michael will just be the first."

Kyle looked at me. *"Are we dreaming?"*

*"If we are, we are having the same dream."* I told him.

"No guys, you're not dreaming," Dad answered our thoughts.

Mom gave a sudden gasp, and grabbed Dad's arm.

"Crap." Dad looked down. Mom's water had broken.

"Matthias," Uncle Daniel said, "You have been granted the power to move a person." Dad looked up at Uncle Daniel. "But only this once, I'll go first." Uncle Daniel then disappeared right before our eyes.

Dad got up and pulled Mom to her feet.

"He's found a spot." He took Mom's hands and they both disappeared. Uncle Daniel appeared back in front of us.

"You two follow me." He told Kyle and Granddad as he grabbed my hand.

"Wait, I don't know how." Kyle was panicking. Granddad looked just as scared.

"Just think of me, think that you want to see me, think you are right beside me." With that, I found myself standing in a dark shadow right down the street from the hospital. Uncle Daniel was still holding my hand. Granddad appeared beside us, and then Kyle.

"*That was so cool.*" Kyle told me.

I really didn't care how cool it was at this moment, although it really was, but I was more worried about Mom.

"*They are taking us to a room. I'll let you know what one when we get there.*" Dad spoke into our minds as we went into the Emergency Room.

"Maternity Ward?" Uncle Daniel told the lady at the desk.

"Third floor," she said as she pointed to the elevators.

We rushed across the room.

"*325,*" came Dad's voice.

The elevator ride seemed to take forever. We all heard Mom as we came up on room 325.

"You go first, then tell us if it's okay." Uncle Daniel pushed me towards the door.

I didn't want to go in by myself, but I understood the reasoning. I peeked around the curtain. Mom was in a hospital gown, but she was decent.

"*You guys can come in,*" I told Kyle.

"She is dilating fast," Dad told us, just as a contraction hit Mom. She moaned and held onto Dad, trying not to scream but you could see the pain on her face. Two nurses came in and told us we needed to go to the waiting room. "We are going to give her an epidural now."

We all turned to leave.

"Kara," Mom said. "You can stay if you want."

I really didn't want to, but she had huffed and puffed to get it out without screaming.

"*You don't have to.*" Dads voice rang in my head.

"*I don't want to hurt her feelings.*" I told him. I walked around and stood in front of Mom as the nurse lifted her gown in the back.

"The pain should be subsiding any second." The other nurse had a huge needle ready. The minute Mom let out a sigh the nurse told her to stay perfectly still.

In just a few minutes, Mom was resting comfortably. The Dr. came in to check her progress.

"You only have two centimeters to go. It won't be that long now, and you can start pushing."

I looked at Mom. I must have gone white.

"You don't have to stay if you don't want. I just thought you might like to see your brother being born."

Was she crazy? After seeing her in all the pain and the needle they used, I didn't ever want kids.

Dad nudged me with his leg. "*Thank her, and go find your brother before you pass out.*"

I gave mom a smile "Thanks, but this is a husband- wife thing. I think I will pass."

She smiled. "Alright then."

I turned and walked as calmly as I could to the door, but I wanted to bolt. The nurse pointed me toward the waiting room where the guys were.

Kyle laughed at me when I walked in. "You look like a ghost, you're so white."

"I don't think I ever want to have kids." Uncle Daniel and Granddad both laughed at me. I really couldn't understand why a woman would want to go through all that pain. I sat down on the couch next to Kyle and leaned over against him.

"Looks like we were both wrong on the date."

"I'm just glad I'm here," Granddad told us.

Uncle Daniel was sitting next to Granddad, but he had his eyes closed and was perfectly still, like he was in a trance. He suddenly smiled.

"He has your Dad's eyes and your Mom's hair," he said as he opened his eyes.

"Is he pale or dark?" Kyle asked.

"Well, right now, he is just red and gooey."

"Oh, yuck! I didn't need to know that."

"How's Mom?" I asked.

"Your Mom is just fine."

I took a deep breath. Mom was good, I had a new brother, and my Uncle and Granddad were here. Life couldn't get any better.

Uncle Daniel laughed. "You said it, girl."

Dad came through the door. "Anyone for seeing their new brother, grandson and nephew?"

Kyle looked up at dad. "Uncle Daniel cheated; he already saw him." Uncle Daniel punched Kyle in the shoulder. "Well, you did."

We all filed down the hall and waited outside the door until the nurse said it was okay for us to go in. Mom was holding David all snuggled up in a tightly wrapped blanket.

"Come on in, you guys." Mom's glow was back to normal, but it couldn't shadow the blue coming from David. But the blue had a silver cast to it almost like blue with an outline of silver. It was different than I had ever seen. Mom situated David and turned him just enough for us all to look at him. He had the biggest ebony eyes I had ever seen. They were wide and looking right at us. He was so beautiful.

"Would you like to hold him?" Mom asked Kyle, who was now rubbing David's little cheek.

"Really?" He was all excited.

"Sit down."

Kyle immediately sat down in the chair beside the bed. Dad took David and placed him in Kyle's arms.

"Hey, little brother," Kyle told him. "I'm going to watch out for you, keep you safe." I noticed Dad looking at Uncle Daniel. I tried to hear what they were thinking, but didn't have any luck. Kyle rocked slowly in the chair and David feel asleep in his arms.

I lay in bed that night thinking. Man, what a day I had had: dreams, discovery, excitement. I was exhausted, but couldn't seem to sleep. Dad stayed at the hospital with Mom and David. Daniel and Granddad had vanished back to England, and Kyle and I had come home to get some rest. I sat up, flipped the lamp on beside the bed, and grabbed my Bible from beside the bed. I knew it by heart, every word. I thought about all that had happened today, then opened it up. Romans 8, Verse 38 seemed to be speaking to me: "And I am convinced that nothing can ever separate us from God's love. Neither death nor life, neither angels nor demons, neither our fears for today nor our worries about tomorrow not even the powers of hell can separate us from God's love."

It seemed my whole day was wrapped in that verse: angels, demons, worry about what might be coming tomorrow.

Kyle appeared beside my bed and I jumped.

"Sorry," he said. "That verse speaks volumes today doesn't it?" He stood there looking at me.

"Come on." I threw back the covers and he climbed in. We had had separate rooms since we were tiny, but I think we had spent most of the time in one bed anyway.

"What do you think is going to happen?" Kyle asked.

"I don't know, but I have a feeling Dad and Uncle Daniel aren't telling us everything."

"Why do you think that?"

I leaned up on my elbow to face him. "When you had David, I saw Dad and Uncle Daniel looking at each other. I think they were talking, but I couldn't hear them."

Kyle was staring at the ceiling. His thoughts were roaming around through all that had gone on throughout the day. He stopped on Kelly. "What's going to happen to Kelly and Rhett?"

I hadn't given that much thought. "I don't know." I really liked Rhett.

"I really like Kelly, too." Kyle said.

Rhett had helped me discover powers I had, so maybe I would still be able to see him. I had a feeling life was getting ready to really change, but not exactly the way I would want it to. I was fifteen, and wanted a boyfriend and all that stuff. But now...

"Now, who knows what tomorrow holds." Kyle finished my thoughts again.

"I sort of liked normal life." I laughed.

"Our life has never been what most people called normal."

"You're right."

We had been home schooled since we were five, and had memorized the entire Bible by thirteen. "You remember the first time we went to church?" Oh what a catastrophe that had been. Dad corrected the preacher during his sermon. We both laughed at the memory of it.

"He didn't take it too well, did he?" Kyle laughed again.

We hadn't gone back after that, well, not till we were twelve.

"How about Youth?" Kyle asked.

Mom took us to a Youth Group, which is where we meet Rhett and April. We knew more about the Bible than the youth pastor, but we had held our tongues, unlike Dad. We went for about a month until Kyle couldn't contain himself one night and put Billy, the youth pastor, in his place over a verse he kept misquoting and taking out of context. Needless to say, we never went back.

"No, we have never been normal, have we?"

I laid back and closed my eyes. Life was definitely going to be different now that we knew all we did. My mind wandered once more to Rhett...

## CHAPTER 4

# CAMELOT

The wind was whipping past me. I could see clouds and blue skies all around. What was I riding and who was I holding on to? At this point, I really didn't care. I just didn't want to fall. I held tighter and squeezed my eyes closed. The winds ceased as I felt us touch down. I opened my eyes and released my grip. The rider in front of me slid out.

"My lady," he said, as he held out his hand.

It was Rhett. He was older and his hair was longer, but it was him. I took his hand and slid from my seat. The huff of the beast grabbed my attention as I looked back to see a mighty dragon. It was huge, with silvery-white skin and bright turquoise eyes.

"Did the ride pleaseth my lady?" Rhett asked as he escorted me up the path.

"Very much so," I answered.

We walked up the path and over a ridge, where the most beautiful meadow opened up before us. A castle sat in the distance. I noticed that Rhett was dressed in the clothes of a knight as we walked toward the castle through the meadow. Just as we were nearing the bridge to cross the moat, he jumped in front of me and drew his sword.

"Wait, my lady, something is amiss. Why is there no guard?"

I felt like I was in an old English movie. Just then, two men jumped from behind the stone fence and attacked us. Rhett was excellent with a sword and fought gallantly. Soon, both men were disarmed and begging for their lives.

"My lady," Rhett said, "their fate is in your hands. What would you have me do? Just say the word, and their lives will be forfeit."

"Please, please, my lady," one of the two begged. "Throw us in the dungeon."

The other man looked at me. "Let him slay us, for the master's hand knows no boundaries." His eyes were sincere.

What should I do? I held the lives of two men in my hand. "Why do you do your master's bidding?" I asked the man who still held my attention.

"I chose the wrong path many years ago and now I travel it where it has taken me."

I looked at the other man. "And you, why do you follow your master."

The man fell to his knees. "I follow the footsteps of my father, and his father before him."

I smiled gently. "Take heart, because today you serve that master no longer. Today you serve a new master. Today you are in the army of the king. Arise, my good men. Take up your sword and follow me."

The one man stood up. He seem to have a sense of pride and stood strong and tall.

"Do you accept my offer?" I asked the other.

"By my life, I swear to serve the king for the rest of my days or until life is taken from me."

Rhett handed each of them their sword. I turned and looked to the meadow behind us as two large, silver dragons landed behind us.

"Today is a new day. Go, take these two mighty servants and go fight for your king."

The two mounted the dragons and flew off into the sky.

"They did not deserve what my lady gave them," Rhett said from behind me.

I turned to face him. "Do we all not deserve a second chance? Would you have had them put to death? No better fighter than one that has been given a second chance."

Rhett bowed before me. "My lady."

I awoke with the sun coming through my window. The clock read 6:00 a.m. Kyle was standing in the doorway.

"My lady," He said with sort of a bow.

"Shut up." I looked around for something to throw at him.

Kyle laughed then turned and left. Why in the world was I dreaming of dragons, knights and Rhett? Maybe that dream was just a normal dream, but Kyle had watched. He usually didn't, if the dream was normal. Then again, nothing seem to be normal lately. I climbed out of bed, got dressed, and headed for the kitchen for some breakfast. Kyle was already dressed and standing with the refrigerator open, looking for food. He looked up as I came in the kitchen.

"I wish Dad was here." I laughed. We were so spoiled by him fixing us breakfast. I sat down at the bar.

"All I want is an omelet with toast and a big glass of milk," Kyle said as he closed the fridge and turned to face me. A plate with an omelet and a glass of milk appeared on the cabinet in front of Kyle. Kyle smiled. "I almost forgot." He opened his hand and closed his eyes as a fork appeared in his hand. "This is so cool."

"Well, what about me?" I asked him. "Are you not going to get me anything?"

Kyle took a big bite of his omelet. "Wow, it's wonderful, almost as good as Dad's."

"Kyle!" I said again.

He looked at me. "Okay, I'll try." he said. He closed his eyes and squinted, but nothing happened.

"Here you go." Dad said as he appeared beside me with food in hand.

"Stop it, Kyle. You're going to blow a gasket."

Kyle opened his eyes. "Why can't I get Kara something? It was easy when I wanted it."

Dad smiled at Kyle as he got me a glass of milk out of the fridge. "It takes practice, son. Especially if it's not for you."

"How are Mom and David?" I asked.

"They're fine. Doc says they should be able to come home late this evening." Dad was beaming.

"We'll make sure the house is cleaned up," I told him.

"Thanks." Dad walked over and picked his car keys off the entryway table. "Had to come home and get the Explorer." We all laughed. "I need for you two to start cleaning downstairs on the storage room. We're going it turn it into the game room, since it's smaller, and use the current game room for your training." Kyle smiled and jumped into a Kung Fu looking stance. Dad laughed. "Son, it is going to be so much more than fighting. You have to get your mind into it."

Kyle stood up tall. "I know, Dad, but to know how to fight is going to be cool."

Dad looked over at me then back to Kyle.

"What is it Dad?" I asked.

He took a deep breath and let out a sigh. "Oh, nothing. I'm going back to the hospital. You two get the house cleaned and work on the storage room. I'll see you around lunch and tell you what time your Mom and David will be home for sure."

I watched Dad as he walked towards the door. His clothes changed and he looked like he had had a shower. He turned and winked at me.

"That is just too cool." Kyle said. "I can't wait to be able to do all the stuff Dad can do."

I was thinking more about why we had to learn fighting. What were we going to have to do that required all the stuff we were going to have to learn? The thought was quite scary. Would we have to face demons? Kyle finished and cleaned up his dishes with just a thought. I, on the other hand, had to wash mine by hand and put them away.

I worked on the living room and made sure the David's room was clean while Kyle cleaned the bathroom and kitchen. It didn't take us long; the house was always clean thanks to Michelle. So, in less than an hour, we were downstairs in the storage room looking at what needed to be done. Since the whole fourth floor was just split into two rooms, the game room and the storage room, moving the stuff would be no problem. There actually wasn't much difference in the two rooms. One was just a little bigger than the other. But unlike the game room, the storage room wasn't kept clean and neat. We worked all morning on moving the boxes and odds and ends to one corner of the room. Then we mopped the floor and washed the windows.

"Well, there's not much more we can do until Dad tells us what to do with all that stuff." I told Kyle.

"You know Mom won't let him change this until she has it painted," Kyle said.

"Yeah, that's what I thought, too; it needs some work." We both laughed. Mom was picky when it came to the way things looked. She always wanted things nice and neat. It always killed her to look in Kyle's room at his wild mess, but she tried to be good about it and let him have his own space, as long as it didn't spill out into the hallway.

I glanced at the clock as we walked through the game room. It was going on noon. Dad should be back soon. Kyle's cell rang as we were heading up the stairs. It was Rhett. I could hear his voice on the other end of the phone. Kyle gave me his "Stay out of my head" look, then ran up the stairs in front of me. My mind wandered back to my dream and Rhett dressed in his knight's uniform. He looked quite handsome. I ran up the stairs and was surprised when I opened the door of the house to find Mom sitting on the couch. Kyle wasn't on the phone anymore and was sitting beside her holding David.

Mom smiled at me. "Doc said we could come on home, since we were both doing so great."

I walked over and sat down on the other side of her.

"Am I ever going get to hold him?" I asked Kyle. He had held him at the hospital and now had him again. Kyle smiled up at me.

"Sorry, Kara," he said me as he handed David back to Mom.

"Here you go." Mom placed him in my arms. His eyes were open and were so large and black. He just stared at me. With his sandy blond hair and black eyes, he reminded me of a certain vampire. Kyle laughed at my thought.

"Share!" Mom said.

"She thinks he looks like Edward Cullen when he's hungry." Kyle's laughter filled the whole house, which caused Mom to laugh too.

"Well, I guess he sort of does." She smiled up at me and winked, then looked at David. "But you're a lot cuter than any movie star could ever be made up to look like," she told David.

"That's just downright insulting to him," Dad said as he came into the room. "Come on, you two, let's go see what progress you made on that storage room."

"Why don't you and Kyle go. I need to talk to Kara," Mom told Dad.

I was glad. I didn't want to give David up so quickly.

"Let's go, Kyle. I'd like to get the room finished today."

"*No fair, you should have to come, too.*" Kyle fussed at me in my head.

"Shut up, Kyle, and come on," I heard Dad say from the hallway.

Mom smiled at me. "You know your Dad will have the room done in less than twenty minutes and be back. He needs to work with Kyle on that stuff not you." She winked. "Your Uncle Daniel says you're like me, which should be interesting. My power worked with emotions. I could do about anything when my emotions were running high… so how's Rhett?" She grinned at me.

"He's fine, Mom." I rolled my eyes. Like I was going to tell her about the turmoil my emotions went through when he was around.

"*You should,*" echoed in my head. "*She can help you focus it.*"

I was not liking it when Dad was in my head. How in the world could I do or think anything on my own anymore? "*I know, Dad.*" I answered him.

Mom looked at me, then said out loud, "Matthias, help your son and let me help our daughter." I had to laugh at her; she had her serious face on. "Men," she said and rolled her eyes. "Think they know it all." We both laughed.

"Now tell me the truth, what do you feel when Rhett's around? Are you nervous? Or do you like him at all?"

I knew Mom was just trying to help, but I was sort of embarrassed to tell her. "Well… I guess he sort of makes me nervous."

"So, you do like him, right?" She laid her hand on my arm as she smiled down at David. "He is so cute."

Okay ! Was she talking about David or Rhett? She was playing tricks, trying to get me to spill my guts on the subject. "Yes, Mom, they both are." I looked up at her.

She smiled real big at me and rubbed David cheek. "When my emotions were running hot, I could feel everything around me."

"How could you feel it?" I asked her.

"It was like I was part of everything and it was a part of me. It was like I held everything in my hands, and I could use it however I pleased, if that makes any sense." She was sort of looking off into space, thinking how to explain it. "Well, it may not make sense now, but when you feel it, you'll know what I am talking about." She focused back on me. "Why don't you invite Rhett over to meet your new brother tonight?" She gave me a little nudge with her elbow then looked off again, thinking.

"What are you up to, Mom?" I asked.

She just smiled, got up, and took David from me. "It's time for me to feed him. Why don't you go see how the guys are doing on the studio? I bet they're just about done." She turned and headed down the hall to the nursery.

Mom was definitely up to something. I got up and went to the door. "*How's it coming down there?*" I asked Kyle as I walked out in the hallway toward the stairs.

"*This is the coolest ever! Come see for yourself.*"

I quickly ran down the flight of stairs and into the new studio. I was amazed. It didn't even look like the same room. The walls were all mirrors. The floor was still the same hard wood, but you could only see it around the edges because of the huge rubber matt. On the end walls in front of the mirrors were lines of metal racks with all kinds of weapons and gear on them. It looked like one of those studios you saw in the movies that the hero always trains in. It was so cool. The door to the now new game room was also a mirror, but it had a large handle on it; it was the only way you could pick it out from the other mirrors along the wall.

"*We are in the game room,*" Kyle spoke in my head.

I walked across the room and opened the door. It sure didn't look like the same room that we had moped and cleaned earlier. Mom was most definitely going to be happy with the changes. The walls were all clean and freshly painted in taupe, and all the molding was white. The floor was now a beautiful redwood. Oh, Dad was good. There were movie posters up, and the pool caddie was hung along with a light over the pool table and air hockey table. The flat screen was gone and there was now a projection screen and a huge sectional. There was even a little fridge and snack bar in the corner. I didn't think our game room could have been improved, but evidently I was wrong!

"So, what do you think?" Dad asked. "Will Mom approve?"

"Oh yeah," I told him as I walked over to the snack bar where they stood drinking bottles of water. "She will love it. I'm not so sure about all the weapons and stuff in the other room though."

Kyle gave me a weird look. "What are you talking about?" Kyle headed back to the studio with Dad and I right behind him. "Dad?" he said as he entered the studio.

"Well, well." Dad said as he walked over and looked at the shelves of weapons.

"Look at this one, Dad." Kyle went to touch one of the large knives, but it disappeared before his finger could touch it. Kyle retracted his hand quickly. "Dad?"

I assumed Dad had removed it before Kyle could hurt himself.

Dad laughed. "Wasn't me." He closed his eyes a second, then opened them again. "Michael says no touching until he's here to show you how to use them properly."

"Sorry," Kyle said to empty air, but he looked up as he did so.

The knife reappeared, and Dad and Kyle walked up and down looking at the shelves of weapons, but neither of them touched a thing. I too took a closer look with my hands clenched firmly behind my back. There was a large range of weapons there, knifes, swords, guns, you name it. I think what amazed me at most was the thought of learning how to use them all…no it was the thought that I might actually have to use them! Yet a question lingered in my mind: why would I have to? Why would we have to use weapons of the world to battle demons? I shuttered at the thought of demons. *Lean not on your own understanding…* ran through my head once more. I know, I know, but it is my nature to want to understand.

I looked up to find Kyle and Dad both starring at me. "What?" I asked them.

"Who are you talking to?" Dad asked me.

I smiled. I really wished I could think without having everyone probing my mind.

"I wasn't talking to anyone; I was just thinking. That reminds me." I turned to Kyle. "Mom wants you to invite Rhett over for supper."

Kyle was already whining in his head. *"What about Kelly?"*

"Oh, good grief, son." Dad was hearing him, too. "Of course she can come."

Rhett and Kelly arrived around 4:00 that evening. Dad had supper fixed and waiting on the table by 4:30. Rhett thought David was the cutest baby ever, but Kelly, well she seemed to be baby shy. From the time she arrived, she stayed as far away from David as possible. It was almost as if she didn't want anything to do with a baby. Rhett, however, asked to hold David. He had several younger siblings handling a newborn didn't even seem to faze him.

"How about you guys go downstairs and watch a movie while we clean up?" Dad told us after supper. I was pretty sure Dad had already called Michelle.

"You have to see the new room." Kyle was telling Rhett as we all got up from the table. "It is so cool."

I wasn't sure which room he was talking about: the new game room or the studio. As we walked towards the stairs, a thought crossed my mind. *"Don't let Rhett or Kelly touch any of the weapons,"* I told Kyle. *"You remember what happened when you tried to touch them. I really won't know how to explain why they vanished if they try to touch them."*

Kyle didn't say a word as we went down the stairs, he just kept talking to Rhett about all the new stuff. Kyle put his hand on the door handle to open it, but stopped and turned to face Rhett, Kelly and I.

"Besides the new game room, we have a new dojo with lots of weapons. I am only going to warn you once: don't touch anything. Our instructor, Michael, is really picky about the stuff and will know if you even think about touching something, so don't, okay?"

I smiled. "*Nice,*" I told him.

*"Of course."* He smiled as he turned the knob and opened the door.

Rhett's eyes got huge as he walked by the many knives, swords, and guns. "This is so cool," he told Kyle. "So you guys are going to learn how to handle this stuff?"

"Yeah." Kyle gave him a big smile.

"What made your parents decide on weapons training?" Rhett asked as he looked at a small hand gun.

"We are going to be learning self-defense, not just weapons," I told Rhett. "You know Dad, he wants us to know a little bit of everything." I smiled at Rhett, who was now looking at a K-bar knife.

"What's this?" Kelly asked Kyle as she pointed and a small black case sitting at the end by itself. Kyle walked over beside her and looked.

"I have no idea. I don't even remember seeing it there earlier."

Rhett and I walked over to take a look at what they were talking about. On the end of the shelves of knifes there was a small black case that looked out of place.

"I wonder what it is." I said to Kyle.

"Open it," Kelly told him.

Kyle laughed, "Not on your life. Michael would be furious!"

"But he's not here." Kelly urged him.

Kelly was doing her best to get Kyle to open the case. I was starting to worry she might try to grab it and open it herself, but Kyle took her hand and pulled her toward the game room.

"We'll find out later. You've got to see the new game room now." He was doing his best to distract her, but she kept looking back untill he pulled her all the way through the door.

Rhett smiled. "Shall we?" He stuck out his arm. I put my arm though his and we followed Kyle and Kelly into the game room.

"Nice!" Rhett said as we entered.

Kelly was staring at the wall of movies. She walked up and down looking. "Which one do you guys want to watch?" she asked as she kept looking.

Thinking about all the training and stuff we were getting ready for, only one movie came to mind. "How about *The Bourne Identity*?" I asked.

"Perfect." Kyle walked down to the T's and pulled it out. Kelly sort of frowned as he walked over to put it in the Blue Ray player.

"I love that movie." Rhett said as he flopped down on one end of the sectional. "Actually, I love them all. Matt Damon is really good. I don't think anyone else could have played Jason Bourne better."

I looked at Rhett, who was now fully reclined and looked quite comfy. He was so good looking. I walked over and sat down about a foot from him.

Kelly sat down on the other end of the sectional but still wasn't looking too happy about the movie selection. Kyle flipped the lights off and jumped on the sectional beside Kelly. I leaned back and relaxed.

Rhett slid close to me. *"Should I put my arm around her, or just hold her hand?"* I found that I had tuned into Rhett as he got even closer to me. *"Maybe I should wait for her to make the first move."* Make the first move, I thought? What should I do? I glanced over to see where his hand was. He had it positioned where I could easily slide mine into it. *"Maybe she doesn't want to hold my hand, but she did at the theater."* I looked over at Kyle and Kelly. Kyle was sunk down and Kelly was snuggled up next to him. He had his arm around her shoulder.

*"Make up your mind before you drive him crazy."* Kyle never looked my way.

I slid over so our legs touched and tried to snuggle up to him like Kelly was doing to Kyle, but I was not sure how. I felt really awkward. Was I doing this right? I couldn't seem to get comfy so close to him. All that was happening was my stomach tying into knots. *"What in the world is she doing?*" Rhett looked at me. I looked back at him and smiled. I was sure glad it was sort of dark because I'm sure my face was red. Rhett lifted his arm and smiled. I slid into the little hole it created, and it was perfect. Finally, I was comfortable and could watch the movie.

Yes, watch the movie, I kept telling myself, but being so close to Rhett was crazy. I wasn't quite sure if I was hearing him or me. *Man he smelled good…I love being this close to her…I wish it would never end… I wish we could do this every night…* It all kept running together in my head. I glanced over at Kyle and he tuned in.

*Why couldn't she be my one and only? I really like her, maybe even love her.* I suddenly took in their glow, still blue and pink, not purple. It was sort of funny, but I had gotten to where I really didn't pay attention to the colors, just like I could tune Kyle out if I wanted. I sort of did that with the auras. I mean, I still saw them, but I just didn't really pay much attention.

Oh crap! I suddenly realized I sort of felt the same way. I really did like Rhett a lot, maybe more than that. He was so great. But were we made for each other? I didn't know. What if we were purple? The thought made me smile. What if we weren't? Would I be able to see it if we were? I mean, I never saw mine when I looked in the mirror. Would I be able tell? I had always seen his, so if he was close, would it be purple? I guessed it should if we were meant for each other. I was afraid to look back at Rhett; what if he was just his normal blue? I closed my eyes. There was no way I could look at him without seeing his aura now that I was thinking about it. I turned my head back to Rhett and slowly opened my eyes.

No color! I couldn't see his color at all. I looked back at Kyle and Kelly. Yep, they were still glowing, but nothing when I looked at Rhett.

*"Do not worry! For the time being, you will see no aura when you're around Rhett,"* came a voice in my head.

"*But why?*" I asked it.

"*Either color will be distracting to you,*" it answered back.

It was the same voice that always gave me a verse. And to be honest, I had always just thought it was…well …I guess the Holy Spirit, but now, I wasn't sure anymore. Whose voice was it? Should I ask? Would it actually tell me?

*"All things will we revealed in time."*

That wasn't the answer I wanted, but I guessed it would have to do for know. I looked at Rhett, and he turned to look back at me.

"Something wrong?" he whispered. "You seem to be distracted."

I smiled at him, but didn't know to say. I sure couldn't tell him the truth. Well, maybe some of it. I really didn't want to lie to him.

"Sorry, I wasn't expecting to be as affected by you as I am." I didn't know if that was a good thing to admit or not, but maybe it would keep him from asking anything else. He smiled back at me and turned back to the movie.

*Affect her? I affect her! This is great. She really likes me. Oh Lord, could you make her mine forever? I promise I will treat her right. I will love her with everything I have or will ever get.*

Wow, hearing Rhett's reaction was insane. He wanted me to be his…forever. He even said a small prayer about it. I was having trouble remaining calm, as if I didn't hear it. Now I really wanted to know what color he was when we were together. Maybe we were meant for each other, maybe not. Maybe I just needed to calm down.

*Distraction!* One word was all it took. Yes, I understood. I didn't need to know, and I could not dwell on it. They could just as easily take him out of my life as they kept me from seeing his color. I was going to have to stay away from him as much as possible. Well, maybe not as much as possible, but just not a lot, especially when Michael arrived.

Michael, hmm, I hadn't given him much thought. What will he be like, I wondered. Will he be like the man I saw with Dad in the meadow? Will he be more like a soldier with battle scars and such? You read in the Bible of angels appearing as men, so will he be just like… normal, maybe? Normal, how could an angel ever be normal?

Sitting here with my mind going in circles, I remembered the last few days. Every thought seemed to bring on a new wave of emotions.

Butterflies seemed to take flight at the thought of our impending training. Happiness ensued with the thought of Uncle Daniel and Granddad coming home. Fear erupted at the thought of being trained or the fact of having to actually need the training. Confusion came with the thought of Rhett, and whether we were meant of each other or not. And then there was the greatest joy at finally having David at home. What a roller coaster I was on. Yes, that was it; my life was like a roller coaster. I was excited, but scared. Couldn't wait to get aboard, but then scared to do so.

When the movie ended, we walked outside with them to wait for their moms to pick them up. Kyle wasted no time kissing Kelly. Rhett just stood there. "*Would she care if I kissed her? Should I try?*"

I stepped close to him. I really wanted him to kiss me. He slid his hands around my waist. My heart was pounding. Slowly, he lowered his lips to mine. My knees suddenly went weak and I would have fallen if it weren't for Rhett holding me.

"Your mom is here," Kyle said from behind us as headlights turned onto our street.

Rhett pulled back and looked at me. "I had a great time." But I wasn't focused on what he was saying. I was focused on what he wasn't saying. *"I think I love her, oh please let her be mine."*

I was speechless. He really did like me a lot, too. Now I wanted to know more than ever if we were purple. This was going to drive me crazy if I kept thinking about it.

Kelly's mom pulled up as Rhett go in with his mom.

"Ooo." Kyle punched me slightly on the arm when they left.

"Oh, shut up," I said, and then headed for the stairs and back into the house.

Dad was waiting at the door. "Kyle, I want you to go with me tonight."

"Where are we going?"

"Well, this is sort of a new thing for me, but I am going to see Ms. Carmichael. She's going to pass away tonight, and for some reason, we are supposed to be present."

"Oh Dad, I don't want to see her die." Kyle took a step backwards.

Ms. Carmichael was the lady that had given Dad the building to put The Village in. She had meet Dad when he was working at another restaurant about ten years ago, right after her husband had passed away. For some reason, she really took a shine to Dad, and soon the two of them had plans for The Village. Ms. Carmichael backed the whole project. Her husband had left her lots of money and property, and she was looking for investments. She seemed to think The Village was a good one. They worked over a year getting the place ready, including the upstairs living quarters. On the one year anniversary of it opening, she gave Dad the deed to the place. She was very special to our family, but I could totally understand not wanting to see her die.

"Neither do I, but we have to go! If it wasn't for her, we would not have all we do, son."

Kyle shook his head. "I know, Dad." Kyle hung his head.

"Follow me." Dad said and disappeared. Kyle followed suit and was gone.

Mom was sitting quietly on the couch. She patted the seat beside her and I walked over and sat down by her. She looked like she had been crying. Her eyes were red and puffy. I was sure it was for Ms. Carmichael. She was indeed a special lady. She had come in the restaurant at least three times a week since the place opened. Of course, Dad never let her pay. I put my arm around Mom and she held me close.

"So sad that we won't be seeing her anymore for a while. She is a grand lady."

"Yes, Mom, she is a special person." It's sad that she had no children, but she has left quite a legacy nonetheless. She backed several of the homeless shelters in the city and built two rehab centers for drug addicts, not to mention her many donations to the city to get parks and recreation areas built. The city will surely miss her generosity.

"Do you know how old she is, Mom?"

"I think she is in her early nineties. She had a long life, and I am sure she is glad to be going home."

David let out a cry from his room and Mom started to get up.

"I'll get him." I jumped up. I hadn't got to spend but a few minutes with him since he came home. Besides, Mom looked tired and emotional.

"Thanks, Sweetie."

I walked down the hall to David's room. It was so cute all decorated with little green frogs. The smell, however, about knocked me out as I entered. Why did I have to pick this time to take care of my little brother? I lifted David out of his crib and took him to the changing table. I was sure glad Mom had made us take a "caring for infant" class, or I wouldn't know a thing about handle him or change his diaper. He was so tiny. Oh, I didn't want to do this. The smell was horrible.

"*At least it's just a dirty diaper. You could be here with me,*" Kyle popped in my head.

"*So, what's happening there?*" I asked him, trying to get my head out of the nastiness I was facing.

"*Not a lot right now. Dad is sitting beside her bed just talking to her,*" Kyle told me while I removed the dirty diaper. Oh, good grief, how could something so small smell so bad? I could hear Kyle laughing in my head. Cleaning this up was no easy task. I wondered why anyone would want to have kids and have to do this all the time. It was beyond me. I felt Kyle's emotions suddenly change from not wanting to be there to interest. "*What's going on?*" I asked him as I tuned in more closely to hear what he was listing too.

"*Ms Carmichael is telling Dad she remembers him from when she was a young girl, something about Spanish Influenza.*"

I hurried and got David in a clean diaper and back in bed, then went to my room so it was quite and I could concentrate on Kyle.

"*Wow, Dad healed her when she was twelve years old.*" Kyle chuckled "*She is really asking more than telling.*" I had to wonder if Dad was going to admit to it or not. But since she was dying, did it really matter if she knew or not? I didn't have to wonder long.

*"He told her it was him, and that he had not realized it was her all these years. But he remembered her. Dad had called her Sally Jo."* Kyle got quite and I strained to see if I could tell what was happening.

"*Whoa.*" Was the last thing I heard him say, then an extremely weird feeling came over Kyle and I felt it along with him. It was something different, something that I had not felt before. Well, I didn't think I had… it was really strange.

"*What's happening?*" I asked him in my head. Silence came back and the wildest sense of peace I have ever felt came over me, if you could say peace was wild.

"*She's home,*" he finally said, *"and it was the most beautiful thing I have ever seen."*

"*What do you mean beautiful?*" I asked him

*"I will tell you all about it when I get home."* Then he didn't say anything else. I got up and walked back into the living room. Mom was sound asleep. I had to wonder what Kyle had seen. Did he see into Heaven? Could he have seen the Maker? I walked back and forth in front of the couch, then I went back to my room. I didn't want to wake up Mom.

What was taking them so long to get home? My mind went crazy. I wanted to know, had they seen Him? I thought of the account of John and Isaiah. John talked in Revelation about seeing the Maker. Well he tried; he really had a hard time putting into words what he saw. He used jewels to describe what he saw, like Emerald and Jasper. He also used thunder and lightning to express what he saw. But Isaiah's account says more about rumbling and light. I finally sat down on my bed. How would I feel about seeing God? Isaiah felt so unworthy to be in front of Him.

Dad's voice in the living room brought me back. I sprinted into the room and found Dad was sitting next to Mom. Kyle was on the chair. I dropped on the couch on the other side of Mom.

"I had no idea that she was Sally Jo," Dad was saying, "the girl I had healed from Spanish Influenza when she was twelve." He glanced up at me when I sat down but went on talking. "She had figured it out long ago. Well, she wasn't real sure, but when I talked about Daniel, she put two and two together." Mom smiled and patted Dad on the arm while he kept talking. "You would think of all people I would not be amazed at what He does, yet, I am."

"So, what happened when she died?" I blurted out. I had been sitting there about to burst wanting to know. "What did you see? Did you see into Heaven? Did you see...?"

"Good grief, Kara, calm down," Mom told me and patted my arm. "Here is your chance, Kyle. Tell Kara what you saw."

Kyle sat up straight and smiled. "Well, Dad was talking to Ms. Carmichael, and suddenly it got so bright in the room that I had to shield my eyes. I had to squint just to see what was happening." Kyle was now sitting on the edge of the chair. "It was sort of like those movies where you see with the ghost-like soul coming out of the body. But it was a very bright orb-like thing that came from her instead of a ghost thing. It was so cool. It floated up and then one came from Dad and they both floated up about two feet in the air, then vanished. The nurse had been standing in the door, but I'm sure she didn't see any of it. When Dad and her stopped talking, the nurse went round the bed and checked for a pulse. Then she tried to tell Dad she was gone, but he didn't say anything. He was just sitting there with his head bowed. She finally reached across and touched Dad's arm. A bright light flashed, and then Dad sat up." Kyle was talking so fast he had to pause and catch his breath. "It was so cool. I had the wildest sense of peace come over me, if you could call peace wild, anyway. The lights where so bright, but like nothing I had ever seen. It was almost iridescent with flecks of every color. They were so beautiful."

Wild sense of peace, strange. I had thought the same thing, I thought.

"So what about you, Matthias. What was it like for you?" Mom asked. This, I really wanted to hear. Now I was on the edge of my seat.

Dad grinned. "Sorry, I am not free to say what happened to me, so Kyle's rendition is all you get."

Well, that was just not fair! I thought. "Dad!"

"Sorry, that's just the way it is. I can't do anything about it. Kyle's account was pretty good, anyway."

"Can you even tell us about the lights?' Kyle asked.

"No, son, I can't, but it was amazing."

This really was not fair. Kyle got to see it, Dad got to experience it, and we just got to hear about it from Kyle, who is not a very good story teller at all. Maybe he could show us like he did the wood and demon.

"Could you show us, Dad?" I asked.

"No, babe, not this time," He answered as he patted my arm.

Well, this was disappointing. I got up off the couch. "I am heading to bed unless you need anything." I looked at Mom.

"I'm fine, Sweetie. Go ahead, and thanks for taking care of David earlier."

"No problem." I said goodnight and walked towards my bedroom. It had been a long day and I was bushed. Kyle followed me and flopped down on my bed.

"Do you think I can show you what I saw like Dad showed us?"

"Let's try." I flopped down beside him on the bed and touched his arm.

"Here goes," He said as he closed his eyes.

## CHAPTER 5

# DISCOVERIES

The night air was cool against my skin and I found myself looking out over the countryside from a balcony. A knock at the door brought my attention to the room behind me.

"Madam," a young woman spoke as she cracked the door and peeked in. "The two men are waiting for you in the throne room."

"Thank you." I told her as I walked towards the door.

The place was strange, but I seemed to know where I was going, thank goodness. I walked down the long corridor and through a large room that looked like a library to another corridor. This one was wider and there were guards lining the walls. Two of them opened the door as I approached. The room was huge. A large purple carpet led all the way up to an enormous looking chair, the throne. Off to the side was a smaller chair draped with blue and pink silk fabric. I was most definitely heading toward the small chair. As I sat, I heard the doors open again. Six men came towards me, four guards and two men in shackles. To my left, someone spoke, and I turned to see who was talking.

"Here are the two men you asked for, my lady," Rhett said as he leaned slightly forward. I looked back at the two men.

"How dare you treat me like a common thief! Release me at once!" One of men said. He stood tall and had an air of arrogance about him. He held out his hands for his shackles to be removed. I just smiled as I looked at the man.

"I will decide if you are a thief or not. Now..." I paused and looked from one man to the other, "you will both have a chance to tell your side of the story. And if you speak while the other one is speaking, then you will be found guilty either way." I pointed at the arrogant, well dressed man. "You shall tell your side first."

"Very well," He said. "Carl Black is my herdsman. He takes care of all my flocks and herds. And why he should say I stole his lamb is beyond me. I picked my youngest lamb to cook so it would be tender for my dinner guest. Where is the crime in that?"

As I watched the man, his blue aura had a strange look. It was as if the inside of his aura had a small hint of red to it.

"It was he who stole it from me," he continued. " He had to have taken a lamb from my flock and called it his, and if it was not from my flock, then he stole it from someone else. It was clearly not his. I would be doing him a service by taking the animal, anyway. He clearly has no means to feed it."

I could tell the man didn't care either way for his servant. "Your turn," I told the Mr. Black. He was very worn looking, dressed poorly, and was filthy.

"It was my lamb, my lady." He fell to his knees in front of me. "It is true that I work for Mr. Cason as his herdsman. He has many herds with many lambs, but as for the lamb he chose for his dinner, it was mine."

I noticed Mr. Black's aura was blue, but in the center where the other man's had a red cast, his had a white tinge.

"It is true I have very little," he said. "And it would have been hard to keep the animal, but I was not planning on keeping it long. You see, my daughter Miranda is to be married soon, and my brother James brought me the lamb for the wedding supper." The older man looked as the doors in the back opened. Two men and a very young pretty girl entered. "My lady, this is my brother James, my daughter Miranda, and John, my future son-in-law."

The three approached. James looked not much better off than Carl but older, the girl was pretty, but poorly dressed. John, however, looked as if he came from a family of means.

"Did you give the lamb to your brother?" I asked James.

"Yes, my lady, for Miranda's wedding."

I stood and looked at all before me. It was time for me to give my judgment.

The arrogant Mr. Cason looked down at Carl. "I didn't know you even had a daughter. She is truly beautiful. I will give you half of all my flocks for her hand."

I almost felt sick to my stomach. How could this man even offer such a thing? He clearly thought he was better than the young man she was supposed to marry.

"No, Papa," the girl pleaded and fell to her knees beside her father.

"Don't worry, my daughter. I would never dishonor you that way."

"This is what is to be carried out," I said. "Mr. Cason will be put in the dungeon for one month. During that time, Mr. Black will be put in full control over Mr.Cason's estate."

"What?" Cason yelled.

"Sir," I said to Mr. Cason. "If you had paid your herdsman a decent wage, this never would have happened."

"That is preposterous!" he yelled again.

"Silence!" Rhett ordered him, and then pointed to a guard. "Take him away."

"Wait," I said to the guard. "In one month when you are released, you will be the herdsman for Mr. Black and work for wages. You will not be given back the estate. Now take him from my sight." Two guards dragged Cason away as he yelled at how unfair he was being treated.

A guard knelt down and released the shackles from Mr. Black, then helped him to his feet.

"Be wise, sir, for in two months you will be before me again."

"Yes, my lady." He bowed then turned with his family to leave. The girl Miranda stopped and turned to me.

"Thank you, my lady." She gave a short curtsy and ran back to her father's side. I smiled and sat back down on the chair.

"What is it, my lady?" Rhett asked as he came around to stand in front of me.

"In two months, we will see if the servant can rise to the challenge of becoming a good Master. If so, he will receive half of his Master's estate; but if he squanders it, he will be put into the dungeon."

"And what of Cason, my lady."

"If he learns to become a humble servant and do a good job for his Master, then he will get his estate back. But he will only get half in either case. If he is not a good servant, he will remain a servant for the rest of his days, working as a lowly herdsman."

I woke before sunrise. Why did I keep having these crazy dreams, and why was Rhett in them? I went to the kitchen, grabbed a bottle of water, and went to the roof. Mom had made it into an oasis. There were lots of planters with beautiful flowers and lounge chairs. The stars where slowly giving way to the glow of the horizon as I laid down on one of the lounge chairs. My thoughts turned to Kyle and our experiment last night. It evidently didn't work. I couldn't remember a thing after touching Kyle's arm. My eyes began to get heavy as I watched the night sky fade.

I was sitting back in the chair in the throne room. In front of me stood Mr.Cason and Mr. Black. Cason was decently dressed and clean. He did not look bad for spending a month as a herdsman. Mr. Black was nicely dressed as well. Rhett handed me a piece of paper listing all the holdings of Cason's estate on it. To my relief and pleasure, Cason's estate had grown in size since Black had taken over. Everything had doubled in one month, and in the second month had almost doubled again, except for the herds. They hadn't grown the first month and had barely made any more improvement in the second, the month that Cason had been working them.

"You have done an excellent job, Mr. Black, and you shall be rewarded. Cason, what have you to show me for your month? Why did the herds not grow? According to this, you were given three times the wages you were giving Mr. Black."

"I am not a good herdsman, my lady, but I am learning." He looked up from the floor that he had been starring at. I was pleased to see his blue aura with not a hint of red in it.

"He is, my lady," Carl spoke up for Cason. "He has been working hard."

I smiled at Mr. Black then looked to Cason.

"With all you did to this man, he stands up for you. He speaks on your behalf. What do you have to say for yourself?"

Cason looked up at Black. "Please forgive me, my friend, for ever wronging you. You have taken care me and my family as if they were your own, and you have made my estate more successful than I ever could have dreamed. I am in your debt forever." Cason dropped to his knees at Carl's feet.

Carl leaned over "Oh please, Mr. Cason, get up. I only did what I thought was right and fair."

"It is settled, then," I announced. "Mr. Black and Mr. Cason are to split the estate. One half of it is still more than you had to begin with," Mr. Cason. "But take note that I will be watching you both. Remember to give a fair day's wages for a fair day's work, and always, and I mean always, lead by example."

"Yes, my lady, I will. Thank you." Carl said. He bowed and left.

Cason looked at me and fell once again to his knees. He buried his face in his hands and wept. I went and knelt down in front of him.

"Good sir, it is time that you start your life anew. Right the wrongs from your past. Make good on every promise you have ever made. Life begins here. Now, go home to your family and serve you fellow man with honor."

He looked up at me with tears still flowing down his cheeks. "I do not deserve any of the estate, my lady. I have treated them all so badly."

"Second chances are hard to come by. Now I suggest you get up and become a new man. Let the old one go; let him die here and now."

I stood up in front of him. "Now, stand up Mr. Cason for you have an estate to manage and it needs you."

Slowly, Cason got to his feet. He turned to leave, but stopped and turned back to me. "Thank you, my lady."

At that very moment, I noticed that his blue aura had a small glimmer of white in it.

I opened my eyes to find the sun coming over the railing.

"*Where are you?*"Kyle popped into my head.

"*Roof.*"

*"What are you doing up there and what is it with you and the Camelot dreams?"*Well, I didn't have to ask if he saw that one now.

*"I wish I knew because they are so weird."* I reached over and grabbed my bottle of water. As I did, I would have sworn I caught a glimpse of someone sitting on one of Mom's planters. But there was no one there now. Chill bumps rose on my arm. Whoa, it was just freaky. I quickly got up and headed back downstairs.

Kyle was sitting on my bed as I entered my room. "What were you doing on the roof?"

"I woke earlier and just went up there to watch the sun rise, but I fell back asleep," I explained, then got my laptop and sat down on my bed. It had been over two weeks since I got online.

"Do you think your dreams mean anything?" Kyle asked me.

"No clue, but they are strange. At least I am not dreaming about demons."

"That's true. Those dreams were freaky and the last one with all the killing was even worse."

I had to agree with him there. I had been seeing the man with the red glow for quite awhile, but until the other night, he had never caused death. Every time I had seen him before, he seem to be, well, maybe traveling. I hadn't really given it a thought until now, but the first time I saw him, he was in a meadow. The next time I dreamed about, him he was on a bluff, and then the next time he was on a different bluff looking out over a city. The first dream I had when he was actually in the city, I noticed the people he was around being angry and hateful towards each other. I guess that's what prompted me to ask Mom about what a red aura meant. But then there was the last dream I had with all the killings; it scared me a little. Now the more that I thought about it and all this training we were going to have to go through, it made me wonder if those dreams were a premonition or something. I was glad I hadn't dreamed about him lately, but now I was having these Camelot dreams, as Kyle called them.

"Do you really think they are premonitions like Mom had?" Kyle asked.

"I sure hope not." I didn't want to even think about any of the killings happening for real.

*"Kyle,"* I heard Dad in my head, *"I want you to go with me today out to the meadow to do some practicing. Kara, you are going to help your Mom today; maybe she can help you some in return. But mainly, I think she just needs some rest. Do you mind?"*

*"No, Dad, that's fine. I need to do some catching up on some online stuff."*

*"When are we leaving?"* Kyle asked.

*"Change and follow me, son. Just think you want to be right beside me."*

As I watched Kyle's clothes change from what I remember him having on last night.

*"See you later,"* he said as he disappeared.

I decided to check on Mom and David before I got engrossed online, so I sat my laptop down and went to find them. She was sitting on the couch feeding David when I got to the living room.

"Are you feeling okay, Mom?" I asked. Since Dad said she needed rest, I figured David must have kept her awake most of the night.

"Yes, I feel fine. Do I look like I feel bad or something?" she asked.

"No, Dad just said you needed to rest."

"That man." She shook her head. "If I toss or turn the least amount at night, he thinks I am not sleeping well and have to be tired. I have almost always tossed and turned. He just hasn't noticed until now because he doesn't need to sleep again."

"Doesn't need sleep?" I asked.

"No, when your Dad was silver before, he never slept or ate. Well, he did eat when other people were around, but it was just to blend in."

I walked over and sat down by Mom on the couch. I didn't like to be in the room while Mom was breast feeding, but I would make an exception this time.

"So does Kyle not sleep either?" I asked since he was now like Dad.

"You know, I asked your Dad the same thing," she told me as she moved David to the other side. "He said that he wasn't. I figured he had told you."

"No, but I did notice he was wearing the same clothes from the night before; I didn't ask about it. Mom?"

"Yeah, Sweetie."

"Can I ask you something?"

"Sure, what is it?"

"Well, I wanted to ask if you thought my dreams were like yours… you know, sort of like a premonition."

"I really hope not, but I am afraid they might be. I know that when I did meet the demon, I was thankful for the dream."

"Why?" I asked her.

"It sort of prepared me for the encounter. I knew what was going to happen and wasn't shocked when it did. Well, at least the first part was the same. I never saw how the dream ended. I guess that was up to me," she added.

"But I'm not in my dreams. I am just watching."

"Maybe you're there to learn what he can or cannot do. Pay attention when you dream about him." Mom was serious; I could hear it in her voice. "I hope you never have to meet this demon you dream about, but if you do, you need to be prepared, and the dreams may give you the advantage you need to defeat him."

Just the thought of the demon gave me cold chills, but the thought of actually having to face and fight him made me feel I felt like I could pass out. The room sort of spun and I got slightly light-headed.

"Kara?" Mom placed her hand on my arm.

"Mom, I don't want to face him." I was flat out honest with her.

"I know you don't, but if there is anything I've learned from my experience, it's that you are not alone, and you will have everything you need to do what you are supposed to do."

I knew what she meant, but it really wasn't that comforting at the moment. Life felt so out of control. A sudden calm washed over me like a wave at the beach. I felt a small hand rest on my arm. I looked down to see David's large onyx eyes. He was staring at me as if to say it will all be fine, big sis, don't worry about a thing.

"I know, Mom." I reached over and touched David's little hand. He grabbed my finger and held tight. "What are we doing today?" I was to change the subject.

"Well, I'd like to get out of the house for a while before I go stir crazy." She smiled as she lifted David up to burp him.

"I'll go change, and then I'll hold David while you change," I told her as I got up from the sofa. "Or would you rather go first?"

"I'd really like a long hot shower first. Do you mind?"

"No, go ahead." I held my hands out for David. She gently placed him in my arms and headed back towards her bedroom.

"Well, cutie, it looks like we get have a little brother/sister time." I placed him on my shoulder and patted him lightly on the back then walked and bounced my way into the kitchen. I didn't care if Kyle had to eat or not; I did, and I was hungry. After a few small burps from David, I rested him in my arm and opened the fridge. There was a bowl of blueberries and some small cups of yogurt. That would do nicely. We went to David's room and retrieved his bouncy chair and I placed him in it on the table. Then got out a bowl and set down to eat beside him.

I quickly tuned in Kyle to see how his day was going. *"...you have to be selfless, Kyle"* I could hear Dad telling him.

*"What do you have to be selfless about?"* I asked Kyle.

*"To do stuff for others, like when I tried to make you breakfast. It has to be a true act of love or something. It's really hard, and I seem to be no good at it. So what are you doing?"*

*"Watching David while Mom takes a hot bath."*

*"Kyle, concentrate! Kara, you need to leave him alone or he will never get this."*

*"Sorry, Dad, I just wanted to check in on him. I'll leave you two alone."*

I finished eating and cleaned up, then picked up David in his chair and went back to my room to get dressed. He had fallen asleep while I ate. He was so cute. I sat him carefully on the bed and went to my closet.

The weather was getting warmer, but it still wasn't shorts weather yet. I once again put on a pair of jeans and rolled the bottoms up. I put on a light blue shirt and then checked my email. I might not go to a public school and have lots of friends, but we did travel some, and I had made some friends that I liked to email. White Turtle was one of my closest friends; she lived on the Cheyenne Reservation in Montana. We had gone out to the Reservation several times when Dad was getting stuff for the restaurant. Dad did a lot of stuff with the Cheyenne and Cherokee Indians because of his Dad being Cherokee and his Mom being Cheyenne. I had always thought that he meant he was descended from the two tribes, not that they were currently part of the tribes. Dad did totally look the part, though. I would have to ask him about it sometime. As I sat there thinking about it, I realized he had always been sort of vague about his family. At least it made since now why he was.

I had two letters from White Turtle. She mainly wanted to know how Mom was and if she'd had David yet. I wrote her a quick reply that Mom and David were home and he had the most beautiful onyx eyes. I added and I hoped we could visit soon, and that I missed her and her brother Red Wolf. I hadn't thought of him lately. He was really cute with his red hair and dark eyes. I smiled at the thought of him.

*"I can only do so much, Turt! You are going to have to buck up and ask her yourself."* Turt? That was what Red Wolf called White Turtle? Had I tuned into Red Wolf? *"She's on the phone now. You better go ask before she gets off."* I thought hard on Red Wolf and White Turtle. What did she need to do herself? *"Mom, I can go and help her. Let me go, please."*

*"Turtle I know you want to help but..."* I could hear Turtle's Mom through her thoughts.

*"But, what Mom? You know I can do this. I'm old enough to make the twins behave, and take care of Aunt Ginny. Please, Mom, you're not able and Aunt Robin is not well enough, either."*

*"Ginny, I'm going to send Turtle to help you."* I heard Turtle's Mom again.

*"Turtle."*

*"Yes, Mom."*

*"Thank you for helping Ginny. If things get rough, call and I'll come help you out."*

The conversation faded in my head. I tried to reconnect, but just couldn't seem to find them again. I immediately went to typing. I wanted to know what had happened to her Aunt Ginny, but how to ask without it sounding really weird? Could I ask how the family was, or how her aunts and uncles were? Maybe I'll just ask how she's doing and what she has planned for the summer. Yeah, that was it. She would have to tell me where she was going and what had happened. I finished up my message and then got off line. I sure hoped she would get online and get her mail before too long.

David gave a little noise and I jumped. I had been so engrossed in finding out about Turtle and Fox that I had forgotten he was even in the room with me. He was just making baby coos, so nothing seemed to be wrong. He was looking around the room, using those amazing eyes. It was as if he was looking at everything and saying, "so this is your room, cool."

"You ready?" Mom asked from my doorway.

"Yep, so where are we going?" I gathered David out of his bouncer and handed him to Mom.

"I think I'd like to go to the Farmer's Market. There are a few that have green houses, and I'm excited to see what they have freshly picked. Now, young man," she said to David, "let's go check that diaper before we leave." She headed towards David's room. I followed and put a few things in the diaper bag, then picked up David's car seat out of the corner. Mom carefully strapped him in and off we went.

The Farmers Market was always a neat place in the late spring and summer with all the vegetables and fruits, but with it being this early, there wouldn't be much there. I was with Mom on something fresh sounding pretty good. The Diefendorf family always had great things. I think they were from somewhere in Germany. I really liked Alina, but her Mom, Ava, not so much. There was also the Parker family. Their produce always looked the best. Mike was very picky about the food he selected to sell. If it wasn't good enough for his table, he wouldn't put it up for sale. What I liked about him and Carol the most was that at the end of each day, they would take what didn't sell and give it to a local homeless mission. They had encouraged a lot of the other vendors to do the same, but there were a few that wouldn't. Mom never would buy from them, and I was glad she didn't. I sort of hoped Alina would be there, but I wasn't sure if they had a green house or not. I hadn't been to the market in a while and would love to see her. The parking lot was bare, maybe fifteen cars altogether. I could see four trucks with produce. The Parkers were there, along with Ida Jenson and her niece, Molly. I could also tell Mark Grant was there, one of those Mom wouldn't buy from, and Alina. I didn't see her Mom, though.

"Good morning, Alina." Mom spoke as we approached her stand. "How are you doing this wonderful morning?"

Alina looked up and smiled. "Mrs. Black, it's nice to see you've finally had your baby. He is so cute! It's a boy, right?" She asked as she walked around and played with David's little cheek.

"Yes. David, say hello to Alina"

Alina wasn't her normal cherry pink, I noticed. She had a slight yellow cast to her.

David was awake and wide eyed, taking in his surroundings. He looked at Alina with intent eyes. He always seem too really concentrate on what was around him. I knew he was too young to really be seeing things clearly, but he was always so attentive to everything around him.

"Alina, how's your Mom?" I asked her. I still didn't see Ms. Ava anywhere, and Alina's worried glow made me wonder if she was sick.

"Yes, how is your mom? I don't see her anywhere." Mom must have been thinking the same thing.

"She's in the hospital. She fell and broke her hip two days ago."

"Oh, that's horrible," Mom said.

"I wished I could be there with her, but I know the doctor bills will start coming in and I can't afford to let anything go to waste."

I could already see Mom's mind hard at work on how to help them. She looked to see what Alina had on the truck. There were tomatoes, onions and some zucchini.

"I'll tell you what, Alina, you take all the produce you have each morning for the next two weeks and deliver it to the restaurant. I'll see that you get paid for it. That way you'll have the rest of the day to spend taking care of your mother."

"Oh, Mrs. Black, I couldn't ask you to do such a thing," She said.

"You didn't ask. I offered."

"But you may not need all those vegtables."

"Don't you worry about that. I'll take care of it. We do need most of it on a daily basis, and what we don't need, I'll send to one of the shelters. Now, head on to the restaurant."

"I don't know how to ever thank you," Alina started loading her veggies back on the truck.

"Let me help you." I went around the side of the stand and helped her load seven boxes of onions, tomatoes and zucchini back into the truck. Mom smiled and walked on up to the Parker's table of goodies.

"I can't believe this," Alina said. "I'm all Mom has now, and with her not being able to speak English, this has been so hard on her. I just don't know how to ever thank you."

"Is there anything else we can do to help out with your Mom?" I asked her. I may not have really liked Ava, but I would sure hate it if it was my Mom and no one would help me out.

"Oh, no, you've done enough already."

Mom came back just as we finished loading.

"I called Matt and he's expecting you," Mom told her. "Which hospital is your Mom in?"

"Cook County. She's in room 435. She's scheduled to have a full hip replacement on Friday."

"Make sure you call if we can help out in any other way," Mom told her.

"You're too kind, Mrs. Black. You have already done too much."

"There is never enough kindness, Alina."

"Alina hugged Mom carefully, since she was holding David. "Thank you so much." Alina told her, then turned and hugged me also.

We watched as she drove away.

"Would you go get the things I bought from Carol? I didn't want to bring them over here before Alina left."

"Sure." I went over and talked with Carol a few minutes. She had Mom's stuff ready to go and waiting for me. Then I headed for the Explorer where Mom was putting David back in his car seat.

"I think we should stop by and see Ms. Ava on our way home. What do you think?" she asked me.

"Is it wise to take David into the hospital where all the sick people are?"

"I think he'll be fine, and she might enjoy seeing a little one."

If Mom was fine with it then what else could I say? "Alright then."

We drove over to Cook County Hospital and parked. When we went in, Mom made a stop by the gift shop and picked up some flowers to brighten Ms. Ava's day. The white flowers were a welcome calm color in the sea of crazy colors going on. When we got off the elevator on the fourth floor, we could already hear Ava fussing at a nurse. She had a very harsh, raspy voice. But something was different; I wasn't hearing her normal fast German. She was speaking perfect English.

"Well, I can't believe it," I told Mom. "All this time I thought she couldn't speak English."

Mom looked at me as we walked. "What are you talking about?"

"Listen to her fussing at the nurse about her bed being too high."

Mom gave me a very strange look as we made it to room 435 where all the fussing was coming from.

"You're hurting me! Stop that. Just go away and leave me alone," she was telling the nurse as we entered her room. The nurse looked up at me with frustration on her face. Her glow was changing from its pink state to a yellow one. The nurse had her moving into a sitting position even with all the protest Ms. Ava was shouting out. Ava looked up as we entered her room.

"The Johns. Great. I need Alina and she is sends guests to see me," Ava said hatefully. "Woman, you're hurting me. Stop it!"

"Is there a reason she has to sit up?" I asked the nurse. "You're causing her pain."

"Finally, someone that can understand her." The nurse let off the button "Where is she hurting?"

Understand her? She was talking perfect English. What was the nurse talking about?

"Where are you hurting, Ms. Ava?" I asked so she would tell the nurse. Ms. Ava looked at me and, for the first time that I could ever remember, smiled at me.

"She is causing pain to shoot down my left side, and my foot is going numb."

I looked at the nurse waiting for her to say something, but she was staring at me as if waiting for me to translate.

"Well," she finally said. "What's wrong with her? Where is she hurting?"

I was confused, Ms. Ava had just told her where she was hurting. Why was she asking me? Wasn't she listening?

"Her left side has pain shooting down it and it's causing her foot to go numb." I told the nurse.

"Tell her I am sorry. I will go get her something for the pain. Here," she handed me the bed controller, "try to find her a comfortable spot." Then she turned and left. I looked up at Ms. Ava, and then over to Mom. Mom had the weirdest look on her face.

"Please lay me back flat," Ms. Ava said, and I turned back to look at her. "That is the only place that doesn't make me hurt."

I smiled and looked at the controller in my hand, then pushed the button that had a little head with an arrow pointing down on it. Mom walked up beside me and held out the flowers to Ms. Ava.

"Thank your mother for me," Ava said. "It was so nice of you two to come see me. I see your mother has finally had that baby. What did she name it? Is it a boy or girl?"

Again I was confused why was she talking to me instead of Mom, who was standing right beside me. I looked back at Mom,who was now smiling at me.

"Are you confused?" she asked.

"Yes, why is she talking to me as if no one can hear her but me?"

"Well, evidently you have the gift of speaking in tongues."

"What?" Tongues? What did she mean by speaking in tongues?

"You understand all she is saying, right?" she asked me.

"Yes."

"Well, she is still speaking German. And when you talked to her, you were, too."

I stared at Mom. Was she serious? She couldn't be. I didn't know German.

"Is something wrong?" Ms. Ava asked me.

"Ah...no ma'am. It's a boy, and she named him David.".

I looked back to Mom. "Are you sure? All I hear is her speaking is English."

"Oh, I'm sure. That was all German."

"Here we are." The nurse came back in the room with a shot. "Tell her I'm so sorry again. I didn't mean to cause her pain." She put the needle in the I.V. tube.

"The nurse is sorry for causing you pain. She just didn't understand." I told Ms. Ava, then turned back to the nurse.

"Ms. Ava said that lying flat is the only way she can lay without hurting."

She smiled as she took the needle back out of the IV. "I'll make a note on her chart so someone else won't make the same mistake. "I'm so sorry," She said again, looking at Ms. Ava. "I am so glad you came in," she told me. "She might have been in pain all day til her daughter arrived. Please let me know if she needs anything else."

"Is there anything she can get for you, Ms. Ava, before she leaves?"

"I am fine, now that I am on my back again," She eyed the nurse.

"No, she's fine. Thank you."

"I didn't know you could speak German? Where did you learn it? Do you have family in Germany or something?"

Great, what do I tell her? "Mom, she wants to know how I know German. What do I tell her?"

"The truth." She looked at me and smiled. "Language is your gift."

I turned back to Ms. Ava. "No, I don't have any relatives in Germany that I know of. I just have a gift when it comes to languages."

"Well, you speak it well; not many people talk very clear that have learned it in the US."

David let out a small cry from Mom's arms.

"He's hungry. Does she mind if I fed him before we leave?" Mom asked me to asked Ms. Ava.

"Mom says David is hungry. She would like to know if it is okay if she breast feeds him here before we leave."

"You tell her to go right ahead; it's nice to see her breast feeding. Most women today don't, and that is so sad. It is a special time for mother and baby." She smiled at Mom.

"Go ahead, she doesn't mind at all."

Mom sat down in the chair over in the corner with David. Ms. Ava just smiled in her direction. Her eyes kept half closing, so I was sure the medicine the nurse gave her must have kicked in. It was only a few moments and she was sound asleep. I sat down in the chair by the bed and waited for Mom to finish feeding David. I wondered how Kyle's day was going, so I concentrated on him to tune him in. I didn't want to talk to him, just to see if he was having any better luck than he was the last time I checked.

*"Here you go,"* I heard Kyle telling someone.

*"It feels good to give, doesn't it?"* I heard Dad tell him. *"Now try to help that one,"* He instructed Kyle. *"That's great, son."*

I wondered where they were and who they were helping, but I wasn't about to ask. I listened for clues. They seemed to helping quite a few people, but I couldn't hear any "thank you's" or any response from anyone they were helping.

*"Dad, what about her?"*

*"No, son, not her. Do you feel the push when you get close?"*

*"Yeah, what is that?"*

*"That is His way of saying, not her or not now."*

Where were they that they were helping so many people? A hospital, a homeless shelter, where?

*"But, Dad, why not her and why not now?"*

*"Son, there is one thing you must learn: never question His decisions. He is the Maker of all things and knows what has happened and what will happen. We can only see the here and now. We don't know who her life has touched or who she might touch that will affect another person. But He knows and it is not her time. Understand?"*

*"Sort of... I guess."*

*"Don't dwell on it, son. There is nothing we can do now. But who knows, we might meet her again in the future and then we can help her."*

"Kara," Mom touched my arm. "So, what are the guys up to?" She smiled.

"They are helping people, but I'm not sure where. I haven't asked and don't intend to because last time Dad told me to leave them alone, I've just been listening to them talk."

As we exited the elevator on the first floor of the hospital, Mom handed me David and the car keys. "Would you go put him in his seat? I need to stop by the admin office before we go."

I took David and headed for the Explorer. If I knew Mom, she was going to see if Ms Ava had any kind of insurance to help pay for her bills. Mom had such a big heart. "Take care of others," she would always say, "and you will be taken care of." She truly believed it with every bit of her being. I think Dad had a lot to do with her way of thinking. He cared for everyone that worked for him and treated them like family. Dad mainly had two rules: treat others how you would want to be treated, and a fair day's wage for a fair day's work. If you didn't work hard, you didn't get paid; and if you were rude, you didn't have a job.

*"So, where are you guys?"* Kyle entered my head.

*"Just leaving the hospital. Ms. Ava, from the market, fell and broke her hip, so we came to see her,"* I told him. *"How about you? Where are you guys?"*

*"We have been everywhere. Africa, Iraq, Honduras, you name it. Any hurting country and I think we've been there."*

*"Africa? What were you doing in Africa?"*

*"Dad and I helped out some people as they were digging a well. Then we went to a shelter in Honduras and served food to some needy kids, then we went to a hospital in Iraq and helped victims from the war. It was so cool. You should have seen us."*

I really wish I could have. Here he was helping out people all over the world, and we were just visiting Ms. Ava in the hospital.

*"You did more than just visit. You helped her,"* Dad said interrupting my pity party. *"You have the gift of tongues. You can reach people no one can because of it."*

*"Tongues?"* Kyle asked. *"What do you mean by tongues?"*

*"She can hear and speak in different languages,"* Dad told him, which, now that I really think about it, was really cool, as Kyle would say.

"*So, where are you now?"* I asked Kyle.

"*We're at home. Are you guys coming home soon?*"

*"I don't know, I'm waiting on Mom. She hasn't come out of the hospital yet. I think she's checking on Ms. Ava's bills."*

*"Most likely,"* Dad said. "*We will see you when you get home.*"

I waited another fifteen minutes for Mom before she made it out to the car. As we drove out of the parking lot, we passed Alina going in.

"I'm glad we left before she got here." Mom said.

"Well, did they have insurance or not?" I asked her.

"They have a little, but not much."

"So…"

"Well, let's just say 95% of their bills will now be covered." Mom smiled as she drove.

"As if their insurance picked up the bill?" I asked.

"Of course. How else would it get paid?" She winked at me. "Did you ever find out where the guys are?"

"There at home now. Evidently Dad has had Kyle all over the world, and I do mean that literally." I told her.

Mom laughed. "I am not surprised. He used to pop all over the world when we were in high school."

Mom ran a few errands and then we headed for home. We sat in the living room all afternoon and listened to Kyle tell how *he* had healed a broken leg on a little boy, and how *he* had taken away a fever from a woman, and how *he* had done this, and that. I was really getting sick of him bragging.

"You realize, son, what you are saying?" Dad asked him. Just before he added another *he had done* to his list of things.

"What are you talking about?" He asked. I thought he might tip over; *his head* had gotten so big.

"Who did all those things?" Kyle paused and looked at Dad.

"Oops, I think I better redo my story, hadn't I?"

"Remember, son, there is a fine line between pride and humility. I know that sounds strange, but you must know where the praise goes, and to whom it goes. Never forget that, or you will pay an awful price. With great power comes great responsibility."

Dad was quoting Voltaire, but most people would have thought he was quoting from the movie Spiderman.

"I get it, Dad; I'm sorry." He dropped his head.

"I am not the one that you need to be talking to," Dad told him.

Kyle shook his head got up and went to his room.

"So, let's hear about your day," Dad said, looking at me.

"Oh no, I'm not saying a thing. You can talk to Mom about how our day went. I'm going to do some reading."

I didn't even want to be tempted into boasting or bragging about knowing another language without knowing it. Kyle had sailed that ship, and I didn't even want near the dock. I got up and headed back to my room. I wanted to do a little reading. I wanted something to get my head and heart in line where it was supposed to be because I really did want to brag just a little, especially after listening to Kyle.

I sat down on the bed and picked up my much worn and very shabby looking Bible. I knew it word for word, but I still read it just to keep from taking it out context or confusing the words of different verses. I opened it and Hebrews; Chapter Eleven caught my attention. I read through it. It was on faith, the faith of Abraham, of Noah, of Moses and so many others. I lay down on my bed thinking, *I must be faithful…*

"My lady, why are you out of the castle without an escort?" a young woman asked as I walked through the orchard.

"The outside called to me, and I came." I smiled at her. She was not in the finest of robes, but they were neat and clean.

"Please let me call for Sir Rhett to escort you, my lady."

"I am fine, Nikki. I wouldn't want to bother him at this early hour."

"Then let me go fetch my brother Ryan. He has been up for hours. Please, my lady, you must not wander alone."

"Oh, very well, get him quickly." I turned and strolled through a row of trees. The sun was coming over the horizon and the morning dew was rising. It was so peaceful and quite. I enjoyed mornings; they were so inspiring to me. Nikki and her brother Ryan came running from the barns. They both stopped and bent over, out of breath. "This…is... my …brother, Ryan, my lady," She finally managed to get out.

"Very well," I told her. "Thank you." The girl smiled, did a little curtsy, and ran back up into the orchard.

"She is right, my lady, you shouldn't be out here alone. It's not safe." Ryan looked a little older than Nikki. He, too, was wearing worn clothes, but he looked healthy and clean.

"The mornings are so beautiful and inspiring to me. I really hate not being able to get out and enjoy them."

"Something tells me you get out and enjoy them quite often, but you are never caught," he said with a coy smile.

I had to smile back at him. I didn't tell him whether I did, or didn't. We wandered through the orchard and over into the woods to the East of the Castle. Beams of sunlight were filtering gently through the trees as we walked. A sudden sound of riders came from the West. Ryan whisked me behind a tree and stood in front of me. He was quite taller than me, but if I had been wearing my full robes, I could have been seen. Two riders flew by, us paying no mind. Ryan stood in front of me until they were out of sight. He looked back from where they came.

"What is it?" I asked him. I could see him thinking.

"That was James and Judas. They are always up to no good. I wonder what they have been into this morning."

"Well, what are we waiting for? Let's go find out." I walked towards the road and the direction they had came.

"Let us stay just off the road, my lady, for safety."

"Very well then."

We had not walked far when we heard another set of hooves. Again Ryan pulled me behind him to hide me. This time the man was in no hurry. He just seemed to be traveling. He was well dressed and looked wealthy. After he was out of sight, we started walking again. Two more times I was whisked behind Ryan while travelers passed us by. One was a guard of the castle and the other was Carlos, the village blacksmith. As we walked around a small turn in the road, we spotted a man lying in the road. He had been beaten badly and left for dead. Ryan ran to the man and began to tear his shirt in pieces to bind the man's wounds. Ryan was so gentle and careful with the man.

"I must get him to the village to the doctor," he said. "I am afraid I have to leave you, my lady. Please go straight back to the castle, stay out of sight of the main road and be safe." He gathered the man up in his arms and headed towards the village at a fast pace. I stepped off the road and back into the woods. Three men had passed us on this road, why had not one of them stopped to care for the man? I wondered. All three of them were men of means. Why had it taken Ryan, a man from the stable, to have compassion where the other three had not?

I woke with Mom calling my name. I could hear her coming down the hall.

"Kara, your dad has had it with Heather. He let her …" She came into my room. "Oh, sorry, I didn't realize you were asleep, but your Dad fired Heather and needs you to work."

"I'm surprised she lasted as long as she did. She has called in sick ten days is the last two months." I told Mom as I got up and walked to my closet to get a uniform..

"Change quickly; he needs you as soon as you can get there." Mom left my room "Kyle?" I heard her yell. "Your dad needs you in the restaurant; change and get there as fast as you can."

"Mom, why does he need me, too?" I heard him whine.

"Just change and go help. Now!"

I changed and ran to the bathroom to check myself in the mirror. I brushed through my hair and washed my face. Now that was better, and I felt better too. Mom handed me and apron as I headed out the door. I could hear her yelling at Kyle as I opened the stairwell door.

"Kyle, what is taking you so long" The word long wasn't even out of her mouth when he appeared on the landing below me. He looked up and smiled, then disappeared again.

"What's taking you so long?" he yelled from the bottom of the stairs.

*"Stop teasing her, Kyle, and get in here,"* Dad's voice echoed in my head.

*"Kyle, take tables Seven, Twelve and Twenty-four. Kara you have Eight, Eleven and Twenty-five. Take at least five percent off. Make it ten if they seem really agitated. They have been waiting a while."*

*"I need my…"* I looked down. My order pad was in my apron along with all the regular straws, napkins, and pens, and I could feel my potholder in the back. "*Thanks, Dad.*"

I quickly knew what kind of night it was going to be by the color of the ladies at the first table. They were hot pink!

## CHAPTER 6

# MICHAEL

The next two weeks went by pretty fast since Kyle and I were working at the restaurant every night. Dad had interviewed three people to replace Heathers. He was leaning towards the older gentleman who had applied, but wasn't sure yet. Mom had told him he should try each of them for a week. He liked the idea and George, the older guy, was the first one he called. He would start his trial week tonight. Next would come the young guy, Tony, who looked fresh out of high school. Then Mary would be the last one to work her week. She was trying to work her way through college, which Dad admired, but she was sort of "overly bouncy" as Dad called it. In other words, he thought she was a big flirt. Dad didn't like big flirts. They got good tips at guys' tables, but their service was typically lacking at family tables.

Almost every night, I had dreamed in Camelot Land, which Kyle teased me nonstop about. While him and Dad traipsed all over the world helping people, Mom and I spent most of our days doing normal stuff, which was fine, but I hadn't learned anything.

"Come on, Kara." Mom was already at the top of the next staircase. "I'm going to beat you, and I'm carrying a baby and diaper bag!"

It wasn't like I wasn't carrying anything. I had four bags of groceries hanging off my hands, and they weren't small or light either. Just as Mom hit the top step, a bottle fell from the bag and she stepped on it and fell backwards. David flew out of her arms. Time froze. I could feel everything around me, the walls, the stairs the groceries, Mom and David. With every ounce of my mind and feelings, I pulled David back into Mom's arms and pushed Mom back to her feet. The groceries just seemed to hover around me and then returned to my hands when time sped back up. Mom just stood there a moment, then turned and sat down on the top step. She held David tightly and just stared at me.

"Thank you, Lord!" she closed her eyes and rocked David.

"Mom." I was now right in front of her. "I understand now what you meant by feeling everything around you." She looked up at me on the verge of tears. "Come on." I picked up the bottle and diaper bag. I could see she was still visibly shaken. "Wait here. Let me take these up, then I'll be back for you and David." I walked on up the two flights of stairs and opened the door without even getting out the key. I guess I was still in the moment, too. I didn't even move from the doorway. All the bags floated to the table. I turned to go back for Mom. I could still feel her and David. I opened the door to the stairwell and stopped at the top step. I closed my eyes for a moment, and then opened them. I brought Mom and David to me without moving. Mom was still in a sitting position with her arms wrapped tightly around David. Her eyes were closed too. I put her gently on the very top step.

"Come on, Mom, you need to come in the house," I told her.

She opened her eyes, "You take David. I'm not sure I can even hold myself up." I could still feel her shaking on the inside.

I couldn't imagine what she was feeling. What if I hadn't been there? What if David had fallen? The very thought of it shook me to the core. I took a deep breath, and then took David. Mom pulled herself up with the railing. She took my arm as she stepped off the top step and into the house. The stairwell door opened and we went through. I had left the house door open, and I ushered Mom to the couch and handed David back to her. He was looking at her with such compassionate eyes. He was only a couple of weeks old, but he was already way ahead of the game. He was holding his head up and rolling over at two days old, and now at two weeks old, he was sitting up by himself. But it was the ability he had with his eyes that always amazed me the most. It was as if he understood your mood and could soothe you when you needed it, cheer you up if you were down, or just sit and listen to you when you needed a friend. It sounded crazy for a baby, but I was sure that, just like the rest of us, he was no ordinary baby.

I was so emotionally charged I still could feel everything around me with such clarity. I realized I could hear too. *Oh, Lord, what if I had been alone. What if I had killed David?* Mom's thoughts were coming through loud and clear. *Lord, you told me I was blessed and David would do great things one day. This was for her, wasn't it? She needed to feel and know what she could do, sort of like the emotions You used to teach me. Oh, thank You for letting me know that was all just for her, and that I wasn't that clumsy. Thank You, Lord, thank You.* I had to smile at Mom; she understood things better than she ever let any of us know. And what was this about David? God had told her David would do great things. What kind of things? I knew he was special. He just has that look about him. Mom smiled up at me and got up off the couch.

"Thanks, Kara. I'm glad you were with me. I don't know what I would have done if I had hurt David." She pulled me into a hug.

"I don't like this kind of training," I told her. She looked at me. "It seems while the emotions are running high, I can read your mind."

"So, who else's mind can you read? How about Rhett? Can you read his mind right now?"

I closed my eyes and… I*s she insane? There is no way…* Ok, I was hearing someone, but was it Rhett? *I already have four reports due. I cannot wait to get school over with. Summer, I can't wait for summer. Maybe Kara and I can spend some time together.* Yep, it was Rhett alright.

"Yep, I found him."

"How about…you're Uncle Daniel? Try to find and read him."

I closed my eyes and thought of Uncle Daniel. Several voices came in and out until I focused on one.

*"Listen, Matt, it's so much more than you just wanting to do it. You have to be selfless. It has to be…"* He was talking to Granddad, but he paused right in the middle of his sentence. *"Kara, what are you doing, checking up on us?"* Oh, wow, he knew I was there. *"Sorry Uncle Daniel. I had a sort of breakthrough and was just trying to find certain people."*

*"Yes, I saw that you caught David. Good job. Keep up the good work."*

*"Hey, Kara."* Granddad came into my mind.

*"Hey, Granddad. So, when are you guys coming over?"*

*"Coming in tomorrow. Will probably be late,"* Uncle Daniel told me.

"Well?" Mom asked.

"Sorry. I was talking to Uncle Daniel and Granddad."

"So, where are they?"

"I don't know, but I'll ask." I told her

*"Uncle Daniel, where are you guys?"*

*"Currently, we are in London. Why?"* he asked.

*"Mom wanted to know."*

*"Okay, tell her we will see her tomorrow,"* Granddad interrupted.

*"Okay, Love you guys. See you tomorrow."*

*"Alright, see you then. Love you, too,"* Granddad told me.

*"Love you too, baby doll,"* Uncle Daniel added.

"They are in London. From what I can tell, Granddad is having trouble being selfless, like Kyle."

"Yes, well, I understand. Culture is all about self-gratification. It's a hard lesson to learn, to give without return, to give without wanting in return; to give because you want to because you must to find the true joy of life."

Mom was so passionate about giving. I looked around the room at all we had. I knew the only reason we had so much was because we gave so much. I estimated that Mom and Dad gave about seventy-five percent of our income away to charities. If they saw a need, they filled it. Mom always said that we wouldn't have a thing if we didn't give. God wants cheerful givers, and she always gave the money with her heart.

"You know if it weren't for …." A knock at the door, interrupted her.

"I got it." I walked over to the door. As I did, I noticed a glowing light that was coming in all the cracks around the door. I opened the door slowly, expecting to be blinded with light when I opened it, but there was only a soft grey glow around the man in front of me. He stood tall and proper. His hair was blond and hung just below his shoulders. He was dressed in blue jeans and a black t-shirt. There was a large tattoo of a lion and a lamb on his left arm, on his right was a tattoo of a large sword. He had black biker boots on and a leather jacket thrown over his shoulder. He couldn't have been much older than me, maybe nineteen or twenty, but yet he had an air about him that made you want to take him serious, even if he did look young.

"Can I help you?" I asked. He smiled and looked me square in the eyes. His eyes were a beautiful turquoise.

"Well, is this not what you were expecting?" he asked as he smiled at me.

*It couldn't be, could it?*

"Yes, it could be," he answered my thought.

"Who is it?" Mom asked from behind me.

I opened the door wide so he could come in.

"Michael," I told her as he came around me into the house.

Mom was still standing in front of the couch holding David, who made a noise and reached for Michael as he walked up close to Mom. Michael laid his jacket on the couch and took David from Mom's arms.

"Glad to meet you, too, little man," He told David. Mom and I both stood there staring and speechless. As Michael held David, his aura got so bright that Mom and I both had to look away.

"Sorry," He said and the light faded.

"Does he know who you are?" Mom asked before I had the chance.

"Yes." He looked up at Mom. "You act surprised. Were you not told he would be blessed among men?"

Mom smiled at him "You know that I was." She sounded a little sarcastic.

"Then why are you surprised at him knowing me? I knew of him before he was ever conceived."

Mom dropped her eyes to David, and then looked back at Michael. "You know the answer to that. I am only human and cannot even comprehend such things."

He smiled at her. "Ah, but to know that, you are way ahead of the game."

I just stood there looking at him. An angel mentioned in the Bible was standing in my living room. Okay, so he looked … well, not exactly what I thought an angel would look like, but he did look like a tough guy, so I guess he did sort of look like I expected. I figured either a tough guy or Oriental to be a master weapons and defense teacher, but you add in the angel thing and I really didn't know what to expect.

"Oh, come on." He looked up at me. "Oriental?" He chuckled. "I could have done that, but I figured you would take me more seriously if I looked like I could take off your head." Michael handed David back to Mom. "Come on, Kara, I want to show you something." He picked up his jacket and headed for the door. "When we get back," he told Mom who was wondering when we were going to get home. She wasn't going to ask, but she had just thought it.

Mom just smiled at me as I fell in step behind Michael. He opened the door and went into the hallway and I followed. As I got to the steps, noticed that I was now wearing jeans, boots, a t-shirt, and a leather jacket. A helmet was tucked under my arm.

"Where are we going?" I asked as we went down a flight of stairs.

"You'll see when we get there," He told me.

Outside the back door was a large motorcycle. I couldn't find a Harley sign, but it sure looked like one. Michael slid his helmet on and got on. "Come on," He said and started the engine.

I climbed on behind him. Now what? I wondered.

"You can put your arms around me if you're scared."

I was and I did. He laughed as the bike took off. I finally relaxed bit and it sort of felt good with the wind whipping past me. It really wasn't scary at all. I loosened my grip a bit and thought I might get a motorcycle some day. I felt Michael chuckle more than I heard it.

*"Come on; please tell me where we are going?"* I asked as he weaved in and out of traffic on the interstate.

*"New York City."*

*'New York City! We're in Chicago. It's going to take at least twelve or thirteen hours to get there. Mom was going to freak."*

*"Your Mom will be fine, and it won't take us nearly that long. I need for you to see something, and you will need to see it firsthand, not in any dream."*

*"Show me what?"* I asked.

He didn't answer. Traffic was whipping by on both sides like it was sitting still. Since I was sitting in a taller seat, I tried to look over his shoulder to see how fast we were going. There was no speedometer, no instrument panel of any kind. I didn't even see keys. I glanced up as we whizzed by a state trooper. Crap! We are going to get pulled over for speeding. I just knew we were going way too fast. But I looked back and the trooper was already out of sight. I felt Michael chuckle again. All the vehicles we passed were just blurs now. We were going so fast that, I couldn't tell if they were even cars or trucks anymore.

The bright lights of New York City became visible when the sun dropped behind the horizon. As we came into the city limits, time slowed down. I noticed the cars starting to catch up with us. Ten minutes later, Michael stopped the bike in an alley in the warehouse district.

"Come on. You need to see this." He held out his hands for the helmet and sat it on the bike when I handed it to him. I followed him out into an empty lot. The Hudson River was to our right and rows of warehouses to our left. There were loading doors on the warehouses. As I looked around, the place sort of had a familiar look to it, but I had never been in this part of New York City. Well, not that I could remember.

"Think and remember," Michael told me.

I looked around and then closed my eyes. Why was this place so familiar to me? I could hear all the sounds of the city. I heard a door lifting and opened my eyes. This was the place in my dream. I looked to my left. There was the old factory where the gang had come out of. Yes, I did remember this place. The lot that and the demon! I turned to the alley where I remembered the red glow coming from.

"He was right there. I remember him," I said and looked back at Michael "Was I dreaming, or did it really happen?"

"It hasn't happened yet, but it will."

"How soon?" I asked him.

"Not for a while, but you needed to see that you have the gift of sight. And it can serve to help you or hurt you."

"How can it hurt me?" I understood it was going to happen, but how could it affect me? I wasn't really there when it happened, or at least I didn't think I was.

"You need to learn several things before you are given that knowledge."

"So, why was I shown this then?"

"You needed to see it was real. You could be told, but until you actually see with your own eyes, it really has no effect." Michael started walking back towards the bike. "I have one more thing to show you."

We rode over a few blocks to some houses. My stomach did flips as we passed guys with bandanas and some low riders. We were most definitely in gang territory.

"*Look to your left,*" he told me as we passed a house slowly. Three men were leaning up against a vibrant blue low rider. They stared at us as we passed. One had huge gauges in his ears and a horrible looking scar. I remembered him from my dream. I hugged tightly to Michael as the man pointed towards us.

"*You're safe with me,*" he said soothing my fears.

How in the world could I be so scared? I was with Michael, the mighty Archangel. A sudden wave of calm washed over me. I felt as if his arms were wrapped tightly around me in a shield of protection. I took a deep breath and relaxed. Michael chuckled again. He seemed to have a great since of humor, but I guess he never felt vulnerable and he knew things that I could not comprehend. I bet we were funny things to him. I felt him chuckle again.

"You have no idea. Humans are untrusting and have very little understanding of anything. If you only could grasp even a small amount of how much He cares for you, you wouldn't do the stupid things you do."

I was taken aback by his honesty. We really were stupid to do all the things we did to ourselves, and to cause so much pain to each other. It had to be sad to the Creator that his creations were so careless with all He had given them. The calm I had felt earlier was nothing compared to the sudden warmth and peace now washing over me like a waterfall.

*"Your family is truly blessed by Him,"* Michael told me as if it was to the response to the warmth I now felt.

Why are we so blessed? Why did He choose us? Questions I thought were valid but weren't going to ask because I was sure they were just silly and trivial to Michael.

We rode silently as we headed back toward home. *"Where are you?"* Kyle popped into my head.

*"On our way home,"* I told him. *"What about you? Where are you?"*

*"Home, waiting on you two. Dad is pacing and cooking. I think he's nervous about meeting Michael. So, what's he like?"*

*"He's really cool, not what I expected but extremely cool. And he has a great sense of humor."* I was sure Michael was listening in, but I wasn't going to tell Kyle that.

*"So, where have you been? Mom said you left four hours ago."*

*"New York City."*

*"New York! What are you doing in New York?"*

*"You remember my dream with the gangs?*

*"Yeah."*

*"Well, it is a real place, I even saw the guy with the gnarly scar, and according to Michael, it hasn't happened yet but is going to."*

*"Why did he show it to you then?"*

*"He wanted me to see it, you know, to see that it was a real place and that the people were real. But as far as why, well, I don't understand if I am supposed to try to change it, or stop it, or just what I am supposed to do."*

Kyle was quite for a few minutes. *"I wish I understood even a little bit of what was going on. I feel like I am in a big maze and can't find my way out."*

*"I hear you, bro; me too."*

Michael was still silent when we pulled up behind The Village. I handed him my helmet and we walked to the door. "I know you feel dazed and confused about all that is going on, but stay faithful and things will become clear in time," He told me as he held the door for me to go through.

I stopped in front of him and looked him directly in the eye.

"I know they will," I told him "but human's time moves slowly and the suspense can kill you."

"It's not the suspense you have to watch out for; it's the demons of this world's influence on the people around you."

"Well, at least I can see them coming." I smiled to lift the mood.

"Only if you are looking closely," he answered as the door now shut behind us and we started up the first flight of stairs.

"I think I can see red pretty plainly," I told him. Auras were one thing I did know and saw plainly.

"Influence doesn't show on the outside; you have to look on the inside."

"What do you mean, show on the inside?" I asked him.

"You remember the herdsman Black and his master Mr. Cason?"

He was referring to one of my Camelot dreams. "Yes."

"Do you remember seeing the red tinge in Cason's blue glow?"

"Yes."

"That was influence. He wasn't evil or possessed by a demon or he would have appeared red to you. He was merely being influenced by evil, and so he had a red tinge. You have to look for the influence. Say you passed Cason on the street; you would not see the red. You have to focus on him to see his motivational influences."

Great! How was I supposed to focus on everyone I pass?

"You're not." He answered my thought. "When you come face to face with someone, or when you are trying to influence the situation going on, then is when you need to focus and see what is really going on."

I stopped on the top landing and looked at him. He stepped up beside me and smiled. "Don't worry, Kara, you will know when it's time." He gently pulled me into his arms and hugged me. I felt all warm and soothed again. He chuckled as he held me. "You humans are truly an emotional breed," he said as he let me go and opened the hallway door.

"You make us sound like were dogs or something," I told him as I walked entered.

"The Master has many creations. You are just one of them."

Dad opened the house door before Michael could get his hand on the handle. "Michael," Dad stuck out his hand.

"Matthias," he shook Dads hand. "You have taught your children well." Michael looked back at me, then to Kyle. "They are learning quickly."

"It's you!" Dad said, looked surprised. Michael smiled. Then Dad looked at Mom and said. "Why didn't you tell me it was Michael at the end of our bed?"

Mom just smiled at him then turned to me. "You hungry?"

I really hadn't thought about food, but as soon as Mom mentioned it, my stomach started to growl. It wasn't until then that I even noticed the wonderful smell of rotisserie quail, one of my favorites, filling the house. "Starved." I told her, and we headed to the kitchen while Michael and Dad talked in the living room. Kyle sat down beside Dad on the couch.

"Training will start at seven in the morning," Michael told them.

"How long will you be with us?" Dad asked.

"I will only be here for three months. Then James will come."

"James?" Dad asked.

"It is not important right now. You will know when it's time."

I sat at the bar listening while Mom fixed me a plate: quail with steamed, marinated potatoes and raw mushrooms, all my favorites. I looked up from my plate to find Michael staring at me.

"Sorry. I didn't stop and get you something to eat."

I smiled as I popped a mushroom in my mouth. Michael's concern surprised me. He had hugged me earlier to comfort me and now he was apologizing for not getting me something to eat. I really did not know just exactly what to expect from him. I guess I thought he would be hard or harsh. Why I thought that, I really couldn't say, but I was most definitely wrong.

Kyle had been quiet up until then. "I don't need to eat," he said now.

Michael looked at Kyle, then to me again. *"This coming from the former bottomless pit?"* I heard in my head. I laughed so hard I almost spit food everywhere. Yes, he was definitely unexpected.

"What?" Kyle looked at me. Evidently, I was the only one that heard it.

"Nothing. Just thought it was funny hearing you say that," I told him.

"And what's so funny about it?"

"You have got to be kidding, right?" Mom said. "A couple of weeks ago all that mattered to you *was* eating."

"She has you there," Dad told Kyle.

"I will see you in the morning, sleep well," Michael said, and then headed to the door. "I will be around." He looked back at Dad then left.

I guess we all had been thinking the same thing, but he answered Dad. As soon as the door closed, Dad turned to me. "So…"

"So what?"

"You have been gone the last four hours with Michael. Fill us in."

Dad asking to be filled in hit me as a little strange. How many times in the last two weeks had he been in my head, no matter if I wanted him there or not, and now he was asking for details? Was he really not aware of what had happened? Kyle had even talked to me, and Dad was always listing to us talk.

"I tried to find you and listen, but I couldn't" Dad answered my thoughts. "I guess Michael didn't want me there."

"Sorry, Dad. It was a weird afternoon." I had finished eating so I walked over and flopped down on the couch. "We went to New York City…"

## CHAPTER 7

# LET THE FUN BEGIN

My screaming alarm clock woke me. I turned over and pushed the button. 6:30, the numbers read, all glowing in green. I was supposed to meet Michael in the studio at 7:00. My thoughts stopped on Michael for a moment and our trip yesterday. How was I supposed to change things or influence them? I got up and walked to the bathroom and wash my face and pull my hair up. As I looked in the mirror, I noticed what I was wearing. Tank top and boxers, not my normal pj's. Why in the world had I put… Wait, I didn't remember getting ready for bed. The last thing I remembered was Michael leaving and Dad asking me where we had gone. I didn't remember anything after that, not anything. I walked back up the hall to my room and got dressed.

"*Kyle,*" I called in my head. "*Where are you?*" Only silence. "*Kyle!*" I yelled in my head. I stepped out my door and tapped on his door.

*"He's fine. He's with your Dad and Uncle."* Michael came into my head. "*Your breakfast is on the bar. Please finish it and come down to the studio as soon as you can.*"

*"Ok,"* I answered him. *"Thanks."*

A large glass of milk, an egg with cheese, and a sliced apple sat on the bar. I ate as quickly as I could, put the plate in the sink, and then headed for the studio. Michael was standing in the middle of the room with his eyes closed when I entered. He was dressed in a black pair of pants with no shirt, which was another thing unexpected.

I found myself admiring his well-formed chest and eight-pack abs when I noticed he had opened his eyes and was staring at me. Crap! What in the world was I thinking?

Michael chuckled, "What am I suppose to look like," He asked, "a middle aged man with a beer belly? I don't think so." He smiled at me.

I smiled back, but dropped my head. I knew I must have had a red face. After all he had caught me admiring him. He was quite handsome in a rough, biker-angel kind of way.

A sudden noise caught my attention and I looked over to find David lying on a blanket in the corner.

"Your Mom is running some errands and I'm watching David." As he spoke, David lifted into the air and floated across the room into his arms. "Now, let's get started," he said. "The first thing you must know is not to think, but to trust."

"What?" Trust not think, what was he talking about?

He grinned. "When you are being attacked, the first reaction is always best. Don't think, just do." He chuckled. "Or do not." His grin got even bigger.

"You're quoting Yoda?" I was completely dumbfounded. He had shown me that he was not what I was really expecting, but quoting Yoda from Star Wars. I had to laugh. I always thought that God had to have a sense of humor. I mean, look at some of the animals He made. It was like He was just playing when he made the duckbilled platypus. But I guess I never really thought His angels would have a since of humor, but why not?

"So, you want me to use the force?"

"Yes, but the force I want you to use and trust is the Spirit. I want you to let it lead you. Let it consume you when you are in battle. It is the only part of you that you can trust when fighting a…I don't like the word supernatural, so let's use the word Devine. Trust it fighting on a Devine level. Let it have full control over you." Michael walked up and handed David to me. "Protect him at all costs. No matter what might happen or what you think will happen. It doesn't matter. What does matter is his safety!"

Michael turned and walked over to the side of the room. I looked down at David, who was staring up at me with those intense onyx eyes. As I looked at him, a strange feeling arose from deep inside me. It was something new, yet it felt familiar at the same time. I looked up towards Michael and saw three objects flying in my direction. Just like in the stairwell, things seem to slow down and I could feel everything around me. I took a step to the left and let the knives slowly pass us, then let time speed up again. The three hit the wall behind us and shattered the mirror with a loud crash. David laughed in my arms. I was expecting him to cry at the noise, but instead, he just laughed.

I turned to find the mirror back in place and the knives gone. I turned to glare at Michael. How dare he put David in harm's path just to give me a lesson? Here he was telling me to protect him, and he himself was trying to hurt him. Michael chuckled, and anger flared in me. I was so mad I picked up a large sword from the shelf with my mind and hurled it at him. I watched as the sword disintegrated in mid-air. Michael never even flinched, but set to throwing anything and everything on the shelves at me and David. I slowed time, but there were too many objects coming to side step, so I curled David in my arms and turned my back to the hurling objects and waited.

"Why did you turn back?" Michael asked. I looked up to find him standing in front of me.

"Never turn your back! Always keep the danger in your sight and never look away! Stand your ground." He sounded sort of angry.

Michael disappeared right before me and the objects that had once been behind me were now all coming from the direction I was now facing. I slowed them again and turned my attention to David. He lifted out of my arms and floated to the ceiling. The many knives and other objects were now mere inches from me. I held my hand up and they all stopped and fell to the ground.

"Good," Michael said from beside me, where he now stood. David drifted back into my arms. "Never doubt what you can do. You will never fail unless you are supposed to. Understand?"

"Sort of, I guess. But how will I know if I am not suppose to do something?"

"It all comes down to that one word you have heard several times lately."

I knew exactly which word he was talking about: selflessness. Michael smiled at me and took David from my arms.

"Your Mom is here."

All the stuff on the floor disappeared and reappeared back on the shelves. The door to the studio opened and Mom walked in. Michael had David's stuff and met her halfway across the room.

"I hope he wasn't any trouble," she said as she took David from Michael's arms.

"Not at all." Michael smiled at her.

"How's it going?" she asked. "And where's your brother?"

Michael answered her question, since I didn't know. "Matthias took him to do some training with Daniel and Matthew."

"Okay." Mom said. "I'll let you two get back to work then. Thanks again," she told him as she turned and left.

"You planned for Mom to leave David, didn't you?"

"Me? Now, whatever gave you that idea?" He gave me a dumb look. "Come here and look at all the weapons. Tell me which one you like the best."

I walked over and strolled up the wall looking at each knife, sword, gun and weapon on the shelves. They were unique in one way or another. I liked the swords, but you needed a lot of upper body strength and they wouldn't be easy to hide. Guns were cool, too, but they were noisy and you needed to fire them accurately. Throwing stars you could hide, but there was the accuracy thing again. I guess out of all the things on the shelves, I liked daggers the best. They were smaller, but not tiny, and you could stab, slash, or just do about anything with them. I guess if you had to, you could throw them. I think I liked the fact that they were just small and cute. I liked one in particular. From hilt to tip, it couldn't have been more than ten inches long; the blade on it was only about five inches long.

"Very nice choice." Michael picked up the dagger. "I am a sword wielder myself, but daggers are nice." He handed me the dagger. "How would you hold a dagger?" he asked me.

"I thought you were going to show me how." I looked up at him.

He smiled. "I want to know how it feels in your hands."

"Oh. Well, how is it supposed to feel? I mean, I can hold it this way..." I held the dagger by the hilt with the blade pointing up. "It feels fine, but you could only use it for poking at someone. But if I hold it this way..." I turned the blade so it was back towards me and turned my wrist. "It seems like this would work better for slashing at someone, or for stabbing someone."

"Very good." Michael told me. "That is the right answer. There are a number of ways to hold the dagger that can make it more productive. Having skill is all in the knowing which way to hold it to the best advantage for the situation you're in."

"Ah, that is the real trick," I said.

A sword appeared in Michaels hands. "Come on, let's see what you can do."

"Against you? With tha? Are you crazy? I can't do anything yet. I thought you were supposed to be teaching me how to use it." I backed away from Michael.

"The best way to learn is by using it." He stepped towards me as he raised the sword up over his head.

I took another step backwards. Was he crazy? I have no idea how to use a dagger, and what chance did I have against someone with a sword?

"Defend yourself, Kara, with whatever means you have. Not only with what is in your hands, but with things you have already learned."

"With what I've already learned? I haven't learned anything yet."

"Do I need to bring David back for you to defend him?"

I looked at Michael with wide eyes. I would do what it took to defend David. "No," I said as I planted my feet.

"Good, now do as if David was behind you and you were protecting him. As I said earlier, be led, follow the Spirit. Let it take the lead and follow it and you will never fail."

Michael suddenly lunged towards me. I side stepped and spun to my left. I had the dagger poised to guard myself. Michael turned and came at me again. I blocked the sword with the dagger so it did not slice my forearm open. Michael circled, and I followed his every move. Like earlier, I noticed I could feel all the things around me in the room clearly. I took the opportunity and lifted three knives from the shelves and sent them toward Michael while his back was turned. The three hurled across the room, and I lunged toward him with my dagger raised. He caught my arm and flung me to the floor.

"Nice," he said. When he turned and I could see the three knives sticking in his back. "Keep your opponent off guard."

He held out his hand to me. "Let's go again."

I took his hand and he pulled me up. "Let me try something small, too." He walked to one of the shelves. When he turned I looked at his back and the knives were gone. Michael picked up a gnarly-looking knife. It had two sharp points on the end with a serrated side and a smooth side. He raised the knife as he sprinted across the room towards me.

Keep your head, Kara, I thought as I stepped to the side. I caught his arm with mine and spun him around, and caught his jaw with the hilt of my dagger. He fell to the floor, but not before he caught my leg and I toppled down on top of him.

"Good, but I win this one."

I pulled up from him. "How do you figure… Oh." As I got up, I could see the hilt of his knife sticking out of my stomach. I reached for it, but it disappeared, just like the ones from his back. I rubbed my hand across my stomach.

"You're not going to get hurt while with me, no matter what happens."

I looked up to find him still sitting on the floor, but smiling at me. This time I held my hand out to him.

"That was a good move, but it was sloppy and that is why I was able to catch your foot. You need to move faster and get out of the way after you strike. We are going to take a break so you can go eat lunch, but be ready after lunch. It is going to get tough."

He was right. After lunch it was nonstop fighting all afternoon. He would get a different weapon every time and come after me. I hit, kicked, and threw things at him to stay out of his reach and to keep him off guard. Each time the battle ended, he would give me a small piece of advice on how to stay out of reach next time. Most of the battles belonged to him, but I won several.

"Let's try some of these now."

I got a little nervous when he picked up a gun instead of a knife. The gun he chose was semi-automatic, and he shot off several rounds in seconds. I froze and time slowed. There were bullets everywhere.

Michael was suddenly behind me talking over my shoulder into my ear. "What is it you feel like you need to do?"

I stuck my hand up as if to stop to the bullets. They disintegrated as the met with my hand.

"Very good. Remember to always follow the Spirit, no matter how crazy you may think it is that it asks you to do. That will be all for today. You need rest, and I need to go see your brother now." He smiled and was gone.

I looked around the room. It didn't even look like we had been in there. All the mirrors that had been shattered from time to time were now back in place; shelves that had been toppled were all neat and tidy. I had learned quite a bit today.

I ate a light supper, showered, and went to bed. Mom had tried to talk to me, but I was worn out. It was as if once I left the studio, I could hardly move. I hadn't noticed being that tired while there. I guess the adrenaline had worn off and I was totally exhausted.

"My Lady, my Lady," I heard a small voice call from behind me. I took in my surroundings as I turned towards the voice. I was walking on a dirt road. On both sides of me the countryside spread out as far as I could see. I had three guards with me. A young girl was running towards me.

"My Lady, please wait!" The young girl was very worn looking. Her clothes were just rags, her face was smudged with dirt, and her hair was long and stringy. I stopped and knelt to be on her level.

"What is it, sweetie?" I could see trails running from her eyes from where she had been crying. I opened my arms and she buried her head in my shoulder. "What has happened that has upset you so, little one?" Tears flowed freely down her cheeks and onto my shoulder. I pulled her back to look at her face. "What is it?"

"They are going to kill my mother," she struggled to get out through her sobs.

"Who is?" I asked her.

"A bunch of men. They came to the house and called her some really bad names and drug her out into the street."

"What is your mother's name?"

"Miriam."

"Guard." I stood to face the men with me. "You two run to the village and find this child's mother before she is harmed. Hold her at the castle until I arrive and get to the bottom of this." I looked back at the child. "Run and my guards will follow you. Take them to your mother and I will be there soon. Can you do that?"

"Yes ma'am," she said, and then darted back up the road.

"Run," I told two of the guards. The girl was already way ahead of them.

The other guard and I followed at a quick pace. When I arrived at the castle, the guards had not arrived with Miriam yet. I paced back and forth in the throne room hoping they had not arrived too late. Suddenly, the two doors in the back swung open and five men came in, followed by the guards and a young woman. The young girl was holding the woman's hand.

As the group came before me, I motioned to a young servant girl to the side of the room to come to me.

"Yes, my Lady." She curtsied before me.

"Mary, would you please take the young girl and give her something to eat. See that she has a bath and some clean clothes as well."

"Yes, my Lady" Mary went to the young girl and knelt beside her to talk to her. The girl held tight to her mom's hand. I walked down and knelt in front of the girl.

"What is your name, sweetie?"

"Kayla," she said quietly.

"My sweet Kayla, this is Mary. She is a good friend of mine. She is going to the kitchen to fix you and your mother something to eat. Would you help her? I promise I will take care of your mother and she will be down to eat something with you in a little while." Mary stood up and held out her hand to Kayla.

"Go ahead, Kayla, I will be down in a few minutes," her mother urged her.

Kayla looked up at her Mom. Miriam gave her daughter a hug. "Make me something good."

"I will." She let go of her mother's hand and took Mary's.

"Now, what is this all about?" I said as I stood. All five men started talking at once. "One at a time. You go first," I said pointing to the short, chubby man who looked like he hadn't bathed in weeks.

"This woman has stolen from my customers and must be punished."

"And you are?" I asked.

"I am Malcolm Dunn. I own the tavern."

"And what has she stolen?"

"She has stolen money from a client." He pointed to the man standing beside him.

"Client? What kind of client? You said customer a moment ago and now client."

"Miriam is one of my working girls, and she stole from her client."

I looked at Miriam, who had stood quietly, looking at the floor.

"Miriam."

The woman looked up at me. "Yes, my Lady."

"Did you steal from this man?"

"Yes, my Lady. I took one extra dollar."

"Why?"

"Malcolm is supposed to give me five dollars out of every fifteen I earn, but has not been giving me anything for the last month, so I took the extra dollar to get Kayla something to eat."

I turned to Malcolm. "Why are you not giving her these agreed upon wages?"

"Her business has been slow and she is costing me money." The man angrily looked at Miriam.

My anger flared at the man and I had to hold my tongue. Miriam had evidently agreed to this arrangement.

"If you entered into an agreement with her on her pay, then you will pay her what you agreed on, no matter how your business is. If you get the same amount, then so does she." I looked at the man standing beside Malcolm. He had not said a word.

"What do you have to say about this?"

"I did not know Malcolm wasn't paying her. I would not have said anything if I had known it was to feed her child. I would have paid her myself for her time."

"From now on, she will be paid for her services directly, and you will be paid when the men leave." I looked at Malcolm. "You will pay her for a month of services rendered."

"I don't have..."

"You have plenty. Now pay her, or she will own the bar and you will be the harlot."

Malcolm pulled a money pouch from his hip, and then pulled out five coins and gave them to Miriam. She didn't say a word, but you could see it was not the right amount.

"Malcolm, shall I hold you until you pay the full amount?" He pulled ten more coins out and handed them to her.

I looked hard at Malcolm. His blue aura had a small red tinge in it.

"What punishment were you going to give Miriam?" I asked Malcolm as he put his pouch back under his shirt.

"Three days in the stock with no food, only water." Malcolm smiled a sly grin.

"That shall be your punishment then."

"What?" He looked up.

"I gave you two chances to pay Miriam the right wages and you still shorted her, so for three days, you shall be in the stocks and she will run your tavern."

"This is an outrage!" he yelled at me. "She shall never run my tavern."

"Very well. Guards, get him out of my sight. Take him to the stocks and guard him for three days. No food or water. And close the tavern and make sure it stays that way for three months."

"Three months? I will go bankrupt! My kids will starve!"

"You should have thought of that before you starved someone else's child." I turned my back to the man, then slowly turned back to him. "I shall give you one more chance: Miriam runs your tavern for a full week, or it will be closed for three months. Choose."

"You said three days."

"Make it two weeks."

"But you said three days."

"Three weeks, take it or leave it."

"Alright, alright, three weeks."

"You cannot enter the tavern while she is running it."

"What!"

"Shall we make it a full month?"

"Okay, okay, I won't go near the tavern for three weeks."

I looked hard at Malcolm again and saw that the red was gone. His head was now low and he looked truly sorry.

"All of you, be gone. Miriam, I would like to talk to you." The men turned and left the chamber.

"Yes, my Lady." Miriam stepped closer to me.

"Can I ask why you are in this line of work?"

Miriam dropped her gaze to the floor. "My husband was killed in a fight at the tavern six years ago. Malcolm had pity on me and gave me a job waiting tables. But one day, something changed. I remember the day like it was yesterday. Malcolm took me in the back room and told me he found a way for me to make three times my wages in one week.

Of course, I was eager to make more money for Kayla, and I so I told him I was in. It wasn't until he locked me in a room with a man for the night that I found out what the job was. Over the years, I just got used to it, I guess. It's not what I wanted for myself, but until recently, I made enough for me and Kayla, but over the last six months I have gotten paid less and less, and last month I got paid nothing."

"I am sorry to hear about your misfortune. But listen to me, Miriam for the next three weeks, the tavern is yours. Run it well and you will earn enough money to get you and Kayla out of this life you have been stuck in. Run it like it is yours. Treat people fairly and honestly. Look at all the things you have seen go on in the tavern. Use what works and get rid of things that don't."

"Yes, ma'am."

"If you run the tavern and it succeeds greatly, who knows, Malcolm may keep you on. Remember not to forget about him and his family. He may not be able to step foot in the place, but it is still his and it is what he lives on, so don't do him as he did you. Treat him kindly. Make sure he and his family are well taken care of, especially during the next three days."

"I will."

"Mom, are you ready to eat?" Kayla came running into the room from the side door with Mary not far behind her.

"Sorry, my Lady. She was getting antsy."

Kayla was in a clean dress with her hair in nice braids down her back. She smelled like rose petals and bread.

"She sure is," I told Kayla. Miriam looked up at me and I nodded at her to go. "I will be watching your progress, Miriam. If you need help, don't hesitate to come ask me."

Miriam smiled and paused as she reached the side door. "Thank you, my Lady."

I walked back and sat down on my chair.

## CHAPTER 8

# NO FEAR

My alarm was screaming when I woke. I lay in the bed thinking about the dream. Rhett wasn't in it, for the first time since I had been dreaming in Camelot. I wondered if that was important or not. It had been a week since I had talked to him, too. I also realized that Kyle wasn't there pouncing on me as soon as I woke. "*Kyle,*" I called for him in my head, "*where are you?*" No answer came back. I closed my eyes and thought hard about Kyle; maybe I could find him. The only thing I found was that I was all of the sudden not alone. I opened my eyes to find Michael standing at the foot of my bed.

"Get up; we have a big day ahead of us. Don't worry about your brother. He's with your dad and uncle again."

"What about his training?" I asked.

"He is being trained, but at night while you're asleep. Now come on, we have things to do. Get dressed and eat," he said then disappeared.

I guess it made sense for him to train at night, since he didn't need sleep anymore. I guess I had just assumed we would be trained together, but it wouldn't have been the first time I assumed wrong. I climbed out of my warm, comfy bed and got dressed, then headed for the kitchen.

"So, I see you're finally up," Mom greeted me as I walked past the sofa where she was sitting. "I guess you'll be training again all day then?"

"Yeah, I think so." I told her as I opened the fridge to look for something to eat.

I heard Mom giggle from the living room. "I think your breakfast has just been delivered," she said.

I turned to find a plate on the bar. Two pancakes, a piece of ham and some apple slices, along with a glass of milk. "I guess you're right," I told her as I got a fork from the drawer and sat down on a bar stool. "So, what are you and David up to today?" I looked back at her. "Where is David?" I hadn't noticed when I walked by that he wasn't with her.

"He's with your dad and brother today, so I have the whole day to myself I guess." She said with a sort of sad tone.

"Sorry, Mom."

"Why are you sorry?" Michael said from behind me suddenly. "She is with us today. David going with Matthias was planned."

I turned to look at Michael and Mom. "She's training with us."

"Yes." He smiled at Mom. "You need to eat, too." He pointed to the bar beside me where a second plate now sat. "I will see you both in fifteen minutes." Then he was gone.

"Well, come on, Mom. You better eat and get dressed. He doesn't like to be kept waiting."

As I watched Mom eating, I wondered how Michael would train her. She didn't have any special ability anymore…or did she? Mom seemed to be lost in thought, too, because neither of us said a word as we finished our breakfast. Once done, Mom went and got dressed, and I waited for her. Together, we then went to the studio.

"How in the world am I supposed to train?" Mom asked as she put her hand on the door handle and looked at me.

"No clue." I told her. "But I'm sure if Michael says you are, then you can." I gave her a smile.

Michael stood in the middle of the room with his back to us as we entered. He never moved or said a thing until we got close to him.

"Stop worrying about what you think you can or cannot do." He turned to face us. "You, of all people, should know not to question that." He looked at Mom.

Mom took a deep breath to relax herself. "I know, but I'm only human."

"This morning, we are going to take it easy. Then later, we'll get to the hard stuff." He turned and looked at Mom. "Starting today, you, like the rest of your family, will have your gifts back for a time." I looked at Mom and her bright pink aura now had a shiny white glow to it. "You were just learning how to use them when you lost them, so now you need to be trained, just like your daughter."

The rest of the day went by so fast. Mom was amazing. She was so much better at reacting to things than I was. She could take Michael down almost every time. Watching her was like watching an action movie; she had all the moves. Michael had commented that he wasn't sure why he was told to train her; she was already good. By night fall I had learned a lot just from watching Mom. I fell in bed after a long hot shower around nine, but she stayed up to wait for Dad and Kyle. Michael had told her the guys would be home soon. I lay there going over things in my head. It seemed like I did that a lot lately, but I'm not sure why. I never could figure out anything.

What was happening? I sat straight up in bed. It took me a few minutes to get my bearings. The clock read 2:00 am. I was breathing hard, but I couldn't remember what I had been dreaming. I looked around my room. I had a feeling that I wasn't alone. Then I felt a sudden calm. Michael appeared at the foot of my bed.

"What's going on?" I asked him.

He walked around to the side of my bed. "Come with me." He held out his hand.

I reached up and took hold of it and instantly found myself standing on the edge of a cliff. I could see clouds below me, but not ground. Michael stood beside me. I still had his hand in mine as I took a step back from the edge.

"Are you afraid you'll fall?" he asked.

Afraid… I don't know that it was fear that made me step back but maybe just a reaction. I knew I was with Michael and he would keep me safe so…afraid…No, I don't think it was fear. "No." I turned to look his in his turquoise eyes.

"Good." He let go of my hand.

The wind left my lungs, along with a scream when he shoved me off the cliff. I felt time slow as I toppled off the edge. My mind raced while everything seemed to be passing me in slow motion. Why had he pushed me off? I turned to look for the ground that I was sure to meet. Clouds were still all around me and I couldn't see anything through them. I was now aware of the fear gripping my heart. Was I going to die? I closed my eyes.

The story of Isaac came into my mind and how his father was to sacrifice him even though God had told him he would make Abraham a great nation from him. Had he known God would stop him, or did he just have faith the God would do what he said, no matter what? The fear that gripped me loosened as I thought of what Michael had told me. I was to protect David, and David was not here. It was not my time to die. A sudden sound of wings above me brought my eyes wide open. I was still surrounded by clouds and could not see the bird, just hear it. I felt arms surround me as I found myself standing back on top of the cliff with Michael's arms around me. He was smiling at me.

"Why?" I asked him.

"You were made for a purpose. Trust in that."

"I know, but why push me from the cliff?"

"You said you weren't scared. You needed to realize that you really are. But just as you also discovered, you have a purpose, just like Isaac."

As Michael talked the clouds around us lifted and I could see the mountains spread out around us.

"You have so much to face yet, and you need to face it without fear, without reservations. You have to react with a clear mind."

I turned to face the cliff once again. I pulled from Michaels arms and stepped directly to the edge. I could now see the bottom. I glanced back at Michael and smiled and then I turned back to the cliff and stepped off. I felt the wind rush past me as I fell. I could see the edge of the cliff getting smaller. Time had not slowed; it now rushed by. As I looked at the cliff's edge, Michael himself stepped over the edge and was now not far behind me. But as I watched two enormous wings appeared at his back, and with two large flaps, he was in arm's distance of me. He held out his hands and I took them. Our decent stopped.

"Look down," he told me.

Just as I did, he let go of my hands and my feet touched the ground. We had been mere inches away when he stopped our fall. I looked back up. He was now standing beside me, no wings in sight.

"I will always be near, but do not test me, just as you must not test the Maker. You have been in my charge since the beginning and will remain that way."

It all made since now. His was the voice I heard growing up. His were the arms that gave me comfort when I was scared. Just like the day we were in New York. I had felt that comfort so many times in my life, but until now, I had not put it together. He had been there, just like today. He had saved me with his hands and with his wings of protection.

Suddenly, we were back in my room. The clock read 2:00 am.

"Go back to sleep, Kara, because tomorrow the real training will start."

Real training? What had we been doing if not real training?

"Fear will no longer hold you back," he told me, and then he was gone.

I leaned back in my bed and closed my eyes.

*"Kyle,"* I called out in my head.

*"Yeah?"* he replied for once. It was nice to hear his voice. It felt like I hadn't talked to him in weeks. "What are you doing awake?" he said aloud, suddenly sitting on my bed beside me.

"Where did you go today?" I asked as he stretched out beside me.

"Dad and I had David, so we visited some of the homeless shelters today. We served lunch at St. Michael's, and then supper with Father Hearting."

"So, you were in the city all day?"

"Yeah. What about you? Did you train with Michael?" Until then I hadn't even thought about Mom.

"You know that Mom has her power back now, don't you?"

"What? No! Well, I guess that explains the big smile she was wearing when we came in, but she never said a word, at least not to me, anyway."

"You should see her in action. She trained all day with Michael and I, and she kicked his butt all over the place."

"Are you serious?"

"Yeah. I think I learned more from her than him. How has your training been going?"

"Okay, I guess. He's tough; sure glad he has a great since of humor. I think he laughs at me more than anything, but I'm just glad he's not yelling at me instead."

"He's good like that, isn't he? Does he give you a helpful hint every time you do it wrong?"

"Yeah." He smiled. "Granddad just says it's his age when he fails."

"Granddad is training with you?"

"Yeah, sort of. He's is mainly just my punching bag. I feel sorry for him sometimes, but Michael assures me that I'm not hurting him. Granddad says I'm not, but it just feels weird punching and hitting him."

"I haven't even seen him or Uncle Daniel yet."

"Really? Well, things have been crazy around here, especially the last few days. What is tomorrow? All my days run together. This not sleeping has good sides and bad."

"Friday… I think. It has been busy, huh?" I figured he was talking about working so much. He was never much on work.

"Working has nothing to do with it," he answered my thought. "It's just the never ending thing. I don't get tired or hungry, but it just never ends. The only time I do have by myself is the few hours when Dad stops to spend time with Mom and David, and it's so late that I can't even call Kelley."

"I don't imagine she would care how late it is. She would just be glad to hear from you."

"You haven't talk to Rhett either, have you?"

"No."

"Maybe we'll get Sunday off and can go do something with them." Kyle got still and quiet for a few seconds. "I gotta go. Michael's calling me. See you later."

I glanced over at the clock. It was going on 3:00. I closed my eyes.

*"Thanks,"* I told Michael in my head. *"I've missed him."*

*"I am not the one you should be thanking; I am just a servant like you."* He was right. I needed to be a little more thankful and let some praises go up.

*"Oh mighty Maker of all heaven and earth..."*

My alarm screaming beside my head woke me once again. I rolled over and reached to shut it off, but it quit before my hand reached the button.

"You better get up before your Mom comes in and drags you out of that bed."

I smiled and opened my eyes. "Granddad!"

"Hey, sweet pea. I wanted to say hi while no one seemed to be paying attention to me." I sat up as he sat down on the edge of the bed.

"So, how you like the angel gig?" I asked.

"Well, I've never felt better in all my life. I have the strength of a twenty-year-old." He raised his arms and flexed his muscles, then laughed. "I must say it's pretty cool. So, what about you? I hear you can do some pretty amazing things."

"I am not sure amazing is the word. Mainly I just feel confused and lost."

"I hear you there. I wish I knew what I was supposed to do. I feel like a lost puppy most the time."

"What are you guys doing today?" I asked him.

"Well, currently we are waiting on Daniel. He was contacted by some guy out west about some kind of job. Not real sure, but Daniel thinks we are supposed to help him, so he has gone to talk to him and we are just helping out at a local shelter serving breakfast. Well, me and Kyle are serving. Your Dad is doing the cooking. Big shocker there." He smiled "Everyone was busy and I snuck off. I've been around for a few days and hadn't got to see you yet." He pulled me close to him. "I miss you, sweet pea."

"I miss you too, Granddad."

"So, here is where you are." Dad appeared in my room. "Hey, honey, how you been?" Dad bent over and gave me a hug.

"Good. I miss you, though."

"Me, too babe. Maybe Sunday we can all sit down and visit for a while. Sort of regroup and see what's going on with each other."

"You promise?"

"No, I better not promise anything I might have to break, but I'll try to make it happen."

"We need to get back, Matt," he told Granddad. I climbed out of bed when Granddad stood up and I gave them both a big hug.

"Love you guys."

"Love you, Kara," Dad said.

"Love you, too, sweet pea," Granddad said just before they both disappeared.

"Kara," I heard Mom yell from the kitchen. "Hurry up; you don't want to keep Michael waiting."

I slid into a pair of pants, grabbed the first shirt in my closet, and ran to the bathroom to wash my face. I then grabbed my socks and shoes and headed for the kitchen.

"Morning, Mom." I sat down on a bar stool and pulled my socks on.

"Was that your Dad I heard in your room?"

"Yeah, he and Granddad popped in to say hi."

"That was nice." She was fixing David some cereal. He was sitting in a high chair by the bar. Man, he was growing quickly. "Are you coming today?"

"No, I'm back in Mommy mode today, so it's just you and Michael again. Today you're going to kick his little angel butt all over the place." She looked up and smiled. "I just know it."

"I doubt it." Michael's voice came from behind me.

"Who knows, I just might," I told him as I finished tying my sneaker.

"We may never know if you don't hurry up and eat," He told me as he walked past me to David. "Hey, little man." He stopped in front of David. "Can I feed him?" he asked Mom. "It will keep me busy while she eats."

"Sure, it will give me a few minutes to get dressed. But you may be wearing most of it by the time he's done." Mom handed Michael the bowl and spoon and darted off to get dressed.

He looked up and smiled at me. "You ready for some real training today?"

"As ready as I'll ever be, I guess."

David was playing with the food and it was going everywhere. More was hitting Michael than was going in his mouth. Watching Michael trying to dodge the projectile cereal was priceless. I got choked twice, I was laughing so hard.

"Oh, my," Mom said as she came back into the kitchen. David blew hard, but this time Mom stopped it before it hit Michael. "David, stop playing with Michael; you're supposed to be eating it."

The glob of cereal hung in the air just inches from the already covered Michael. He stood up, laughed, and was instantly clean. "You ready?" He asked me.

"Yep, let's go. I am feeling lucky today. Maybe I can get you, too." I winked at Mom and David.

Michael opened the house door, and as we stepped into the hall, I found I was wearing jeans and boots. I had a helmet tucked under my arm again.

"So, where are we going this tme?" I asked.

"We could use some more space, so a road trip is in order."

The ride on his bike wasn't long, but nothing took long on that bike.

"Today it is going to get tough," he said as he took my helmet from me.

Michael had parked at the end of a large meadow. Trees were on one side and a large rock wall was on the other. Michael pointed towards the tree line. Three men stepped out into the meadow. They all looked like gang members, with their leather jackets and gloves. One of the three carried a baseball bat. The others didn't seem to have anything, but I was sure their weapons were just concealed.

"The object is to get to him before they do." He pointed to a young man standing between me and the three men. "And keep him safe at all costs." The young man's back was to me but he looked like... no it couldn't be. He turned and I was starring at Rhett.

"Go!" I heard Michael yell.

The three started running towards Rhett, and I took off at a hard run. What in the world was Michael thinking, bringing him here? I reached out with all my might and flung the three men backwards towards the tree line. What was Rhett going to think? The three men got back up and started running again. I got to Rhett and as I pushed him behind me I noticed his turquoise eyes. Ah, Michael was not the only angel here. I felt the knife leave one of the man's hands before I saw it. I deflected it easily enough and again flung them backwards towards the tree line. One of the three pulled a gun and started shooting as he ran to my left. The other two went to my right. I slowed time just as the bullets left the barrel of the gun. The two men to my right had split, and they now came from all directions. The bullets disintegrated just inches from us. I felt three throwing stars being let loose and turned my attention to the man for only a second, then felt the ball bat hit my head.

I woke with Michael standing over me. "It's hard to focus on more than one, isn't it?"

He held out his hand and pulled me up. The four men were nowhere in sight.

"Called in a few friends, did you?" I asked him.

He smiled at me. "They had you fooled at first."

"Only until I saw those turquoise eyes. Do you all have turquoise eyes?"

"No, not all of us." He started with his helpful hints. "You need to feel everything around you. You felt the knife and the stars, but the bat was an object you already knew was there, and it got past you. If you already see it, connect to it. Know what that object is doing. Own it." The four men appeared again. This time they were all standing together in jeans and black t-shirts. "You ready to go again?"

"So, who am I protecting this time?" I asked, but did not take my eyes off the others as they slowly walked towards us.

"Me," he said. The voice was not his though. I dared not look at him and take my focus from the four, but I knew if I did I would find Rhett standing there.

"Fine, then; stay behind me."

I watched the men as they split up and start to circle us. I reached out with every feeling I had. I didn't want to be caught off guard again. I felt of each of them and as I did so, two of the four let knives go. This time I needed to do the unexpected and I let the knives get a few inches before I stopped them and pulled them out of the air. Now I, too, had weapons. The one that was now behind me fired a gun as the one in front of me charged us. I pushed Rhett to the ground and sat on his chest as I let one of the knives fly towards the man rushing us and leaned back as the bullets flew over us. The man rushing us dodged the knife, but was struck with the bullets. He immediately vanished. Only three left. The two on either side of me came at us. I jumped up and pulled Rhett up, and then pushed him behind me. The one with the gun walked towards us, firing as the other two closed in from the sides. This time when I put my hand up towards the bullets, I only shifted their direction and the man to my left fell and was gone. Two left, I smiled. I stood facing both of them. They were only ten feet from each other. They looked at each other and started running towards us, one flinging knives and the other firing his gun. They meet in five long strides and were now side by side. I held my hand up to the knives and bullets and they just fell harmlessly to the ground a foot in front of us. The onslaught continued as they ran. They were now ten feet from us, and the ground was littered with weapons and bullets. I turned with my hand still lifted towards them and with the other pulled Rhett close to me and hoisted us into the air. We hovered for a moment, then I pulled us across the meadow out of their path.

For the first time, I turned and looked into Rhett's eyes. I almost lost my breath when I realized Michael not only had taken his form, but had not made the mistake of not changing his eyes. I found myself momentarily distracted. I hadn't realized just how much I had missed Rhett and how much I wanted to see him and to feel his... Michael was now the one I was suddenly holding. Our feet touched the ground and I let go of him, stumbling backwards. I fell and my heart was pounding so loudly it was all I could hear as I looked up at Michael. He held out his hand to me.

"I think you might could have won that one," he said as I took his hand.

When he pulled me to my feet, I found us standing back near the bike. The sudden comfort of Michael's invisible arms surrounded me and my heart slowed. It wasn't until then that I noticed I still held his hand. I let go instantly.

He chuckled as he handed me a bottle of water. "Five minute break."

I took the water and sat down over against a rock. I took a drink, then closed my eyes and leaned my head back. All my mind could see was Rhett's eyes at first, but then Michaels. My heart began to pound again. What in the world was happening to me? It was Rhett that had stopped me in my tracks, so why was it Michael's eyes that I kept seeing in my head? This was not good. I opened my eyes to look at Michael, but he wasn't there. I glanced around the meadow and I didn't see him anywhere.

"Michael." I got to my feet.

"Yes." His voice was right behind me. It scared me so that I jumped like I had seen a mouse. I heard him chuckle as I turned to find myself face to face with him.

He took a step back. "Sorry, have you had enough today?"

"No, I'm okay," I assured him.

"You may be almost impossible to hurt, but being physically hurt is not all you have to worry about. Just like looking into Rhett's eyes had an effect on you, you need to know you are vulnerable in other areas."

"You weren't kidding when you said the real training would begin today, were you?"

"No, I wasn't. Your next lesson will be one of the hardest you have had to face so far, but I don't think now is the time."

"Harder than facing four angels? I think I can handle what you have." I smiled at him. I was ready for anything he could dish out.

"You're not purple."

"What?" Purple? What was he talking... Rhett was now standing before me again. My heart skipped a beat when I looked into his beautiful brown eyes. Okay, I wasn't ready. He stepped close to me; our faces were inches from each others.

"Don't let," he leaned even closer, "your heart overcome your common sense, Kara." He said it so smoothly. "So, what do you think?"

"About what?" I struggled to get out. The last time I had been close to Rhett I didn't know if I wanted him to kiss me or not, but now, that was all I wanted.

"You and me. I want you, don't you want me?"

Yes, my heart screamed, I do want you. I closed my eyes and the gap between our lips in one motion, but when my lips should have touched his, they touched... nothing. My eyes opened to find no one there. I found myself alone in the meadow again. Oh crap, what had I just done?

"You failed a very important test." Michael's voice filled the air. I turned, but he was not there. Well, what did he expect; I was only human. He wanted me to fail, wanted to humiliate me. The sickness of what I had just tried to do was now being replaced by anger. How could he do that? How could he play with my emotions so easily?

"You knew I would fail, didn't you." Anger was taking over. "I thought I was yours to protect, not hurt!" I turned in the meadow hoping to find him, but he was still not there.

"You need to learn to control your emotions."

"I thought my emotions were what made me strong. Is that not how you first got me to use my power, by putting David in harm's way by manipulating my emotions?"

"That is how I awakened you to what you can do, but you must realize that you can be controlled by them as well if you are not careful."

"Why will you not show yourself?" I screamed into the air. "Are you afraid of my emotional state? Some mighty angel you are." The chuckle I heard only made me that much angrier.

I could feel everything in the meadow with such clarity, and with my anger raging, I reached out and pulled trees from their roots and toppled rock walls. The meadow was beginning to look as if a tornado had come through it.

"Show yourself!" I stood in the midst of the rubble. "Show yourself, or I will destroy the whole forest!" I shouted. I was so angry at him.

"Do you want really want to see me?" his voice rang in my ears. I suddenly felt myself being lifted into the air. The meadow melted out of sight as I heard the unmistakable sound of his mighty wings.

A hand appeared around my chest. It had an appearance as if cover by millions of small prisms and all the colors reflected in them. It was so huge that I was like a Barbie Doll in its grasp. Was this Michael's hand? I knew that when I looked at Michael, I only saw a man, but not until I saw this huge hand did it really sink in that he was a mighty angel of the Lord. My anger immediately melted into fear. Fear of the very angel here to protect and train me. Why had I provoked him? Who did I think I was? I closed my eyes as the tears began to fall.

"I'm sorry," I managed to whisper into the wind. It immediately calmed and the wind ceased. When I opened my eyes, I again found myself standing in the meadow. Michael now stood before me as if nothing had happened. He smiled gently and opened his arms to me. I found that I could not have stayed out of them even if I had wanted to.

"I'm so sorry," I whispered again as my head lay on his shoulder.

"Not nearly as sorry as I am." He held me tightly. "But the lesson is not over just yet." I looked up to find Rhett holding me in his arms once again. I tried to step back but he held me tightly.

"I love you, Kara."

My heart started beating wildly. No, it's not real, I told myself even as Rhett lowered his lips to mine. Yes, my heart sang; no, my head screamed! Just push him off! No, you want him, you need him. A war raged within me. When our lips parted, the tears were rolling freely down my face and I dropped my head.

"Look at me, Kara." It was Michael's voice, not Rhett's. How could I look at him? He lifted my face and repeated my name. Slowly, I opened my eyes. "Yes, I knew you would fail this test. But just like me taking you to New York to see it was real, you needed to feel the emotions that would take a hold of you and tear you apart if you did not understand them. I am sorry that you have to learn in such a harsh manner, but telling you will never replace putting you in the situation."

The sobs were now physically wracking my body and tears poured down my face. Michael's mighty arms of comfort couldn't seem to calm my hurting heart. Michael pulled me back into his arms and let me cry.

"Let's get you home; I think you've had enough for today."

The ride home seemed slower. I held on to Michael and thought of Rhett. It was probably good I hadn't talked to him all week.

"The rest of the day is yours," Michael told me as I got off the bike.

I turned and looked at him. "Thanks," was all I could managed, and then turned and walked towards the door.

"Kara."

"Yes." I turned back.

"The training you face is for you, and no one else."

I stopped and had a vision of Rhett and me kissing, but as I saw Rhett, he vanished and Michael became the one I was kissing. I understood perfectly that would be a little hard to explain to someone else.

"I see your point," I told him, then turned and left him sitting on his bike.

Mom was feeding David his lunch when I came in. I sat down at the bar and asked, "What are you doing this afternoon?"

"I'm going to see Alina and Ms. Ava."

"Do you care if I tag along? Michael gave me the rest of the afternoon off."

"That would be great. Everything okay?" she asked.

"This morning was really hard. He called in four other angels to fight me."

"So, how did you do?"

"Well, they got the drop on me the first round. The second time, I did better, but they still won."

I almost said something about him turning into Rhett, but then that would have brought up stuff I really didn't want to talk about to

Mom. I sure didn't want to say or let anything slip about the second part of the lesson, so I figured silence was best. I got a plate and fixed myself a sandwich. After lunch, we went to Alina's. Ms. Ava had been to rehab with her new hip and was resting when we got there.

"Mom always takes a couple hour nap when we get home from rehab," Alina told us as she showed us into the living room of their small apartment. Pink was most definitely Alina's color. If only she knew how well her pink shirt and pink aura made her look so beautiful.

"How has she been doing?" Mom asked her.

"She grumbles a lot, so nothing really has changed." She smiled at me. "I had no idea you spoke German, Kara. Mom told me about you coming to the hospital. So, where did you learn it? She said you spoke it very well."

I looked at Mom then to Alina. "I just seem to have a gift for languages."

"Alina!" Ava called from the other room. "Who are you talking to?"

"Just a minute, let me go check on her and I'll be right back." Alina told us as she got up. I could hear her perfectly fine, in English just as before, while Mom heard German.

"She just wants to know who's here," I told Mom. It was only a few moments when Alina and Ms. Ava came back into the room.

"Kara, how are you and your Mom? Oh, I see you have that baby with you. What was his name again? My mind is not as sharp as it used to be." She rattled off as Alina helped her set down on the couch beside me. It was nice to see that she was a nice color of pink as well.

"David, and we are all fine. It's nice to see you doing better," I answered her.

"I think you speak German better than I do," Alina told me. "I thought Mom was exaggerating when she said you spoke perfect German, but I see she wasn't." All I could do was smile at her.

Mom hadn't said a word when I realized we were talking German, so she had no clue what was being said. "Sorry, Mom, didn't mean to leave you out. Alina was telling me how well I spoke German, and Ms.

Ava asked how you were and what David's name was because she had forgotten."

Mom smiled. "That's okay. I sure wish I had the gift of language, too."

"You don't speak German, Mrs. Johns? So, where did Kara learn it?" Alina asked Mom.

"She has the gift of tongues. You know you read about the gift in the Bible several times, but Kara truly has it."

"But I thought speaking in tongues was all that jibber-jabber talk. You know, those churches where people run up and down the aisles."

"Yes, that's what most people think, but what the Bible teaches is that tongues are being able to hear and speak other languages that are not common to you, ones that were not taught to you."

"Well, that makes much more sense."

"What are you talking about?" Ms. Ava asked Alina.

The afternoon was spent talking about our belief in God and His amazing love for us. It was truly great. Mom is a natural witness; me, I am still learning. By the time we left, the angels of Heaven were rejoicing. I must say it was an experience I will never forget.

## CHAPTER 9

# BACK TO REALITY

Mom and I headed back home. I tried several times to find Kyle, but never found him. As much as I hated him being in my thoughts all the time, I hated it even more when he wasn't.

"So, what are the guys up to?" Mom interrupted my thoughts.

"I wish I knew," I told her. "Most of the time, I can't find them."

"I wonder why?"

"No clue, and I can't believe I am going to say this, but I miss Kyle in my head."

"I am not surprised. You two are close. I am sure it's strange for you. Have you asked Michael about it?"

"No, but I will." I closed my eyes.

"*Michael, why is it that we can't talk all the time?*" I waited a few minutes. "*Come on, I know you're there.*" I thought he might answer, but silence was all I received for all my attempts. I so wanted to understand what was going on. It seemed life was going from one extreme to another, but why? What was the purpose?

When we got home, I helped Mom get David and all his stuff back up to the house, and then went to my room. I pulled out my laptop and got online. I hadn't had much time lately, so I thought I would check my mail while I could. I had mail from White Turtle. She was staying with her Aunt Ginny, who had gotten very sick and had twins, so she had gone to help her for the summer. Her aunt had married outside the Indian Nation and lived in Kentucky. Turtle didn't really say what her aunt had gotten sick with, but since she was staying the summer, it must be fairly serious. She talked about the twins being hard to deal with, but she was managing. She was hoping that her aunt would be better by the end of summer, and that maybe she could stop by and visit on her way back home. I sent a short reply telling her that I hoped her aunt got better soon, and that a visit would be great. I would love to see her.

"Kara!" I hear Mom yell from the living room.

"Coming!" I logged out and headed up the hall.

"Would you watch David a few minutes? They're having some kind of problem downstairs."

"Sure," I told her. She handed off David, and went out the door.

"So, little man, what shall we do?" I walked back to David's room and sat him on a blanket on the floor. All his toys were neatly on the corner shelf. I closed my eyes a second to focus, then reached out to feel the room and everything in it. I opened my eyes and lifted three blocks off his shelf and held them in front of him until he reached for them, then I dropped them in his lap. I continued this with one toy after another, putting them in front of him until the floor was covered around him with toys. I then picked up the ones he wasn't playing with and returned them to the shelf. I heard Mom come back after about twenty minutes.

"Kara," she said as she came to the door. I looked up at her. "They need your help downstairs. You know your Dad hired George, Tony, and Mary since you guys are in training and haven't had time to work. Mary is having troubles, especially with the family tables. Would you be willing to go down and help her tonight, sort of train her?"

"Sure, let me change."

"Just hurry." Mom cleaned up the toys without touching a one.

I ran to my room, dressed and headed downstairs. Jake, one of the chefs, was waiting for me in the prep area.

"Kara, I am so glad you could come." He turned, "Matt, call Mary in here, please." He looked back at me. "You may want her to follow you, or you follow her, it doesn't matter. Just help her with some good tips on how to serve."

"No problem," I told him as a girl came into the kitchen.

"You wanted to see me?"

"Mary, this is Kara. She is the best waitress around. She is going to help you out tonight, give you some pointers."

Mary looked over at me. "That would be great. I guess I'm not very good at this yet."

"First thing I need to know is what tables we have tonight," I asked her.

"We have the blue ones, all the even numbers, twelve through twenty-four," she told me.

"Well, then, let's get started," I told her as I loaded my apron with straws, napkins, and order tickets.

The first table had three men at it. She had already gotten their water, but had not taken their order yet.

"How long have they been there?" I asked her.

"I was just getting ready to take their orders when Matt called me to the kitchen."

"I will watch you on this one and give you pointers where I think you need them, and then you can watch me on the next one," I told her.

"Have you decided what you would like?" she asked when we got to the table.

"Well, I'm not so sure," one of three said.

I leaned up and whispered in Mary's ear. "Did you ask them if they had been here before?"

"Have you guys ever been here before?" Mary asked.

"No, it's our first time," the one with blond short hair answered.

"Todd, a guy from work, said it was excellent," the chubby, short guy said.

"Offer them a sample platter," I told Mary.

"Would you be interested in trying our sample platter then?"

"Tell them a little more about it," I urged her and she looked back over her shoulder at me, bewildered.

I stepped in. "Our sample platter has grilled bison, rotisserie quail, and marinated rabbit on it-- along with fresh raw veggies and grilled corn on the cob. It's really good, and if you have never been here before, it's a good choice."

"That would be great," the chubby guy said. "I don't see a drink menu on here," he said, still looking at the menu.

"That's because the meal you order comes with its own specific drink. The drink that comes with each meal is to enhance specific flavor of the food. For example, the sample platter you will get comes with a very light tea so that each flavor comes through."

"That sounds good to me. I'll have the sample platter," the blond said.

"Me, too," said the chubby guy.

"I'll make it unanimous and have the same," the third, dark haired guy added.

"Wonderful, I'll put these orders in for you." I smiled and took their menus.

Mary and I then left the table and headed to the computer to put in their orders to the kitchen.

"It's all in knowing the menu well, and reading the customer. If they look like they have no idea what they're doing, then they probably don't. Just think of what you would like to know when you go out to a new restaurant."

"I never thought of it like that," she smiled at me.

I placed the order and we headed back out to wait on another table. This one had a couple with three children at it. "You take notes on this one and then you do the next table, okay?" Mary nodded in agreement. "We need to take the water out before we even ask them what they want." We went to the drink station and picked up two glasses of water and three unbreakable plastic cups of water for the kids. "Welcome to The Village. My name is Kara. I'll be your waitress this evening." I told them as I placed the water on the table. "Have you ever been here before?" I asked the couple.

"Oh, yes, several times," the man answered.

"Well, we are glad you're back, then. Can I get the kids some coloring books and crayons?"

"That would be great!" The woman said with a smile.

"I'll be right back with them, and then take your order." I went to the supply desk and picked up three books and crayons for the kids. "Here you go." I gave each kid a book and crayons. The smallest was in a booster chair and had the cutest smile. "Now then, what can I get for you tonight?" I looked to the couple.

"I'd like the wild bison," the man said.

"I think I'll have the quail, and I would like the rabbit tenders for the kids, please."

"Yes, ma'am. I'll get this right in for you." I took the menus. I leaned over and picked up a crayon that the smallest kid had dropped. "Here you go, cutie."

Mary and I went and placed the order on the computer. "The thing about families is to keep the kids busy so the parents can relax a bit. Tell some corny jokes to the kids, drop by and color with one of them a second. When you're able to keep the kids from driving the parent's nuts, you'll find that they are most generous with tips. A general rule of thumb is just being attentive to the customer. If they look down, tell them a joke or just keep the conversation up and lively. Make them feel like you're glad to see them. Give complements, always be polite, and say thank you and you're welcome. It's really not that hard."

"For you it doesn't seem hard, but I'm just not getting the hang of it. I mean, I get along with college guys easy enough, but I just can't seem to relate to the others."

"You can do it, look there." The next table was an older couple. The Marshalls to be exact. They were a fun old couple. "You can work on your technique with them while I take the food to the first table."

"I can do this!" Mary got two glasses of water and headed towards their table.

I picked up the sampler plates and headed back to the table with the three guys. "Here you go. I'll be right back with your drinks." It only took a few seconds to get their drinks and return.

"Not everyone likes these, but they are the best sellers here. That's why we put them on the sampler platter. But we also have a wonderful rabbit stew and salad that is quite popular."

"I like this," the dark haired one said. "It has a great flavor. Not sure what it is, but I like it."

"It's rabbit," I told him. "It has been marinated in four herbs for about six hours, and then it's seared to hold in the flavor. Can I get you guys anything else?"

"No, I think we are good."

"All right, then I'll be back in a few to check on you. Don't hesitate to yell at me if you need anything." They smiled and I left the table to go check on Mary. She was talking to Mr. Marshall when I got there.

"No, sir, I'm not having very good luck," she was saying as I arrived.

"Kara," Mr. Marshall said as I walked up.

"Hello, Mr. Marshall, how have you been?"

"Just fine, darling, how about you?"

"Been fine. How is Mary, here, doing?"

"She's fine. Not as good as you, but I think she can be if she will just relax. She seems a little tense."

"Oh, Harry," Mrs. Marshall said. "She's doing fine."

"Thanks," Mary told Mrs. Marshall.

"Don't worry, sweetie, you will do just fine as long as you remember one thing."

"What's that?" Mary asked.

"Just be yourself and have a good time." Mrs. Marshall patted Mary's arm. "I waited tables for twenty years. It was hard at first, but once I learned to relax and be myself, I had some of the best times. It was where I meet Harry." She winked at her husband.

"Thanks for the advice." Mary told her. "Now, what can I get you to eat?"

The night went on and Mary seemed to finally understand that if she would just relax and be herself around her patrons, as if it were her friends, then she was pretty good and waitressing. She told me in the two weeks she had been working there, she had barely cleared fifty in tips, but that night, she had cleared over a hundred. I left the restaurant around ten and headed up to the house. As wild as it sounded, I had sort of missed the craziness of the restaurant. Maybe it was because it felt normal while nothing else had lately.

"So, how did it go?" Mom was sitting on the couch when I came through the door.

"I think she'll be fine now. She just needed a little inspiration."

"Well good. Your Dad will be glad to hear that."

"Have you heard from Dad today?" I asked her.

"Yeah. He popped in once to tell me that all four of them would be working in Montana. They will be working for a man restoring a cabin up in the mountains. He said he'd fill us in later."

I wanted to wait around and talk to Kyle when they got back, but I was beat. I took a long hot shower and climbed into bed. Michael's lessons for the day came flooding back, mainly the ones about my emotions. As I was thinking about them, my phone vibrated on my night stand. I picked it up. It was Rhett.

"Hey, Rhett."

"Kara, so how's your week been?"

"Well, it's has been long and hard." I didn't lie, it had.

"What have you been doing?" he asked.

"Our training started this week, and the instructor works us hard."

"Oh, yeah, I forgot about that. So, have you learned how to use a gun or sword yet?"

"Well, we are focusing on self-defense right now, so I really haven't done anything with guns and stuff. I did, however, defend with a dagger, but that's about it for weapons so far. So, how has school been?" I wanted to get of the training subject.

"Today was our last day before spring break. I'll be so glad when it's summer break and we're out for two months instead of just a week."

"We finished a few weeks back, but I am ready for warmer weather. You'll be a junior next year, right?"

"Yeah, and you'll be a senior. Man, I wish Mom would home school us."

"Not if your Mom was anything like mine, you wouldn't."

"Kyle says she's tough on you guys."

"She is, so I'm glad this is our last year," I told him.

"What are you doing this weekend?" he asked. I was waiting for this question.

"I am not sure. Uncle Daniel and Granddad are in for a little while, so I'm hoping to spend some time with them. But with all the training and stuff, who knows if we will even have the weekend off."

"I can't imagine your Dad working you on Sunday."

"That's true, but the training schedule is not his, so who knows." Rhett's call was pushing my emotions in to overload. I was so physically and emotionally drained my eyelids stared closing. "It was sure nice to hear from you Rhett, but I'm exhausted. I trained this morning, helped mom this afternoon, and then worked a full shift at the restaurant, and I am beat."

"Oh, my goodness, why didn't say so. Get off here and go to bed then."

"I'm already in the bed and my eyes do not want to stay open. Goodnight and thanks again for calling…"

## CHAPTER 10

# LINAGE

The sun woke me instead of my alarm. I looked over towards the clock. Oh crap, it was going on eight. I jumped up and ran to the closet and threw on some clothes. Michael was going to be mad. I ran up the hall and into the living room. He was sitting on the couch playing with David.

"Morning," he said. "Sleep well?"

I flopped down in one of the chairs. "I guess. What are you doing here watching David?"

"Your Dad and Mom are spending the day together and we are on David duty."

"What about Kyle?" I asked.

"He is with your uncle. They have accepted a new job and he will be helping them for the summer. Today, they are just gathering the supplies they need to take. Everyone will be here tomorrow before they leave."

"Is Dad going for the summer, too?"

"Yes, that's why your Mom and Dad are spending the day together."

A whole summer without Dad, without Kyle. This was not going to be good. I was missing them horribly and it had just been a week. How was I going to handle a whole three months?

"I'll keep you busy," Michael said. That really didn't make me feel better. Slowly I began to feel all warm and calm. I smiled at Michael.

"Thanks."

"No problem." He bounced David on one of his knees. "The weather is warm and I say we get out of the house and do something today. What about you?"

"Sounds good; what shall we do?"

"Well, there is a place I would like to show you." He stood up. Great, another place to show me, I sure hoped it was not like the last place that involved gang members.

"It's not." He answered my thoughts. "Let's go." He walked towards the door.

"Let me go…oh, never mind," Michael had already changed my clothes, and I was even holding a breakfast wrap and milk. I did, however, wonder about our mode of transportation as we walked down the stairs. I knew we weren't going on his bike. Well, at least I didn't think we were. I heard Michael chuckle in front of me as he pushed the outside door open. Our Explorer was sitting in its regular parking spot. He opened the door and put David in his seat, then climbed in behind the wheel. He fasted up just like any normal person and started the vehicle. I fastened my seat belt and waited for his next move.

He laughed. "What are you expecting us to do?" he asked.

It was sort of funny I guess. "I don't know."

He pulled out onto the street and headed south. I watched the traffic as it passed by, oh so normally. Soon the businesses melted into suburbs and then into crop lands.

"So, where are we going?" I looked in the back seat to check on David. He was just looking out the window like I had been.

"I love creation, so I am taking you to one of my favorite spots. Heaven is beautiful, but it is not the same as here. Earth has beauty all its own. It was once even more beautiful, but it still has its charm."

"So what's Heaven like?" I asked him.

"For all the words you have, I don't think any of them even come close to describing it." he said.

"That's it? You're not even going to try?"

"You have read the descriptions in the Bible, and they are as good as any," he told me.

Well, that was disappointing. I turned and looked back out the window. The scenery was now going by in a blur. I looked over at Michael and smiled.

"It would take all day if we went at normal speed."

"And did everyone else decide not to travel this road today?" I asked, noticing that we passed no other cars. He just chuckled.

As time moved slowly and the scenery moved by faster I wondered how far we were going. Not long after that we entered Shawnee National Forest, and he slowed. We passed small towns and houses, and then turned by a brown sign that read Rim Rock. The parking lot was just basically a gravel turn around. Michael parked and got out.

"You coming?" he asked as he got David out. I got out and followed Michael up the trail.

We walked for ten minutes before the path made a sharp turn, then went down long stairwell in between two rock walls. You had to weave in and out of a few rocks then it lead out to more stone steps that took you down into a valley between large stone walls. It was very peaceful and serene. There were large, tall trees reaching out of the gorge. At the base of the stone stairs was a large overhang. It would have been a great place to camp.

"Oh, it was." Michael was in my head, but answered me out loud. "This was a sacred spot for many Indian tribes and a hiding place form soldiers at one time. A lot of animals would stay here when the weather got harsh, so it was a favorite hunting spot for trappers."

"I guess you have seen it all." Being a timeless being has its advantages.

"I guess you could say that." The trail forked in two detections at a large opening. Michael handed me David, and then pulled out a large blanket and spread it out on the ground.

"Come on and set down; David's getting hungry."

He patted the blanket beside where he now sat. I sat down beside him as he handed me a bottle to give David. I watched as he straightened out his legs and leaned back on his arms. He really seemed to enjoy the quietness of the place. It was very peaceful and restful, and I must admit

I liked it, too. As I fed David, Michael lay back and closed his eyes. If I didn't know better, I would have thought he was taking a nap. David finished his bottle, let out a few burps, and then went to sleep. I laid him on the blanket between me and Michael. The sun was peeking through the branches and felt warm on my face. I sat there looking at the beauty around me. Straight in front of us was a small stream running beside one of the rock walls. There was moss and other greenery growing on the wall. Although it was half brown from the winter, you could see it ready to liven up and get lush once again. Everywhere I looked, buds were ready to burst out and show what they had hid all winter. David made a small noise that brought my attention back to the blanket and to Michael, who was intently staring at me. He smiled and pushed up to his elbow.

"Spring is the beginning of life again. It is always so wondrous."

"So, why are we really here?" I asked. Surely we hadn't come all the way just to sit here.

"You could use a couple of days rest before your martial arts trainer gets here Monday. I thought this was the perfect spot to relax."

"Martial arts trainer? I thought you were doing all the training."

"I have been training you with your special abilities, but now it's time for you to learn the human side," he told me. "I will still be here, but you are going to be trained by a normal human instructor in the training studio for the next two months. You won't be allowed to use anything I have taught you." He smiled. "In other words, when you now go into the studio, you are like any other person learning martial arts. Well, you will learn a little quicker, but that's all."

"You mean I can't move anything, right?" If I had all this power and had been trained to use it, I wondered why was I going to have to learn not to use it?

"You're human from a human world." He was answering my thoughts again. "If you go mind throwing knives at normal people… well let's just say you don't need that kind of attention. You need to handle everything you can as humanly as possible, and then only after you cannot find any other way, use your abilities."

"As humanly as possible," I repeated him. "You make it sound as if I'm not human."

"Genesis Six."

"What about it?"

"What do the first four verses tell you?"

"It talks about the sons of God finding the daughters of men fair?"

"Verse Four, what does it say to you? Who is it talking about?"

I quoted the verse in my head. "*There were giants in the earth in those days; and also after that, when the sons of God came in unto the daughters of men, and they bear children to them, the same became mighty men which were of old, men of renown.*"

"Yes, that's what it says; but who is it talking about? Who are the 'sons of God' it refers to?" He looked at me intently.

I sat there thinking about it. Who was it talking about? It says the sons of God. Was it not referring to men? Men of renown it also said. Oh, my gosh, sons of God, members of the high court they were called in Job. It was talking about angels. I looked at Michael. Was he telling me I was part angel?

"Yes and no. Women are men's helpers; angels the Creators. So no, you're not angelic, but yes you are in a way. Many years ago, and I am talking thousands of years, there was an angel in your linage. It comes with a blessing and a curse. As a woman, you will only ever have one daughter, but you will have special abilities, too."

My mind went crazy. "Auras. Mom could see them and so could her Mom, but what about the rest of the stuff. I mean, Mom could only move things at one time in her life, and I'm just now learning." I was excited on one hand, but just like always, oh so confused on the other.

"Kara, listen to me."Michael placed his hand on my arm. "The Maker has always had a plan for the abilities you have. Not every woman in the world can handle what has been placed on your shoulders. That is where the linage comes in. And I know you think your mom's abilities were taken from her, but actually, she has always had them. She was just not allowed to use them. Not unlike your grandmother and her mother. The ability to do great things was there, but they were not called to use them."

His eyes spoke comfort and I could feel his invisible arms around me like always, but this was hard to swallow. There was an angel great, great and more great somewhere in my past, and it gave me power for my future. Intense! One daughter...yes. Mom was an only child and so was her Mom. But had Kyle and David. I am not an only child. My mind kept jumping form one thing to another trying to figure it all out. Angel for a…my mind came to a sudden halt. Could Michael be…

"No, I am not," he said firmly. He almost sounded offended. He pulled his hand from my arm and sat up. "There are many angels with children, male and female. But yours is …well, let's just say a special case. Your mom was given sons because of Matthias, and each of them is special because of him. Don't try to understand it all; just have faith that it all has a purpose."

"Does Dad have an angel great-grandfather somewhere in his past too?"

"No, he was chosen for his task, but is special because he did the bidding of his Creator; and because of that, he was given sons."

"Who is he, my great, great…oh, you know who I mean. Do you know him, or is that a silly question? Will I ever meet him?" My mind swirled with questions and thoughts of angels. Who was he? Verse four talked about men of great renown, but he was only given daughters. Why? Why was he given only daughters? Was it a gift or punishment?

"Yes, I know him and I hope you never have to meet him. But I will be there if you ever do, I promise." Michael told me with the utmost concern in his eyes. "We have been here long enough." He got up and reached for David.

"Wait, you just can't leave it at that. You just told me I was special, but that you hoped I never had to meet the angel who made me so special." I stood up beside him. "Come on, you're not getting off that easy. I need more information."

He left David on the blanket and stepped close to me. "Kara, listen! I know this is extremely hard, but some things you will understand and some you won't. And that is because of your linage. You need to know about it, but as far as who, and the details, that is not important now."

"Why is knowing about it, but not knowing the details so important?' I asked.

"You are going to see and hear things that would, well for a lack of a better term, freak others out. You already know you're different and now you have a little more knowledge on why things are possible, you will be able to accept them easier. Not that it has been hard on you yet, but there will be a time that you will question it all."

"Questioned what? My faith?" I felt so lost in all this.

"No, your sanity." Michael told me as he picked up David and handed him to me so he could pick up the blanket.

My sanity, what did he mean I would question my sanity. I followed Michael up the trail until it came back into the lot where we had parked. We passed several cars pulling into the parking lot as we left. I sat there silent as he drove. Why was my life so hard all of the sudden. Why... why to everything, why was I born into this family, why me, why now, why, why, why?

"Michael."

"Yes." he answered as he turned at another brown sign. This one read Garden of the gods.

"I feel so lost."

"I know you do. I wish I could make you understand."

"Why can't I?"

"It is simply not time for you to."

"But why is it not?"

Michael pulled into another parking lot; this one was paved.

"Come on." He got out, "I want to show you something," he told me as he got David out. I climbed out once more and followed after him. We walked up the trail through the woods. At the top was a cliff of rocks that you could walk right out on and see for miles.

"Sit down and just enjoy what you see. Let your heart feel the glory all around you. Let it take hold of you and consume you."

I sat down out on the edge and let the sunshine warm me. I almost felt as if I was waiting on something. I pulled my iPod from my pocket and put my ear buds in. I hit shuffle. Okay, Lord, here I am. What is it you want from me? As a song came on, I had to smile. It was Psalm 24: "Who may ascend the hill of the Lord, who may be found in Your holy place? Only those who are clean and pure in their hearts can make it to where You are. So do what You will, do what You want. We have decided to trust You only, we want to be whatever You're wanting, You are the Lord of my life."

This was so Him, only He would give you the words with His own. My eyes closed and my hands lifted in the air as the chorus played. *"Lord, not my will, but Your Will; let this be my cry!"*

I felt Michael's hand on my shoulder. "Open your eyes," he said.

When I did the scene that appeared before me took my breath. I no longer looked just off a small cliff in Illinois, but I was on top of the world it seemed, looking down onto the most beautiful place there ever was. I had no words to describe the beauty that spread out before me.

"This is what it was like before the Fall of Man." The scene changed back into the one that was before me.

"Yes, it is beautiful; but it is nothing compared to what it was and what one day it will be again. The plan has been laid since the day of the Fall and you are just one small piece in the big puzzle. But each piece is vital to the completion of the whole puzzle. And even though you can't seem to make sense of the pieces, you know what the end will be like. You know what the end puzzle will be."

Revelations 21 came into my mind: "*Then* I saw 'a new heaven and a new earth,' for the first Heaven and the first earth had passed away, and there was no longer any sea. [2] I saw the Holy City, the new Jerusalem, coming down out of heaven from God, prepared as a bride beautifully dressed for her husband. [3] And I heard a loud voice from the throne saying, 'Look! God's dwelling place is now among the people, and he will dwell with them. They will be his people, and God himself will be with them and be their God. [4] 'He will wipe every tear from their eyes.

There will be no more death or mourning or crying or pain, for the old order of things has passed away."

"Yes, I know what the end game is and I will do anything and everything humanly possible to do what I am supposed to do. I also know that I don't understand, but it's something I just have to have faith about. That is the true test here, isn't it? To do what I am supposed to do; follow His lead and be true to Him."

Michael smiled and sat down beside me. David was in his lap.

"Lunch." He handed me a small brown bag. Inside was a chicken sandwich, some cut up carrots, and a bottle of water.

"You don't miss a thing, do you?" I asked him.

He laughed. "Yeah, like the first time I took you on a trip?"

The rest of the afternoon passed by peacefully, and we got home just after dark.

Kyle, Granddad, and Uncle Daniel were there. Granddad scooped David out of Michael's arms as soon as we walked through the door.

"I'll see you Monday morning," Michael told me, then turned and left.

"Hey, stranger," Kyle said as he got up off the couch and gave me a hug. "So, where have you been all day?"

"Soaking up the sun in Shawnee National Park," I told him. Well, it was the truth. I had sat on the rocks and soaked up some sun.

"We've been working all day, and you were out playing in the park. That's no fair."

"Fair?" I punched him. "I still have to *do* things, not just think about them."

"Alright, you two." Uncle Daniel stepped between us then gave me a hug. "So you're learning lots of things?" He asked me.

*You have no idea* went through my head.

"No idea," he answered my head. "What has Michael been teaching you?"

Oh, crud, I forgot that Uncle Daniel could get in my head. I cleared my head; didn't want to say anything I wasn't supposed too.

"Well, I dare you to try and hurt me, and you will find out. I'm pretty good at defending myself." I smiled and tried to keep my mind focused on lessons that were safe.

"I might just put you to the test," he teased me.

"I bet I can get the best of you," Kyle interrupted.

"I'll take that bet. Let's go down to the studio. I'll kick your little scrawny butt all over the place."

"Sounds like a good lesson for the both of you." Michael was suddenly standing between us.

"Are you sure about that?" Granddad asked.

"They can't hurt each other as long as I am there," Michael told Granddad.

"Well, that's not going to be any fun, then," Kyle teased.

"Let's go." I marched toward the door and my clothes changed as I went.

"I didn't think you could change things," Kyle said from behind me.

I stopped long enough to look back at Kyle. "I can't. So, I guess you just changed me and you both." He had on the same thing I now did: black soft pants and a grey t-shirt.

"No, I didn't." He looked down.

"Hey, brainless." I laughed and pointed to Michael, who was now wearing the same thing.

"Oh," was all Kyle said.

"I am not going to miss this!" Uncle Daniel said as he followed us towards the door.

"Come on. You can stay in the TV room and David will be safe," Michael told Granddad, who then smiled and followed, too.

Uncle Daniel and Granddad went into the TV room, which all of a sudden had a window looking into the dojo. Michael stood between us in the middle of the room. "Okay you two, you are in a safe zone, so don't hold anything back. You both have unique gifts, so use them." Then he went into the other room.

"You ready, sis?"

"Bring it!" I told him as we slowly circled one another.

"You know, I have endless weapons and can kick your butt." He smiled.

"Give it your best shot."

A gun appeared in his hands. I smiled and felt the room. When the bullets stared flying, so did the knives from the shelves.

That evening, Kyle and I lay on one of the benches on the roof starring at the stars.

"What a week."

"You said it." I agreed with him.

"You were so amazing downstairs."

"You were, too. I think it was like Neo verses the Master Chief, or the Terminator." We both laughed. "So, what are you going to be doing in Montana?" I asked him.

"Well, Uncle Daniel was contacted by some old guy about redoing his family's cabin in the mountains. He says it is so far up that there are no roads, and all the supplies have to be air-lifted in."

"No roads…really?"

"That what he says. It will take us two days to hike in, or we can take horses and it will only take a day. I think we're taking the horses."

"Well, that's cool."

"Yeah, I'm not looking forward to no running water or electricity, though."

"Taking horses… Why are you not just doing that thing you do?" I asked. I wondered why they were not just appearing there, but actually taking horses.

"Dad says we have to be legit for the people that will be bringing us stuff."

"Well, I guess that made sense. What are you actually going to be doing to the cabin?"

"Uncle Daniel hasn't given us all the details yet, but he said he would fill us in tomorrow," Kyle told me.

"What are you going to do while we're working hard, sit on your butt?" Kyle teased.

"Not likely. Michael said that starting Monday I was going to have a real marital arts teacher teaching me."

"Really? I thought he was teaching you that stuff."

"So did I, but he says no. Says I need to learn to do it without the special stuff. So as of Monday, I'll be a normal karate student, or kung fu, or… well, I really don't know what I'll be learning. All I really know is that I will be doing it on my own."

"Oh, that sucks. Hey, wait a minute," Kyle sat up. "You mean you haven't learned any normal self-defense at all? So if I could have caught you, I might could have won?"

"You wish." I smiled.

The fight earlier had ended in a draw. Kyle couldn't get anything he threw or shot at me within five feet of me, and he would just vanish every time I sent something his way. But if he would have actually gotten his hands on me, he might have won. I stayed well out of his reach, though. Luckily, he can't appear in mid air, and I can hold myself as high as I want.

## CHAPTER 11

# THE HARD TRUTH

My eyes opened with the sun shining in my window. I was so glad Sunday was finally here. I wanted to visit with everyone. I felt like I had been away from them the last week, I'd been so busy. I could smell bacon cooking and knew Dad was fixing breakfast for Mom and me. I pulled back my blanket and got out of bed, then noticed I was wearing boxers again. I couldn't remember even going to bed last night. Last thing I remembered was Kyle leaving me on the roof. There had been several times lately that I couldn't remember going to bed.

"Finally, you're awake." Kyle came in and flopped down on my bed as I opened my closet doors.

"Some of us don't have the luxury of not needing to sleep," I told him.

"Mom says we can invite Kelly and Rhett over for supper."

I stared in my closet, but my head wandered to Rhett. I wasn't sure if I wanted to see him or not.

"Why not?" Klye asked.

"I get so emotional when he's around."

"I thought that was good."

"It can be, but it can also be a bad thing."

"How do you figure?"

I turned and sat down on the bed beside him. "Just think, Kyle. When you care for someone, they could be used to hurt you."

"Oh my gosh, Kara. You're not serious are you?"

"Yes." I looked at him. "I don't want Rhett to be hurt on account of me."

"Really, Kara?"

I looked at Kyle. "I am serious. We're not being trained because it's cool, but because we are going to have to use what we are learning."

"You're looking at this all wrong, Kara. You have power; you can keep him safe."

"Ok, Kyle, how about this one: I don't want to be hurt by Rhett."

"Rhett would never hurt you."

"Let me let you in on a little secret here. Demons have influence over people. Don't you remember the gangs? The demon just had to be near them to have influence over them. Just think what might happen if he had influence over Kelly. Wouldn't you do just about anything to keep her from getting hurt? Well, if she was under an evil influence, you couldn't protect her from, what she might do to you or anyone else."

"I hadn't thought of that." Kyle looked at me.

"Well, I have. This week I have all kinds of training and lessons, and I won't soon forget that one."

"So what are we supposed to do? Just break up and turn our backs on them?"

"No, but you know just as I do that Kelly is not your mate. So have confidence in that, and let her go gently."

"And what about Rhett. Do you know if he is purple or not?"

"He's not; we're not mates, either."

I got back up and went to my closet.

"Okay, tonight will be the official break-up night." Kyle got up off my bed. "I am going to be gone all summer. It wouldn't be fair anyway"

"At least you'll have that excuse. What am I suppose to tell Rhett? I really like you, but I just don't want to see you anymore?"

"You weren't really going out anyway."

"Do you really think that will matter to him?"

"No." He walked to the door. "This day is starting to suck," he said and left.

I pulled out a pair of shorts and shirt, then went and washed my face and got dressed. I thought of Rhett the whole time. I really had liked him; he was such a great guy. I saw his dark brown eyes with that tint of green in them when I closed my eyes. I opened my eyes, and for a split second, I swore I saw Michael's face. I looked around my room, then cleared my head and went towards the kitchen.

"Well, she's up," Granddad said as I sat down on one of the bar stools.

"Yeah, I'm up." I smiled at him.

"Hungry?" Dad asked.

"A little," Dad handed me a plate with bacon, eggs and toast. "Thanks."

"What's wrong, sweetie?" Granddad asked.

"Nothing, it's just been a long week." I smiled at him as I picked up a piece of bacon and put it in my mouth.

"I know what you mean; it has been a life-changing week."

"So, what all have you and Michael been up to?" Dad turned and set his spatula down.

"Let her eat her breakfast first," Mom piped in from her spot on the couch. "Why don't you tell us about this place in Montana?" Mom looked to Uncle Daniel.

"Sure, I can do that. Mr. Grady has lived in the edge of Glacier National Park all his life, but his family has a place further up in mountains that he would really like to restore. It was his great-grandfather's homestead originally."

"So why is he trying to restore it?" Kyle asked.

"He told me he had wanted to do it for years, but now that he's retired, he could actually do it."

"So he's going to be helping out?" Mom asked.

"Yes, some of the time; I think a lot of the time he will just be over-seeing that we get, what we need when we need it."

"Sounds like a lot of hard work," Dad told Daniel.

"It will be."

"Oh... it sounds so... fun." Kyle dragged out his words and sounded so not thrilled.

"Sounds like a good time to me," Granddad piped in. "Time with family."

"When are you leaving?" Mom asked.

"We're supposed to be at Mr. Grady's at noon tomorrow," Daniel told her.

Dad had taken David from Mom and was now carrying him around, playing with him. I was sure Dad didn't want to leave him. I guessed he could come back at night and visit if there was no one around to notice him missing.

"Is there going to be more than just you guys there?" I asked.

"Yes, it's going to be a ten man team." Daniel looked at me.

"This is not going to be fun." Kyle walked around and nested his head on my shoulder. "Want to trade places?"

"Ah buck up, Kyle; at least you won't get tired or hungry," I told him.

"Oh, whoopee, that makes me feel better... not."

"Oh come on, you'll be out there getting strong, maybe even getting a few muscles. Who knows, by the time you come back you might actually have some pecs." I teased him.

"I could use a few more muscles." He flexed his arm. "By the time I come back, the girls will be flocking to see these bad boys."

We all burst into laughter and Kyle grinned.

"So what do you have planned for the summer?" Granddad asked Mom.

"Plans? I have a baby and a restaurant to watch over." Mom looked at Dad.

We all knew Dad had taken care of the restaurant and Mom wouldn't have to lift a finger, but it was her way of saying she would stay busy.

"So, what about you, Kara?" Granddad asked.

"Michael said I would get a real martial arts trainer starting Monday. So it looks like my summer will be full of training." I clapped my hands like a little kid. "Oh, goody."

"Okay, back to my question," Dad looked at me. "What have you two been doing?"

"Training, what else is there?" I asked. "Well, mainly I've been getting my butt kicked, but I've won a few and I am getting better."

"Michael has taken you a few places, hasn't he?" Dad asked.

"Yes, we went to New York, then out in a meadow somewhere for training, and then yesterday we went south to Shawnee Nation Forest. Didn't really do anything there; just sat and enjoyed the sun."

"What was in New York?" Uncle Daniel asked.

"A warehouse lot," I told him. "A place I had a dream about. He wanted to show me that it was real."

"Why?" Granddad asked.

"That's what I'm not sure about. He said I might be able change something or influence what was going to happen or something. I'm just not real sure yet. Of course he gave me the, 'It will all be revealed in time' speech, so I'm still confused over the whole thing."

After a moment, dad asked, "Well what shall we do today? We have the whole day, and I suggest we spend it together."

"I agree!" chimed in Mom, "But I did tell Kyle that Kelly and Rhett could come by later."

"Don't worry about that, Mom." Kyle smiled at her. "Family is more important."

"Who are you and what have you done with my son?" Mom walked over and gave Kyle a hug.

"How about some hiking?" Dad suggested. "We can make a whole day of it, if you're up for it?" He looked at Mom.

"I'm game," Mom said.

"Kara," Dad looked at me, "you up for it?"

"Of course." We hadn't done any family hiking in a while, and it was always one thing I loved.

"Sounds like we have a plan then," Daniel said.

Mom loaded David's stuff and I packed some sandwiches, then we loaded up in the Explorer and headed to Starved Rock Park.

Dad carried David in a back-pack as we hiked. I really loved nature. It was sort of crazy now, though. Everywhere I looked, I could almost see things that weren't there. Flowers that were just now budding, ready to burst open, I could see in full bloom with more vibrant colors then I had ever seen.

We spent lunch in Mom and Dad's meadow, which was very interesting to me now that I knew the real significance of why they thought so much of the place. I climbed up on a rock at the end of the meadow and watched Dad and Mom sitting on their rock. Uncle Daniel and Granddad had David and were sitting on a blanket playing with him. And Kyle, well I didn't see him. I looked up and down the meadow then closed my eyes. Let's just see if I could find him. I reached out and felt of the meadow and the surrounding area. I was quite amazed how far out I could feel if I tried. It didn't take me long to find him. He was sitting on the bluff behind me. I looked over my shoulder at him high on the bluff. He was stretched out on a rock with his shirt off.

I looked back toward the others and then closed my eyes to think. I really wondered what God had in store for us. Why us? I mean, I knew what Michael had told me, but still, what was the purpose? What was going to happen? Why did we have to be trained? Was there really a demon out there looking for us, for me? How were we supposed to protect against a demon? Was there something in us like Mom that would just come out at the right moment to save the day? My mind swirled. How was a mere mortal supposed to deal with a superna… divine creature, whether it was good or bad?

I thought of Ephesians 6:11-13: "Put on the full armor of God, so that you can take your stand against the devil's schemes. For our struggle is not against flesh and blood, but against the rulers, against the authorities, against the powers of this dark world and against the spiritual forces of evil in the heavenly realms. Therefore put on the full armor of God, so that when the day of evil comes, you may be able to stand your ground, and after you have done everything, to stand."

I knew the verse well, and it was truly speaking to me. He was answered my question. The fight was not mine; I was only a mere pawn, a small piece of the bigger chest game. I had a part to play in His game, and He was equipping me for my task. I had to smile. He was so good. A calm comfort came over me. I loved when Michael did that. A song filled my heart. I suddenly got the sense he was near.

*"Kyle."* I heard him in my head. I turned to see him standing beside Kyle on the bluff. Kyle sat up. "*You have many gifts you don't know about yet, but know is the time to learn of one.*" Michael now had a guitar in his hands. "*You have the gift of music.*"

I got up off my rock and walked to the edge of the bluff and lifted myself to the top.

"Music?" Kyle was saying. "What do you mean?"

Michael handed Kyle the guitar. "There are many ways to minister to people; one is through music."

"But I don't know how to play."

Michael put up his hand. "Explain to me how you can go from this spot to that one. Explain to me how you can heal?"

"Okay, I get your point," Kyle told him. He put the guitar in his lap and looked at Michael.

"Here," he handed him a pick. "Now close your eyes. Kara, what song do you hear? Hum a few notes so Kyle will know."

"Glorified," I told Kyle. "You know," I started to hum.

Soon Kyle was playing along.

"Sing," Michael told me, and then he disappeared.

> "Praise belongs to You,
> Let every kingdom bow,
> Let every ocean roar,
> Let every heart adore You now."

I closed my eyes and lifted my hands to the sky. As I sang, I noticed more voices joining in. Mom, Dad, Uncle Daniel and Granddad had joined us on the bluff.

"Praise belongs to You,
What can I do but sing,
The greatest joy I've found,
Is to lay a crown before my King."

A feeling came over me that was like none I had ever felt. The joy and peace that I felt was indescribable. It completely consumed me.

"I've come to worship,
I've come to lift up your name
For You deserve this,
Life laid down, like the one that You gave,
I have but one voice,
One heart and one sacrifice,
So would you take this life lay down and be Glorified."

As we sang song after song and my heart soared.

*"Look."* I heard Michael in my head and felt his hand on my shoulder. I opened my eyes to see the valley below us full of angels. Some were kneeling, some laying flat, some had their hands lifted. Others just stood there. I glanced around at my family. Everyone had their eyes closed and hands lifted.

*"Wherever there is true praise and worship, there will always be angels present."* Michael whispered into my head. *"And today, you have done more than just sang in praise, you have captured the eye of the Creator, and the angels came to worship as He stands behind you and listens."*

Stands behind us. The thought scared me. I now felt Michael's hand in mine. I looked up to see his fingers entwined in mine. He now was standing shoulder to shoulder with me with his hands raised. He looked me directly in the eyes. His calm enveloped my fear and my eyes closed as I sang along with my heart.

I had no idea how long we stood and sang, but the moment we stopped, I heard what sounded like a flock of large birds take flight. I opened my eyes, but saw nothing. Michael was no longer beside me either.

We had evidently been there for hours. It was now dark. It sure had not seemed like it was that long. I think we all left there with a sense of awe. I guessed I was the only one that Michael had shown the angels to, or at least no one else mentioned them.

"What angels did Michael show you?" Dad asked me from the front seat.

"You really didn't see them?" I asked.

"Angels?" Kyle piped in. "What angels?"

"While we were singing, the whole valley filled with angels." I smiled as I recalled the sight of it in my head. Then I wondered if I should tell them about…

"Tell us what?" Uncle Daniel was now listing in.

"How many angels were there?" Kyle punched me in the ribs.

"Hundreds."

"Tell us what?" Uncle Daniel repeated his question.

"We weren't alone."

"We had an audience of One"

"Are you kidding me?" Kyle looked at me.

"No. Michael told me He stood behind us."

"Back in the meadow you were thinking, questioning about why things were happening to us, and you knew what Michael had told you, but that didn't explain everything. So, what has Michael told you?" Dad asked.

My thoughts went to Michael. Was I supposed to tell them what he had told me or not? *"Michael what do I do?"* I asked in my head.

*"This is why I have kept your minds separate for your training, but it is up to you whether you tell them about the linage."* I heard Michael clearly in my head.

"Kara." Kyle poked me.

"What?" I looked at him.

"Are you going to answer Dad or not?"

"Michael told me why we are set apart. Well, Mom and me, anyway. It's in our linage."

"What are you talking about?" Mom asked.

"You read in the Bible about the sons of God finding the daughters of man pretty. And you read about legends of old. They are referring to Angels and women."

"What?" Kyle looked totally confused.

"Like Samson, Kyle," I told him.

"Are you saying that there is an angel in your family linage?" Uncle Daniel asked me.

"Yes, that is exactly what I am saying."

"But not all of …" Mom started.

I knew what she was thinking. "The power has always been there, Mom, but not everyone learned they had it or how to use it. And you never lost yours; you were just kept from using it."

"But why?" she asked.

"Because we have been set aside for a task. I don't know what it is yet, but I know that there is a task in the future that only we can do."

"Is it your task, not ours?" Dad asked "Your twins turn five today and today their training must start for they have been chosen for a great task."

"Yes, I remember that night well, too." Mom smiled at Dad. "You never forget an angel appearing at the end of your bed."

"So, what is our part in all of this?" Granddad spoke for the first time in the conversation.

"I have no idea," I answered him.

"Neither do I," Daniel told him.

It got quiet then. I think everyone started thinking on their own.

I lay my head over on Kyle's shoulder and closed my eyes.

*"Did Michael tell you who the angel was*?" Kyle asked in my head.

*"No, he wouldn't tell me."*

"*Are there others? I mean, there must be, right?"* Kyle asked.

*"I guess. I never have really thought about it before, but I'm sure we're not alone."*

Kyle's question made me wonder. Were we alone on this task or would we come across others like ourselves?

## CHAPTER 12

# INFLUENCE

I woke to Michael's voice. "Kara, come with me." Michael held my hand and I found myself in a strange place. "What is it you see, Kara?" he asked.

I looked around me, but didn't recognize anything. The streets were almost dirt and the houses looked small and dirty. There were men with guns on the streets, and most wore wraps on their heads. Their blue auras looked normal. The only woman I saw was covered head to toe; all that showed were her eyes. She was bright pink.

It looks like we're somewhere in the Middle East, but I'm not sure."

"Look at them closely, Kara; what do you see?"

I looked again. I looked for influence. The older was solid pink, but the younger one was different. What I saw was not red or white. What I saw was a turquoise cast, the color of Michael's eyes. It wasn't bright, but like an outline or shadow.

"What is that?" I asked him.

"It is the sign of a warrior. And yes, like my eyes." He looked at me.

"Warrior?"

"Yes, one chosen to carry out tasks that is beyond the normal for human kind. She, too, has a linage not unlike yours."

The two of them walked up the street past several houses with large gates and guards, then turned and went in one of the gates.

"There are many people you will come in contact with over your lifetime that you will influence; the woman is one of them. One day you will meet her here, and you will influence her journey in life," Michael told me.

Then, in the next instant, I found that I was back in my bed and Michael was sitting in front of me.

"How will I influence her?" I asked him.

"It's not the time for that answer, but you will know it by the time you meet her. You will dream of many people, and in those dreams, you will be given all you need."

"Did you show me this in response to Kyle's question earlier?" I knew the answer already, but I wanted him to tell me for sure.

"You know it is. You are not alone. You feel somewhat like the woman, alone and unsure. Not that you question who you are, but it is the future and purpose that hinders you from becoming all you can be." Michael reached up and touched my cheek briefly. "You have many things to learn, and many great things in front of you." He smiled. "And know this and let it give you comfort and confidence; you will complete each task given you."

I found myself lost in his eyes for a moment, and when I blinked, he was gone. My clock read 4:00, so I turned over, closed my eyes and tried to go to sleep.

"What are you doing awake?" Kyle said suddenly from behind me.

I turned to find him now stretched out on my bed behind me. "I had a visit from Michael," I told him.

"I find it strange that one minute I can read every thought in your head, then the next I can't. Why do you think he does that?"

"I guess some lessons are just for me and some are just for you, so he keeps us apart during those lessons."

"So, what was he teaching you so early in the morning?" Kyle rolled up on his elbow and looked me in the eyes.

"That we are not alone in our task. It was sort of an answer to the question you asked in the car earlier. I evidently will meet several of these people, and he was showing me one of them and how to tell who they were."

"Why are you going to meet them?"

"I guess, just like us, they are wondering about what is happing in their lives, and for some reason, I'm going to have to help them along their path."

"Why you? Why isn't an angel seeing to them, like they're helping us?"

"Easy answer?" Michael was now standing at the end of the bed. "Most people have had no dealings with angels and would…'freak out', as you guys say. You two are special and have been raised with the Word in your hearts. Not all people have had that, and they are not ready to see and accept it. These people need a little help to open their eyes to what is really happening in their lives."

Kyle sat up. "Why are you showing Kara these things and not the rest of us?"

"Because they will affect her most. You are a healer and she is the warrior. She will lead the battle and you will heal the hearts, minds and bodies of those broken by the battle. You will be a team, but she will lead the way."

I was a warrior? Did I have an aura like the woman he had shown me? I wondered.

"You do have an aura like hers, but she is a different kind of warrior than you. She has taken many lives, and will take many more before you meet her."

"You're talking figuratively, aren't you?" The thought of meeting a killer frightened me.

"No."

"What woman?" Kyle asked.

"In the future, you and Kara will meet a woman. Kara will use her influence to lead her in the right direction. You will be there to help heal her mind from what she has learned in the past."

I was still stuck on her being a killer.

"Don't worry, Kara, she is doing what she was meant to do. Killing is her path now and that's what she is doing. When the time comes, she will have another path. Don't be afraid. Remember the cliff and have confidence."

"Cliff? What cliff?" Kyle was so in the dark.

As I looked to Kyle, I saw Michael disappear out of the corner of my eyes. "I was thrown from a cliff in one of my lessons." I smiled at him.

"Thrown from a cliff? Why?"

"Remember the story of Isaac?"

'Yes, he was to be sacrificed, but at the last minute, a ram was provided."

"Why?" I asked

"God was seeing if Abraham was faithful, even if it meant he would have to sacrifice his son."

"Yes, that's it. If I hold nothing back and fear nothing, then all will be provided, just like the ram was provided."

"But what did being thrown from a cliff have to do with that?"

"I had reservations, fears about falling. I had to learn that I have things to complete, and that I shouldn't fear the things I can't see or understand."

"So how..."

"Once I understood, I walked up to the cliff and stepped off." I smiled at him. Kyle looked at me. "Michael has huge wings you can't see, but they are there, let me assure you. I've seen them."

"Whoa!" Kyle smiled. "Cool."

"You know, he really doesn't look like we see him, either. I haven't seen all of him, but I have seen his hand. He must be huge because I was the size of a doll in his hand."

"Really?"

"All right." Michael was again standing at the end of my bed. "You need your sleep. You have a busy day tomorrow"

"So, what do you really look like?" Kyle asked Michael.

He just smiled at Kyle, "She needs her sleep, Kyle."

"Oh, come on, Michael," Kyle sort of whined.

"One day, Kyle, but not today."

"Not fair!" Kyle straightened up.

"You can pout all you want, Kyle, but today is not the day, so go on."

Kyle disappeared from my bed, then Michael did, too. I lay back down and closed my eyes, but I knew it was not going to be easy to go to sleep.

"Michael." I said into the air, and then I felt his calm, soothing effect…

"You need to wake up Kara or you're not going to get to say bye to the guys," Mom said from my doorway.

I opened my eyes and looked at the clock; it was going on 6:30. I had to be in the studio-slash-dojo at 7:00.

"I'm awake." I sat up. "Are they flying or just…showing up there?" I asked her.

"I think they are just showing up, or they should have already been on a flight. Your dad cooked breakfast for you, so you better get in there and show him some love." She smiled at me from my doorway, then turned and left.

I climbed out of bed, washed my face, and then got dressed quickly and headed to the kitchen.

"Morning." Dad said and hugged me as I entered the kitchen. "I'm going to miss you, sweetie."

"You, too, Dad."

"I made you some breakfast." He pointed to the bar where a plate of three pancakes topped with syrup and bananas lay.

"Thanks, Dad." I kissed him on the cheek and sat down to eat.

"You want milk?" he asked.

"Yes, please."

Uncle Daniel and Granddad were sitting in the living room playing with David, but I didn't see Kyle. I tuned him in.

*"I'm sorry, Kelly, I just think it's for the best,"* I heard him say.

*"But it's just for the summer, right."* I could hear Kelly in his head. She sounded a little upset.

*"We'll see. I don't know what's going to happen, and I don't want you sitting around just because I'm gone."*

*"But breaking up just because you're going to be gone for the summer is a little drastic, don't you think?"*

*"No, I don't think it is. I want you to go out and have a good summer, and if you meet someone, well, then you won't have to feel guilty because I'm gone."*

*But I am not going to meet anybody, Kyle. It's me and you forever."*

*"Not forever, Kelly."*

*"What? You don't think we can make it?"* I could hear her upset turning to anger.

*"Listen, Kelly, we are a little too young to be talking about forever."*

*"No, we're not!"* Yep, she was angry now.

*"Maybe this is good, because I think we are. I'm not ready for anything serious. I want to live first. I want to go out and have a good time, see the world, make my mark. What is it that you think we were doing?"* Kyle asked.

*"Well, evidently, I am a little more mature than you. It looks like this was a good thing. If you're scared of commitment, then you are definitely not for me. I want someone who will commit to our relationship. I am not just some fun thing to play with!"*

*"Commitment? Oh, good grief, we are only fourteen, not thirty."*

"Kara." Mom touched my arm.

"What?" I looked at her.

"Finish eating and stop eavesdropping on your brother."

"What's he doing?" Dad asked.

"Matthias!" Mom looked at Dad.

"He's been up there a long time," he told Mom in his defense.

"He's breaking up with Kelly," I told him.

"Really, what for?" Mom asked.

"He's going to be gone all summer; it wouldn't be fair to her." I smiled. I wasn't going into details; those were between him and Kelly.

"Probably a wise thing," Dad said after a moment.

"What time are you guys leaving?" I asked, changing the subject.

"We are supposed to be at Mr. Grady's at noon. We'll leave by eleven so we have plenty of time to gather up what we need," Uncle Daniel said cheerfully as he came up behind me.

"You really like these kinds of jobs, don't you?" I asked him.

"Of course I do. I've been doing them for over a hundred years."

"I still can't quite grasp that you both are older than me, and one of you is married to my daughter," Granddad said as he came in with David in his arms.

"You think it's hard for you," Mom laughed. "How do you think is for me, being married to someone older than my Dad?" Everyone laughed at that.

It was quite weird, I had to admit. My dad was older than my granddad.

Kyle came through the door as we were all laughing at the whole thing. I could easily see he was still thinking of his conversation with Kelly. I wonder how their conversation had ended.

"You, okay?" Mom asked him.

"Fine." He looked up at her.

"You're missing out on all the fun of picking on Dad and Uncle Daniel about being older than Granddad," I said, trying to get his mind off Kelly.

He looked up at me. *"You were right; I shouldn't have let it go on this long. I knew she wasn't the one, but I just didn't see..."* Kyle was in my head.

*"Kyle, I didn't know she was serious about you, I just knew it wasn't right, and didn't want her hurt or you hurt,"* I answered him, but I still felt bad for them both.

"So," Kyle said, looking at Dad, "when are we leaving?"

"*Kara!*" I heard Michael in my head. Crap! I looked at the clock it was going on seven.

"I've got to go, guys." I jumped up and started hugging everyone. "I'm sure going to miss you."

"You, too." Dad hugged me and gave me a kiss on the forehead.

"It seems I haven't been here but just for a day or two, and now we're off again." Granddad said and hugged me tightly.

"He's right," Uncle Daniel agreed as he bear-hugged me.

"I'll walk you down." Kyle put his arm around me as I walked towards the door.

"Love you guys."

"You, too." I heard as the door shut behind us.

The door had no more than shut when Kyle pulled me into a hug. "I don't want to go," He whispered in my ear. "Being apart for three months will be miserable."

"I know. The last few weeks have been bad enough." I held him tight.

I was going to miss him something fierce. We had really never been apart before. Well, not for more than a few days, and the thought of three months...well I was trying not to think of it.

We walked slowly down the stairs and saw Michael standing just outside the studio door.

"You will be able to talk some, and he can even come back on occasion," He said looking at me.

Kyle hugged me again and looked at Michael, then headed back towards the stairs.

*"Love you, Kyle."*

*"Love you, too,"* He said as he hit the second flight of stairs.

"Don't worry, Kara." Michael put his arm around me and gave me a hug. "The summer will pass fast and he will be back before you know it." He opened the studio door and I walked through.

There was a woman standing inside. She was a little shorter than me, about Mom's height. She had brown hair, and looked like she might have oriental blood somewhere in her genes.

"Kara, this is Carolina Cho."

I smiled at Michael, then at Ms. Cho. I noticed Michael had changed the room. There were no more shelves lining the walls. The mat on the floor was different, too. The whole room sort of had that Zen feeling. There was only one wall with mirrors now; the other three were covered in what looked like bamboo, and there were a few potted plants in the corner. It looked good; it had a sort of have calming feel.

"So, are you ready for some hard work?" she asked me.

"As ready as I will ever be," I told her.

"Good, then let's get started with some yoga. Nothing like it to get you warmed up and flexible. Have you ever done any before?"

"Yes, Mom teaches classes every week."

"Great, then this should be a breeze."

Some of her yoga was a little different than what Mom taught, but I was sure some of the poses had to do with whatever she was going to be teaching me.

"Michael says you are a quick study and a good student. He also says you will learn fast, but you take it one step at a time and don't overdo it. Teachers can be a little pushy." She looked at Michael, who was now in a downward dog stretch like we were.

"I just said she was gifted." He smiled.

Great. This was just what I needed: pressure to learn fast and do it just perfect. I gave Michael a smile. I was sure he was in my thoughts or at least I hoped he heard that. I was surprised that he was here for this part of my training. I never thought about him really showing himself to anyone else, although the gang in New York had seen him.

"So, what are you going to teach me? Michael really hasn't told me," I asked as we moved into a warrior's pose.

"I teach a little differently than most martial arts instructors. I combine the arts I know, so there is really no name for what I teach. You will learn parts of Karate, Kung Fu, Jiu-Jitsu, Judo, Tae-kwon-do, and Aikido. Each has its own uniqueness, but I have found that when you combine them, they are more complete."

Oh, good grief. I felt over-whelmed just hearing her talk about them.

*"Don't worry, Kara, with me here, you will learn twice as fast,"* Michael said in my head as he glanced my way.

*"Am I indestructible, too?"* I asked sarcastically.

*"Not until she leaves."* He smiled at me.

"Now, the first thing you must learn is how to breathe. In martial arts, breathing is essential." Ms. Cho spread her legs and stood in that stance that you associate with martial arts.She put her hands on her legs. "Breathe in through your nose and out through your mouth. Come on, follow my lead."

I mimicked her stance and placed my hands on my legs like hers.

"Close your eyes and just concentrate on breathing. In through your nose," she said and then inhaled deeply, "and out through your mouth." She exhaled. "Good," she said, "keep it up."

I heard her come over close to me.

"Now open your eyes. Pull your hand in like this." She pulled her hand close to her sides palm side up, but in fists. "This will be the first stance. Always come back to it. Now I'm going to go through a series of moves. I want you to watch first, then you can go over them with me slowly. Okay?"

"All right."

The morning went by quickly. I was surprised at how much of what she had shown me I remembered easily. We had spent hours going over stances and movements. It was just like an elegant dance, and I really liked it, so far anyway. Michael had excused around 11:00. He told me he needed to help Dad for them a few minutes, but he was back before she left at noon.

When he returned, he told me to go eat and to be back at 1:00.

Mom had lunch waiting when I got back up to the house. "So," she asked as I sat down at the bar, "how's it going?"

"Good. I guess, but this is just day one."

"That's true." Mom smiled.

"I'm supposed to be back at one. I think Ms. Cho is just going to be here in the mornings. So, I guess it's just Michael and me this afternoon. Most likely, this afternoon will be a lot harder than this morning," I told her.

"You're probably right. What do you think about the teacher? It's a woman?"

"Yes, Ms. Cho is about your height, with short brown hair and green eyes. She looks more American than Asian, most likely third or fourth generation. But she knows her stuff; she knows three or four arts and mixes them together."

"Sounds like she's going to be good."

"I guess so."

"I don't think Michael would have picked her if she wasn't."

"I'm sure you're right." I picked up my sandwich and took a bite.

"I'm going to visit Alina and her Mom this afternoon. I don't know what Michael has planned, but I thought I better let you know just in case you come back and I'm not here."

"Okay, tell them I said hi," I told her.

"I will. Don't have too much fun this afternoon." She laughed as she went through the living room towards the bedrooms.

I finished lunch and carried David down to the Explorer for Mom, then went back to the dojo. Michael was sitting in the middle of the room like he was the first day we started training; barefoot, pants and no shirt. I admired his physique just like then, too. He was handsome, for an angel, who really didn't look like that at all. I remembered his huge hand around me with its pearly shine, with flecks of all colors. I really had to wonder what he really looked like. I was sure it was a sight to behold.

"When you're done daydreaming, we will get started."

He was still sitting on the floor with his eyes closed. I walked over and stood in front of him. He opened his eyes and looked up at me.

"You know, you wouldn't be nearly as distracting if you just wore a shirt."

"Fine." A black t-shirt suddenly appeared. "Better?" he asked.

"Somewhat." The only way he would not be good looking is if he was an old man, but I didn't mind. I think I would rather him be a little distracting than ugly and old.

He laughed and got up. "We're going to work on what Cho taught you this morning, but we are also going to go further by exploring the," he smiled, "Miyagi part of the lesson."

"You and your movie references." I laughed.

"First position."

All afternoon, we explored every position and what it could be used for in defense and in offense. Around 5:00, Michael gave me some kind of drink for supper.

Just when I felt like I was close to information overload, we finally stopped and did about thirty minutes of yoga to end the day with. I had never done partners yoga. It made me feel extremely awkward because I was either lying on Michael, or he was on me in some weird way.

Mom was in David's room rocking him to sleep when I went in the bathroom to shower after our session was over. I was so tired; it was now going on 8:00. I stood in the shower and let the hot water soothe my aching muscles. I think I ached more from the intense stretching than the karate.

When I lay down on my bed, I figured I would be asleep in second, but to my surprise, I was wide awake. My body didn't want to move, but my mind didn't want to sleep.

"Kara!" Mom whispered from my doorway.

"I'm awake."

"So?" she asked.

"Well, I may not be able to kick butt yet, but a few days like today and I'll be able to… well, that is if I am able to move."

Mom laughed. "Which was rougher, this morning or this afternoon?"

"This afternoon, by far." I told her. "It was crazy. Have you ever done partner yoga?" I asked her.

"A few times. The stretching is really intense. Did you do some?"

"Yes. Cho warmed us up with yoga this morning, but Michael ended with partners tonight. I didn't know I could stretch that far."

"You may not be able to move in the morning. You'll be sore for sure."

"I already am!"

"I better let you get some sleep. See you in the morning, Kara. Love you."

"Love you, too, Mom."

I closed my eyes, but I just couldn't fall asleep. As I lay there, I got feeling that Michael was close. I opened my eyes to find him lying beside me. The ceiling of the room was like the night sky. I could see all the stars and the moon shining brightly.

"What do you think of when you look at the sky, Kara?" he asked.

I looked up at the skythat was now my bedroom ceiling. "How amazing it is. It's just crazy to think of the billions of stars and galaxies that are out there."

"But it is just a veil," he said.

"I guess you would see it like that, but to me, that is what makes it even more amazing. Michael?"

"Yes."

"Is there anything that amazes you?" I looked over at him.

He rolled up on his elbow to face me and smiled.

"I never have understood the human race and what the Creator sees in them, but you…well, I guess I'm finally starting to understand, because it is you that truly amazes me."

"Me? How in the world do I amaze you?" I asked him.

He rolled onto his back again. "I don't know how to explain it to you."

"Try."

I watched as he closed his eyes for a few seconds and then opened them again. "No."

"Why not?" I wasn't expecting him to say no. I sat up and looked down at him.

He opened his eyes and looked at me, but didn't say anything. His blond hair wasn't pulled back, and flowed over the pillow around his face. His eyes looked different to me. They were still turquoise, but they looked almost as if the color was moving around in them. It was like looking into the raging sea on a stormy night. Did they always look like that? I couldn't remember them doing that before. I loved his eyes and looked at them every time he was near.

"Why not?" I repeated as I rose to a sitting position beside him.

"Not now."

"Everything is 'not now' with you. If not now, then when?"

"When the time is right."

I looked at him; he was starting to aggravate me.

"Lay down on your stomach." He sat up.

"Why?" I asked.

"Kara, please, don't question me; just do as I ask."

"Fine." I lay down.

I got the feeling there was more going on than he was letting me know. I felt his hands gently touch my shoulders. He massaged up my neck and down my back. I closed my eyes.

"You're right, there are so many things going on here that you can't understand," he said, "and won't understand for a long time yet." He sounded as if he were mere inches from my ear. "I would love to tell you all I know, but I can't."

"Well, that stinks," I said softly, feeling relaxed now.

"I know, but it's necessary. I know that doesn't help, either, but you are key to a great many things, and knowing too much will only stress you out."

"I think I'm already stressed out knowing I don't know."

"You may think you are, but trust me, you're not."

I no longer felt him touching me, but I felt his calmness consuming every part of me.

"*One day, Kara, I will hold nothing back from you. One day, you will understand,*" He whispered in my head as I suddenly fell asleep.

## CHAPTER 13

# FOOL OR PURPOSE

The next few weeks flew by. Every day, I learned a new discipline in the martial arts. Each night Michael worked with me on learning the proper way to use them, and each morning Cho was impressed. Then each evening, Michael would soothe me to sleep. The weekends weren't much different. I still had class on Saturday, but Sunday I got to spend with Mom and David. We spent most of those mornings at one of the homeless shelters. Then in the afternoon, we would go to the park. David was growing fast. He was doing something new each week. He was now walking if we held his hands. It was crazy. He was only a few months old, but he was leaps and bounds ahead of other babies his age.

I sat on the roof one Sunday evening enjoying the weather and the stars. Tomorrow would start another week. *Kyle."* I searched for him in my head. *"Are you there?"* I hadn't talked to him since he left. Mom said she had seen Dad a few times and he said they were all doing well.

*"What's up, you miss me, don't you?"*

*"No."* I told him.

"*Liar.*"

"*I just wanted to know how things were going.*"

"*Fine, and I miss you, too. It's too quiet here without your incessant talking about how you look.*"

"*Ha ha! What are you doing?*"

"*Well, for starters the place is really cool, and Mr. Grady is adding all kinds of cool stuff up here. So far, we've added some solar panels. We completely gutted the kitchen and rebuilt it; it looks really good. He's making the house really livable, even though there are no roads. Everything is being flown into a meadow just down the mountain, and we have to pull it up with horses. But the coolest part about being here is what Dad is teaching me at night."*

*"At night!"*

*"Yeah. When everyone goes to sleep, Dad and I go out and he teaches me how to hunt."*

*"Really? Hunting?"*

*"Yes, and it is so cool. I've learned how to track and snare rabbits, which we've had for lunch or supper, but this coming week, we're suppose to start hunting bigger things, like deer and elk."*

*"That so cool."* I was glad to hear Kyle was having a good time.

*"No, what's really cool is that he's teaching me the Indian style of hunting: no guns, no modern stuff, just bow and arrows, which he has been teaching me how to make."*

*"It sounds like you've been busy."*

*"Every moment of every day has been packed with something."*

*"So, what are you doing now?"* I asked him.

*"Hauling water. The house is built over a cave, and it has a natural spring in it. We hope to get it pumped to the kitchen before long, but the hand pump had to be special ordered and hasn't come in yet. How's your training going?"*

*"It's tough; I spend about twelve hours at it, six days a week."*

*"Twelve hours a day!"*

*"Yep, the first six are with Cho. She's really cool and makes it all fun. But then the last part of the day I spend with Michael, and he can be all business sometimes."*

*"Yeah, right, Michael hard on you? I doubt it."*

*"What do you mean by that?"*

*"He acts worse than Rhett around you. By the way, have you talked to Rhett yet?"*

*"No, I haven't. What do you mean Michael acts worse than Rhett?"*

*"Are you that completely blind?"*

My head started to spin. How in the world did Michael act like Rhett? He wasn't human. "*You're kidding, Kyle, right?*"

*"I have to go. Dad's calling; I'll talk to you later."*

*"When did Dad calling ever stop us from talking. Kyle?Kyle?"*He never answered back.

I lay back on the rooftop patio lounge chair. My head was still spinning. He couldn't be right, could he? I mean Michael was always close to me when he was around, and a few weeks ago I did see something in his eyes when he was lying on my bed. Okay, maybe there was something to it. I mean angels fell for women. It was in the Bible, and I was proof. I had one in my linage

"It's forbidden for angels to be with the daughters of men."

I felt his presence just seconds before I heard him. "That's why you don't hear of it anymore." Michael stood at the side of my lounge chair.

"Forbidden, but does everyone go by..."

"Only once has any angel dared to go against Him. That angel and woman were cursed." He looked at me. He was talking about me and my linage.

"So, who was the one who broke it?"

"No, I am still not telling you who he is." He sat down on the edge of my chair and reached up and pushed my bangs from my eyes.

"Why do you do that?" I took hold of his arm.

"Do what?"

"Flirt with me." I still held his arm.

"I didn't know I was."

"So, I see angels can lie."

"What? No." He pulled his arm out of my hand.

"Can you honestly tell me you don't have feelings for me?" I sat up so we were face to face.

"You amaze me. I have already told you that."

"Yes, you've said that, but what do you mean when you say the word 'amaze'?"

"I have had little use for the human race. They have always caused the Creator pain, so I have had as little to do with them as I could all these years. That is, until you came into existence."

"Keep going, that hasn't explained it yet."

"I was given the task of watching over you and training you, and in doing so…" He paused.

"In doing so what?" I locked eyes with him.

"No." He stood up and backed away from me.

I got up, walked to him, and took hold of his arms with both of my hands.

"Do you want me to have to leave?" he asked me. "I am not finished with you. Please don't make me have to leave you untrained."

I let go of his arms and backed away from him. "Then stop flirting with me." I turned and left the roof.

My heart was doing flips. Did he really care for me, was I just reading it wrong? Dang it, Kyle, why did you have to put these thoughts in my head. I had been doing just fine with Michael. Oh, Lord, I hope I hadn't drawn a line--or worse, stepped over one. My mind wandered back to kissing him. No, no it was only a test, a test about Rhett. It was nothing to do with Michael and me.

"What's wrong?" Mom asked I as I flopped down on the couch.

"I've screwed up big time," I admitted to her.

"How?" she asked.

"I talked to Kyle earlier and he said something I had never really thought about, and now I can't get it out of my head."

"What did he say?" She looked at me.

Did I really want to tell her this? "He said Michael…" I couldn't even say it.

"Michael what?" Her look had got intense.

"He said that he was acting like Rhett does." I hoped she caught what I meant; I didn't want to have to spell it out.

Mom laughed. "Oh, good grief. He was sent to help you. He has to get close to you, talk to you, and touch you. And, no, he is not doing it like Rhett would, why do you say you screwed up?"

"Well, I sort of accused him of flirting with me."

Mom fell back on the couch in laughter. Should I tell her he didn't deny it, although he didn't confirm it, either? Well, maybe he did; he just did it politely.

"Kara," she said, "don't worry about it. I don't think he will hold it against you." She giggled again.

It was sort of silly sounding, now that I thought of it. Here was a mighty angel like Michael, and I accused him of flirting. Yeah, it was silly, wasn't it? Yeah, it was.

"You better get some sleep. You have training in the morning. I guarantee Michael will be there and won't even act like you said a thing."

I sure hoped she was right. "Thanks Mom. Why do I ever listen to Kyle. You'd think I would learn my lesson."

That evening, I showered and lay down. I still couldn't get Michael out of my head. I hoped I hadn't offended him. Man, I was silly. Why had I let Kyle sway my thoughts? I knew better. What was wrong with me?

"Please forgive me, Michael." I finally broke down in tears and said it out loud. I felt his warmth and comfort instantly.

The light was coming through the door where a line of people stood. And suddenly, Kara found herself sitting at a table looking at woman.

"Sorry about that, Kailia; my twin forgets his place here. We better get done. It looks like the line is already getting long outside," I was saying as I pointed to the door and the line of people. Where am I? I wondered.

All the men and women I could see were dark skinned. The women had shawls around their faces and several of the men had turban-like things on their heads. I looked around at the building we were in. It was small and had several make-shift rooms set up. I saw a couple of men and another woman working nearby. Why did Kailia look so familiar to me? I looked at each of the men as they brought me supplies and various other things. There was one white man among the group, and he was wearing a Red Cross arm band. He was bright blue and seemed to be in charge of things. Kyle was there too, and I noticed he had on an arm band, as well. He also looked older. I had to smile. His hair was longer, and not its normal mess. The older lady was quite pink, but several women in the line I noticed were yellow and orange. The men were brown and green. There were a lot of sick people here. There was a guy helping Kyle and I heard someone call him David. He was blue, but not as bright. I looked closely and saw it: a slight red cast. He was being influenced. I looked back to the young woman I had talked to. She was very bright pink with a spot of blue on her belly. I could see something else as well: turquoise. Now I remembered her; she was the warrior.

Kyle brought a bunch of supplies and sat down beside me. "*Sorry, sis, I just thought she might want to know.*" He told me in my head.

"Let's get started." The one guy I thought was in charged announced.

People started coming in one at a time. I asked each of them what was wrong or where they hurt. By lunch, I had already talked to well over a hundred people. I sat down by the warrior, Kailia. I had heard the older woman named Ruth call her.

"Have you got any names picked out?" I asked her.

"I haven't really given it a lot of thought yet," she told me. "Should I be picking out boy names or girl names?"

"Boy ones." I looked at her. "Yes, definitely boy ones."

"So, what are you plans when you get back to the States?"

"Well, I don't know." I smiled. "First thing I plan on is seeing my little brother."

"How many siblings do you have?" she asked me.

"There are just us and my little brother David; he will be seven this year. Man, I have sure missed him a lot. But as for real plans, I don't make plans because I've learned my life is not my own."

Kailia looked at me. "What do you mean?" she asked.

"Each moment of this life is just like a mission. It has all been planned out for us."

"Mission? What are you talking about?" The question on her face I expected, but the look of shock made me wonder about her, why she was here.

I laughed. "Sorry, am I confusing you?" I asked Kailia. "Come on, let me show you." I got up and threw my trash away. Kailia followed me. "I see your confusion, and I understand things aren't always what they seem to be. No one understands that better than me." I smiled at her. "But what I'm saying is not what you're thinking. Look around here; all these people, all this pain and suffering. It's not without a purpose."

"What purpose could there be in these people suffering?"

"If life were perfect and there were nothing to overcome, no challenges, what would there be to live for?"

"What?" Kaila looked at me.

"The Maker has sent me here for a purpose. I'm here to help these people with medicine and supplies, and you're here to help them in a whole different way. The Maker I refer to is the Creator of the Heavens and earth, Kailia."

"Oh, you're referring to God."

"Yes." I smiled at her.

"I find it so hard to believe He would allow people to suffer like this."

"That's just it, without suffering, people would not believe. Without evil, where is the place for good? Without need, where is the place for help?" I placed my hand on Kailia's arm. "I see the struggle in your eyes every time we meet. I know you have been sent here to help in ways I could never help. Ways most of us couldn't help. But know that you were sent here for a purpose. Even if it's not what you understand to be so. He did send you, make no mistake about it."

"It's time to get back to work," David yelled from the door.

"Okay, coming," I yelled back.

"He's not all bad." I looked at Kaila "He just has some bad influence. Now, Karen, on the other hand, I would not trust at all. Come on, we need to get back to work. We can talk more later." I smiled at Kailia.

Just before sunset, the clinic closed and we headed back out the door. Kailia and I walked at the back of the group.

"Kailia?" I slowed to let the group get ahead.

"Yes."

"I'm sorry if I confused you earlier. I just have so many things going on in me that I forget that not everyone is ready to hear what I have been sent to tell them."

"Sent?"

I laughed. "Sometimes I forget that people were not raised like I was, and their faith is not as strong as mine."

"What do you mean 'sent'?" Kailia asked me.

"Have you ever had a dream that affected you so much that you felt compelled to do something because of it?" I asked her.

"No."

"Well, I did, and that's why I came here. I had a dream when I was about fourteen of a woman. She needed to know that her life was more than what she had been taught, more than how she had been raised. She needed to know that her life wasn't her own, but it did not belong to whom she thought it did. She needed to know that God Himself put her where she was." I stopped walking and looked at Kailia. "I have no Idea what this is supposed to mean, but I know I am supposed to tell you. Oh, this sounds nuts, but here goes. Your gifts were given to you for a reason. There is a reason you are the best in your field. Do not fear anything or anyone. You will succeed in the task at hand, but remember to call out to Him, for He hears the very desire of your heart."

"Call on whom?" She stepped close to me. "No one knows I'm even here."

"God does." I smiled "And you have been chosen by Him to be a warrior."

"What are you two doing back here?" Kyle walked up to us.

*"Kyle, we need to talk. She needs your encouragement when I'm done. Don't go far."*

"Come on." I started walking again. "Just think about it, Kailia"

## CHAPTER 14

# AMAZING

I woke with my alarm beeping loudly. I reached over and shut it off, then lay back and replayed the dream in my head. This warrior, Kailia, is the one Michael had shown me before, and now I knew what she needed. I smiled, I had told her that my younger brother was seven, so I knew the events in my dream were still seven in the future. Would I remember it that long? I almost laughed. If I was being prepared, then I would remember.

I got dressed and ate, and then went to the dojo. I was early. It was only 6:30 when I opened the door. Still, Michael was sitting in his usual spot in the middle of the room. I sat down, crossed my legs, and closed my eyes.

The woman Kailia appeared before my eyes. Her aura was bright pink with its turquoise as usual, but she was not pregnant and, as I watched, she changed. She went from Middle Eastern looking to a Gothic-looking white girl. She had blonde hair with black tips, and her eyes were now green traced in black eyeliner. She had tattoos, piercings and black fingernail polish. I was getting confused. Was this the same woman, or a different one? The aura was the only thing that hadn't changed. Something Michael had told me about the warrior entered my mind. She was a killer. It sort of explained the change, yet it didn't. This woman didn't just change in style, her facial features and skin tone had changed, too. Was it possible? That was a silly question; anything is possible when it comes to God. Was there more I was supposed to do for her, or was this just information I was being given to understand what was going on. Most of what was going on I didn't understand, so why was I to understand this?

"Good morning." Ms. Cho said from behind me.

"Morning." I opened my eyes to find her and Michael both standing behind me.

"You ready to get started?" Michael asked me.

"Yes." I sure hoped he wasn't mad at me for being so stupid yesterday.

"Let's do yoga out on the roof this morning. Would that be okay?" Michael asked Cho.

"Sounds great," she smiled. "The fresh air will be wonderful."

"I'll grab some mats and meet you up there," Michael said.

"I'll show you the way." I walked towards the door with Ms. Cho right behind me.

"How beautiful," Cho said. When we got to the roof top patio.

"Mom went all out since we have no yard," I told her.

Michael came up right behind us. "Here we go." He handed us both a rubber mat, then moved a few chairs out of the way for us to have space.

"We should come up here every morning if it's not raining," Ms. Cho said as she unrolled her mat.

The day was filled like all the rest with new stances and movements. Ms Cho was again impressed with my advancement and ease of learning. She said that at the rate I was learning, I would a black belt by the end of the summer, that is if she went by belts.

Lunch came and went, and once again I was alone with Michael. To my great relief, he hadn't said anything about the previous day's silliness. I did feel, however, that he was going light on me, as if waiting on something. About 4:00, he looked up at me from the floor that I had just made him kiss with a nice little round house kick. He smiled, then looked towards the door. Rhett was standing there quietly beside Mom.

"We'll cut it short for today. See you in the morning." He got up and walked over to Mom, said a few words to her, then they both left.

"Wow, that was cool." Rhett walked over from the door. "I hope it is okay that I dropped by. I did try to call you, but you never seem to answer your phone anymore."

"Sorry, I am just so busy right now I don't have time for anything. Michael has me working out almost twelve hours a day.

"Oh my gosh, isn't that a little extreme?"

"He doesn't seem to think so." I smiled at him.

I picked up my towel and wiped the sweat from my forehead.

"So, what belt are you?" he asked.

"I don't know. Ms. Cho, my teacher, doesn't use the belt color system; but she did say that if she did, I would be a black belt she thought by the end of summer."

"I believe it. You're fast and can really move."

"Thanks."

"So, how is Kyle? I haven't heard from him either. April said he broke up with Kelly and left for the summer."

"Yes, he's in Montana working on a house with Uncle Daniel and Dad. Sorry that neither one of us has had time to talk. Things have just been crazy around here. David being born, Uncle Daniel and Granddad coming in, then all this new training-- I have barely had time to breathe!"

"It sounds like it. So why all the training?"

"Well, I am not all that sure myself. I just know that they want me to be prepared."

"Prepared for what?" he asked.

"How about we grab some water and go up to the roof?"

"Sure."

I grabbed a couple of bottles of water out of the fridge in the game room and we headed for the stairs. "I really don't know what I am being prepared for. I feel like one of those guys in the movies that are being trained to go out and save the world." I laughed.

"Ah, Neo, it's good to meet you." He laughed.

"Yeah, exactly."

We walked out onto the roof and sat down in some chairs. I sat down in a single one on purpose; I didn't want him to get any notions about making out. And I really needed to sort of break things off, even though we weren't officially dating.

"So, what have you been doing this summer?" I asked trying to get his mind off training and maybe down a different avenue.

"Not a lot, but we are going to Cancun next week for vacation."

"That sounds great."

"I guess."

He wanted to ask me something. I could see it in his eyes, and he was fidgeting with his water instead of drinking it. Oh, please don't let him ask me to start going out again, I thought.

"Kara."

"Yes." I looked at him.

"You have time to go to a movie sometime with me?"

"Rhett, I really don't. I haven't had time for anything…and I really think," how could I say this, "you should, well, look for someone else." There, I said it, but I felt horrible about it.

"Are you breaking up with me, too?" He stood up.

"We weren't going out. Well not really, but yes, I guess so."

"But why? Did I do something wrong?"

"No, I just feel it is unfair to you. I don't have time for anything; especially a boyfriend right now. It would just be wrong to lead you on because I really don't know when I'll have the time again, and I don't want you sitting around waiting, not that you would, but I wouldn't want it anyway."

"But isn't it my decision if I want to wait or not?"

How could I get this across to him without hurting him?

"Rhett," I said standing up to look him in the eye. "I think it's better to end it now before we both get any more attached. Who knows, maybe when things calm down and get back to normal, if that ever happens, then maybe if you're not seeing anyone else than we can pick back up. But for now, I really think we just need to let it go."

Rhett pulled me into his arms and put his lips to mine. I wanted to kiss him and did, but the whole time my head yelled, 'What are you doing? This is not helping!' I finally pulled back.

"I knew it, you don't want to do this, so why are you?"

"I'm not ready for this kind of relationship, Rhett." What else could I tell him?

"I'm not asking for a physical one. I'm not ready for that either, but where is the harm in kissing someone? Or having a boyfriend?"

"I can't do this, okay. Not now." I took a few steps back. "Please, let's just be friends for now and…"

"Yeah, sure, whatever." I could hear the hurt and anger in his voice as he walked towards the door.

"Rhett..."

He stopped with his hand on the door and turned and looked at me.

"I really like you, and I am not trying to hurt you, but things being the way they are right now…"

"Things the way they are?" He walked back towards me. "Kara, I know you're busy. I know you're training, but what harm can there be in us being a couple? I really care for you."

"I know you do, Rhett, and that is one of the main reasons I have to do this."

"What do you mean? It's because I care?"

"Crap, I hate this." I looked towards the sky and closed my eyes. I took a deep breath, then opened them and looked at Rhett. He had taken a step back from me and his eyes were wide with awe.

Suddenly, he dropped down on one knee and bowed his head.

I looked behind me and Michael stood there. He looked the same, but yet quite different. He was in all white and quite a bit taller than usual. He looked like what you thought an angel would look like. His robes were so white they almost glowed. He smiled and winked at me, then walked around me to Rhett.

"Get up." Michael told him.

Rhett stood up and looked at Michael.

"Do not be afraid, Rhett, for I have come so that you may know that great things are going to happen, and you must let Kara go. I see your heart and know that it is good but where you can see no harm, there can be influence placed that could greatly complicate what should not be complicated. Please go and be at peace."

Michael then disappeared and left Rhett and me standing there. Rhett smiled at me, gave me a hug and left without a word. The door had just shut when Michael reappeared beside me in his normal jean and t-shirt.

"He's a good kid." he said. "Don't worry about him. He'll be just fine. This I know for a fact."

"Why do things have to be so complicated?"

"You mean exciting? Why is it that humans want excitement, and when they get it, they don't see it?"

"I guess we don't look at adversity as excitement."

"Ah, but you should, each thing that happens in your life has a purpose, and whether it is just the act of going to the store, talking to someone, or saying 'not now,' each of them has the potential to be an adventure."

"I guess you're right, but we just don't see it that way. If we are turned down or we think something doesn't go our way it just ruins everything."

"I know. You're the most selfish creatures created, and yet He loves you like no others."

"Why does He, do you know?"

"No. If you had been my creation, I would have already destroyed all of you."

You could hear the seriousness in Michael's voice. He had already said he didn't understand humans and didn't really care for them, but until now, I didn't really know how honest he had been.

"I'm sorry if I disappoint you." I looked at him.

He turned to face me and smiled as he reached up and pushed my bangs to the side of my face. "You are not a disappointment to me. You are different. You have something no other human has."

"And what's that?" I asked him.

"Me." He grinned.

"Ha Ha Ha."

It seemed like the next few weeks flew by. I talked to Kyle a few times and he was still all excited about hunting, even more so when he killed his first elk. Dad had popped in a few times, and David was now walking and jabbering and me. I was all but done with my classes. Cho had said she was about out of things to teach me, and that I could probably beat her if we had a match. I must admit I did think I could take her.

I guess most of all, I was looking forward to the last week in July. Kyle and I would be turning fifteen, and they were supposed to be back that week so we could celebrate.

"So, what do you want for your birthday?" Mom asked me as we sat eating supper that evening.

"I just want Dad and them to be home," I told her.

"They're supposed to be back next weekend, but I thought maybe we could go out on Friday and surprise them. What do you think? Your Dad said next week would just be clean up and most of the men would be gone by Wednesday, so if we got there on Thursday..."

"That would be great! I'd like to see the place. Kyle has told me all kinds of things about it and it really sounds cool."

"Of course it all depends on if you're done with classes, and if Michael says it's okay."

"He should. We're basically done with training, and he hasn't kept me late in two weeks."

*"Michael,"* I asked in my head, *"can we go?"*

David suddenly reached out and Mom and I turned to find Michael standing behind us.

He picked David up from his highchair. "Sounds like a great idea," he said, "but I think you should stay the whole next week. Mr. Grady won't mind."

"Great!" Mom said, "A family vacation!"

"You coming with us?" I asked him.

"Yes. I think you and Kyle need a rematch."

"I think I can take him."

"I don't know. He's learned a lot from your Dad these last few months."

"About hunting," I said.

"Yes, but hunting is a game of skill, and it will take skill to beat you."

"What are we talking about?" Dad's voice came from behind Michael.

"Dad!" I jumped up and gave him a huge hug.

"Kara is wondering if she can now kick Kyle's butt," Mom told him as she got up togive him a hug.

"I don't know," he said "He's become quite the brave."

Dad took David from Michael and Michael pulled me toward the door.

"Come on," he pulled on my arm. "Let's give them some time." He glanced back. "Would you like us to take David?" he asked Mom.

"No, he's fine, but thanks."

"Just let me know if you want us to come get him." He smiled as he opened the front door and ushered me out.

"Where are we going?" I asked him.

"To the roof." He headed for the stairs.

We both grabbed a lounge chair and lay down under the stars. I looked over at Michael; he had his eyes closed. "What are you thinking?" I asked.

He opened his eyes and turned his head to look at me. "As time unfolds and I learn more about the future, I am amazed at the things that will come to pass."

"I thought you knew the future."

"Yes and no, some things I know, some things I don't. I'm only given what I need, like you."

I had never really thought about that. I just figured he knew it all. It was crazy to think he was sort of in the same boat I was.

"Sort of sucks, doesn't it?" I laughed.

"I guess it does, but for as much as we are alike, we are totally different."

"So tell me, how are we alike and how are we different?"

"We were both created in the Maker's image and made for a purpose."

"What do you really look like?" I asked him. I had seen his hand and it was enormous.

"Mainly like this, but larger."

"Are all angels alike?"

"No. Each was created for a specific reason, so like humans, there are differences."

"You're a warrior, a sword wielder, right?"

"Yes."

"Will you show me?"

Michael sat there a moment, then stood up and held out his hand. He pulled me into his arms and looked up. I heard the sound of his mighty wings as we lifted into the night sky. I watched as his wings came into focus around us as they pushed the air down and we went higher. His chest grew before me and I felt like a Barbie doll once again. His hair now tumbled down around me and was bright and shiny like the sun. The wind became so strong I closed my eyes and held tight to his hand, which now held me.

When the wind ceased, I opened my eyes. He sat me gently down on a rock. Michael was like nothing I had ever seen. Mighty and fierce came to mind as I looked at him. He looked at me with eyes like a raging sea, all turquoise and violent. His face was close to what it always was, but much larger. What he wore reminded me of a Roman soldier, minus the helmet. His hair was now in a long braid down his back, between his enormous wings. They were a grey green color, but sleek and smooth. They looked more like a dragon's than that of a bird. His sword hung to his side and was taller than I was. His skin had almost a green cast to it, like he was covered in emeralds. He was quite magnificent standing there.

He reached down and ran his finger under my chin. I felt so tiny standing there.

"Wow, you are…" I couldn't find the right word. "amazing." I decided on his own word for me.

He smiled and picked me back up. I closed my eyes and held onto his hand until the wind ceased. When I opened my eyes, his arms were wrapped tightly around me and I was tightly wrapped around him.

"You're amazing," I repeated, and then let go of him and stepped back.

"I think the same thing about you."

"But I'm nothing compared to you."

"You are everything." He smiled and touched my cheek with his finger. He instantly pulled it back as if when he touched me, it had burnt him. The expression on his face changed and he stepped back.

"Your lessons with me are done." He turned and was gone instantly. I couldn't see him anymore, but I swear I heard his wings.

I walked back and sat down in the lounge. Something had changed. I had seen it in his eyes, felt it in his touch. What, though, I wasn't sure. Maybe I was wrong, maybe it was nothing…yet I got the strangest feeling...

"Michael?" I said in to the night sky "Is everything okay?"

I never got an answer and finally gave up and went back downstairs. But instead of going home, I went to the game room and laid down on the sectional.

"Kara." I opened my eyes to find Michael standing over me in all his magnificence. "The time has come for me to leave you."

"What? We still have another couple weeks."

"I have taught you all I can, and it's time I get back to the war."

"War, what war?"

"You know the war I talk about. It is ever constant and it's time I got back to it."

"But I thought you were going to always be watching over me."

"I will be. I will fight for you until the end of time." He ran his finger down the side of my face and changed before my eyes to the man I was used to seeing. He walked around the side of the sectional and pulled me up and into his arms.

"Fight for me, what are you talking about?' I asked him.

"I have to go, but I am always close." He let go of me and turned away, but then quickly turned back and held his hand out. A small chain dangled from his hand.

"Keep it with you at all times." He smiled. I reached for the chain and as soon as I took it, he was gone.

I looked down at the necklace. It was silver with a small charm on it. Two figures, one larger holding a smaller one. The detail was amazing: his wings and uniform, my small figure and short hair. It was most definitely us. I fastened it around my neck. It was the perfect choker size. I rubbed my finger over it, then walked into the dojo to look in one of the mirrored walls. The little charm fit perfectly in the little spot at the base of my neck. I wondered what I should tell Mom about it; I knew she would ask. As I looked in the mirror, I suddenly noticed a figure behind me. I turned to face the stranger. Who was he, and what did he want?

"I am Gabriel." He looked at the necklace then back up to meet my gaze. "What Michael has given you is special. Never go without it."

Gabriel had dark brown shaggy looking hair and the darkest blue eyes I have ever seen. His sliver grey aura would have told me he was angelic even if he hadn't mentioned Michael. Otherwise, he looked quite normal in his jeans and a t-shirt.

"Why is it so special?"

"I will be your next teacher," He told me.

"I thought James was to be my next teacher." I was sure I remembered Michael saying James would come next.

"Things have changed," He said simply.

"So when do my classes start?" I asked.

"They start now…

I found myself standing in a yard in front of an old house. There were two men and a woman working on cleaning it up. There were literally piles of garbage everywhere. The two men were a nice color of blue, but looked rough. The woman was a bright pink. I looked even closer for influence: the two men had none, but the woman had a tinge of red. It was so small I almost missed it.

"Can I do something for you?" The woman looked up to find me staring at her.

"Would you like help?" I asked.

The woman smiled. "We could always use help. There are gloves, trash bags, and shovels in the back of my truck." The woman came up and walked me to the truck. "I am Lorain." She took off her glove and stuck out her hand. "I'm Kyle." I looked behind me, startled I didn't even know he was there. He shook her hand, then I did.

"Kara." I told her.

"So, what are you doing to the place, besides cleaning it up?" Kyle asked her.

"I plan to restore it." She pulled two sets of gloves from a bag in her truck bed.

"My Uncle and Granddad restore old houses, too." Kyle, told her.

"Really?" She asked.

"Oh yes, they've been at it for years. You may have heard of them, DMJ Restoration?"

"Yes, I have heard of them. They are supposed to be one of the best in the business," she said as she handed him a shovel.

"Oh, they are."

"So how did you two end up here?" The woman handed me a shovel.

"We were down at St. Michael's shelter and overheard a man telling another about being kicked out of his house and you offering him a job and a place to stay if he helped clean up," I told her.

"Ah, yes, there were four men staying here. Two left and didn't return, but two stayed." She looked to the two men cleaning.

"This is an awful rough neighborhood for you two."

I looked at Kyle. We were still young, and so this couldn't be too far in the future.

"I told Dad we were coming to check out the place, and we are more capable than we look." Kyle told her.

"As long as you're on the house grounds, you're safe. But don't venture out in the neighborhood without me or your Dad." Lorain told us.

"Are you going to talk all day or help?" one of the men said as he walked by us to drop his bag into the large dumpster sitting beside the truck.

"Looks like we better get busy," She said. "This is John, by the way, and that's Nathan."

"I hope you're ready to work because she works you hard," John said.

"I'm up for any challenge." Kyle smiled at John.

"Then let's get busy." Lorain headed back into the lot and we followed.

I opened my eyes to find I was laying back on the sectional in the game room. Gabriel wasn't anywhere in sight. I got up and went back upstairs to the house. The lights were out, so I quietly got a shower and headed to bed.

CHAPTER 15

# MICHAEL'S BROTHER

I woke to my alarm going off and I wondered if I needed to go downstairs. I knew my lessons with Michael were over, but had he told Cho? I decided better safe than sorry and got dressed and went to the kitchen to eat. The house was still quiet, so I ate and was headed back down the hall when I heard David.

I went to Mom's bedroom door. She was still asleep, so I went to check on David. He was awake and standing in his crib looking at the door.

'Hey, little man," I said as I picked him up. "You hungry?"

I took him back to the kitchen, put him in his high chair, and then got a jar of fruit and mixed it with some cereal. I also got him some milk in a Sippy cup. Once he finished breakfast, I cleaned up both of us, left Mom a note on the table, and headed downstairs with David in tow. It was 7:00 sharp when I walked in. Cho and Michael were sitting on one of the benches, talking.

"Mom's still asleep," I told her, "So I am watching David this morning to give her a break."

"That's okay. This is my last day here and I really have nothing left to teach you, so I was just going to get my stuff and say goodbye," she told me.

"He's so cute." Cho tickled David in my arm's he giggled and wiggled so much that I had to put him down before I dropped him.

Cho and I talked a while and she gave me a few final pointers on keeping the upper hand, and then left.

As soon as Cho left, I turned to Michael, but he spoke before I did. "So, you met Gabriel last night?"

"You know I did, but I thought James was supposed to be my next teacher. Why the change?"

"Timing," he said. "Gabriel teaches mainly in the mind, so you can be anywhere, and right now, that's going to be to your advantage."

"Why is the necklace so special?" I asked him

"It has a message, a warning to any demon that sees it. It will let them know that in facing you, they are facing me. But don't make the mistake of thinking it will stop all of them because it won't. It will, however, make them think twice before they bother you. Don't worry about it, Kara. If you need me, I will come."

"You promise?"

"Is that not just what I said I would do?" He touched the necklace. "I promised to watch over your until the end."

"The end of what?" I looked at him. "My life, or time itself?"

"Both." He smiled and gave me a quick hug. "I have to go," he said, and then vanished.

By the time I got back to the house, Mom was up and getting some breakfast.

"Sorry, I should have come got him," she asked.

"He's fine. My classes are over. I'm officially trained."

Mom reached up and touched my necklace. "Wow, that is gorgeous."

"Michael gave it to me last night when he told me I was done with his part of my training."

Mom came a little closer and looked at the charm. "Looks like you're well protected." She smiled at me. "Is he still going to Montana with us? When's James coming?" She had remembered him telling us James would be next, too.

"I don't know. I guess he's still going, but James is not coming right now. Gabriel is teaching me next instead. Not real sure why the change.

Anyway, I meet Gabriel last night." I hadn't lied because I really wasn't sure.

"Do you think we can still go next week, then? I talked to your Dad and he liked the idea."

"Michael said we could, but I'll ask Gabriel just to be sure." I wondered when I would see him again. He never told me exactly when we would be training or how, but Michael had said his training was mainly in the mind, so maybe that's what he meant when he said it would work to my advantage.

"What are your training times with him?" Mom asked.

"I don't know, he didn't say, but I think it is mainly going to be dream training, if that makes sense."

"Not really, but not much does make since to me anymore, so I just go with it. I guess what I really want to know is how are we supposed to plan our days and trip?"

"No clue."

"Great, so what do we do?"

*"Plan your trip."* I heard Gabriel in my head. *"My training is different, so you don't have to be anywhere specific."*

"Just go for it, Mom; Gabriel just told me it was fine."

"Good. Go get your laptop. Let's get some plane reservations made."

We spent the rest of the morning planning the trip and got the flight reserved for the next Thursday afternoon. I think we were both excited. Even David seemed to understand something was going on and he was quite happy, too. The rest of the day flew by with plans and washing laundry and getting things in order for our trip. That night, I lay in bed thinking on Monday the 25th, Kyle and I would be fifteen. Mom had asked what I wanted for my birthday, but since we were going out to see the guys, I really didn't know of anything else I wanted.

My mind wondered to Turtle. I wondered how she was and how her Aunt Jenny was. I closed my eyes and concentrated. I hoped I could find her and tune her in. Voices came and went. It was like turning the radio station channels, trying to find your favorite DJ. I wasn't having much luck. I guess my mind was still stuck on the trip and it seemed the only person I could find was Kyle.

*"Supper was great, Dad. Who knew that raccoon could taste good!"* I heard him.

"*You ate Rocky Raccoon?*"I asked.

*"Yes, and he was scrumptious."* He laughed.

"*Sounds like your hunting is going good."*

*"I bet I could take you easy now. I'm as stealthy and deadly as a cougar on the prowl."*

This time I laughed. *"I'll take that bet,"* I told him.

*"You don't stand a chance."*

*"You just keep telling yourself that."* I smiled to myself. I was pretty good at being silent and deadly myself. "*So, Mom asked me what I wanted for my birthday earlier. Dad asked you yet?"*

*"Of course, he's been asking me all week."*

"*Wel?"* I waited for his answer.

*"I don't know. I have everything I need, and the last three months have been so great that I really don't want anything."*

*"Who are you and where is my brother?"*I knew better than that. There was always something he wanted. Although with his new power, he really didn't need for anyone to get him anything. All he had to do was think about it and it was his, which wasn't fair. I couldn't do that, but on the other hand, he couldn't do nearly all the cool things I could do.

"*Nope, I'm way cooler,*" He interrupted my thought.

"*Not even close, brother. I have you beat hands down.*"

"*Got to go, sis. Dad's calling."*

I hate to admit how much I had missed him the last three months, but I really had. Even if he was in my head, I just missed him. He was the other pea in my pod.

"Well, I see we didn't run you off," Lorain said as I found myself walking up beside her truck.

"Of course not," Kyle answered her from beside me. "We even brought an extra pair of hands."

I turned to see who he was talking about and saw Dad smiling with his hand outstretched. "Matthias Johns at your service."

"Nice to meet you." Lorain shook Dad's hand. "We can use all the help we can get."

Dad looked at the house and smiled, "This used to be a grand house. I'm glad to see it getting restored."

"Are you their Dad or Uncle?" Lorain asked.

"Dad, but I used to help their Uncle." Dad had that look on his face when he smiled. He remembered the place in its glory days, not just seeing it in some picture.

"I use to be the M in DMJ, but now the M is my father-in-law. Luckily, he is a Matthew, so the M still fits," He told Lorain and laughed.

"Maybe you wouldn't mind giving me a few pointers."

"Daniel was the restorer and I just took orders, but I'll help out any way I can." Dad was looking at the house like he had fond memories of it. "This house used to hold lots of secrets."

"Really? What can you tell me about the house?" Lorain asked.

Dad strode up the walk to the door. "May I?" He paused at the door.

"Please." Lorain followed him. Kyle and I did, too.

Dad opened the door and we all walked into a grand entrance, or what used to be the grand entrance. It was just a mess and pretty rough- looking now.

Dad stood looking over the place, and then walked to the left and into another room.

"This part was the parlor, but up there was the library." He pointed to what looked to be a banister and bookshelves. "There was one of those ladders that rolled along the tall shelves. But that's not what was so special about the library. It used to hold a special office and two hidden rooms. Even though we are in the North, slave owners still sent people to retrieve their runaway slaves, and Mr. Mayer would hide them and smuggle them to Canada." Dad sounded like he knew first-hand, and he most likely did.

"How do you know so much about the house?" Lorain asked.

"Any house Daniel wanted to restore, he made sure he knew the history, too." He smiled at her and winked at me.

Dad carefully climbed the slender staircase to the rows of bookshelves. He walked to the end, and then turned and took three long strides back. He then turned and faced a slender shelf and pushed it backwards. He pulled out his cell phone, and turned on the light, and went into the darkness. Lorain quickly went up the stairs and followed.

"I'm not missing this." Kyle headed for the stairs. I wasn't about to either, and followed close behind him.

I turned on my cell phone light and went into the opening. We found Dad standing in front of a large desk. Evidently no one had discovered the house's secrets. The room looked like Mr. Mayer had just left his office and would return at any time. Of course, there were two inches of dust on everything, but other than that, it looked like a normal furnished room.

"I can't believe this," Lorain was saying. "Millie didn't tell me about this room."

"Millie?" Dad asked and looked at Lorain.

"Mayer's granddaughter, James's daughter."

"I bet she don't know about the rooms. James was just a young boy when his Dad ran the hidden rooms." Dad turned and walked over to the corner of the room and carefully moved a small table and rolled back the rug to reveal a trap door. "There are two rooms under this one, both very small. They're about the size of a closet, but slaves didn't care to be crammed together for a few days if it meant freedom. The bottom room has a small door that leads into the coal chute, just in case they needed to get out and not go through the house."

"Hey, anybody in here?" I heard Nathan yell.

I went to the office entrance then out to the shelves. "Up here."

"What are you doing up there?" he asked.

"Finding secrets out about the house." I smiled at him and John, who was standing next to him.

"Secrets? What kind of secrets?" John asked.

"Did you know this house was used to smuggle slaves to Canada?"

"But wasn't this considered the North? If my history serves me right, the North didn't have slaves," Nathan said.

"Ah, yes, but that didn't stop Southern owners from sending hired men to bring their runaway slaves back." Dad emerged behind me.

"You're Matthias Johns, aren't you?" John asked.

"Yes," Dad looked at John.

"He owns The Village," John told Nathan.

"Really?" He looked at Dad. "You have the best food in town!" He met Dad at the bottom of the stairs and stuck out his hand. "Nathan."

"Nice to meet you, Nathan." Dad said and shook his hand.

I got the feeling right then that I wasn't here for Lorain, like I had previously thought, but for Nathan.

My eyes opened and looked at my clock. It was 4:00 in the morning. I closed my eyes again but couldn't fall back asleep, so I got up and went to the roof. Gabriel was waiting.

"Good morning," he said as I sat down on the lounge chair beside his.

"Morning." My mind wandered to Michael. I already missed him. I wondered how the battles were going and if he could get hurt.

"He's fine. Don't worry about him. He was created for battle," Gabriel told me. "Now we need to talk about Nathan."

"But I want to know why he had to go to war suddenly?"

Gabriel turned to face me. "He has always been at war. This was not a new battle."

"Yes, I know, but he said..."

"The battle just has new meaning for him now."

"What do you mean?"

"When Michael was created, you could say he had a brother. There were two created at that time."

"Michael has a brother!" Gabriel just looked at me. "Sorry, go ahead."

"Yes, but his brother... Well, he didn't do what he was supposed to and turned against his Creator. Michael blames humans for that."

Turned against God. Was his brother Lucifer? I wondered. Surely not, but...

"Yes." Was all Gabriel said.

"Well, that explains why he really doesn't like us. He blamed us for his brother's fall."

"Yes. He has never really cared for humans, but he has always followed the Maker's bidding, no matter what he was asked to do, even fighting against his own brother. But he only about half-heartedly fought, as you would say. But because of you, the battle has new meaning for him."

What did he mean by that, I wondered.

"The Master knew what he was doing when he gave Michael the task of watching over you and training you. Michael has learned why the Maker sent the Lamb, and now he understands why He loves the human race so much."

"But it still…"

"It has been thousands of years since the Maker has allowed an Angel to get this close to a human." Gabriel looked at my necklace. "But because of his closeness, the war is now personal to Michael. He has a reason to win every battle, to keep demons at bay, to put his brother in his place."

My mind was stuck on the *Angel get close to a human* part. He was talking about Michael and…and me.

"Kara." Gabriel touched my arm and brought me back from my thoughts. "Why this is so significant is because Lucifer is the angel in your linage."

My head began to spin and I had to lean back in the lounge chair to keep from falling over. I was Michael's brother's great-great…well…oh, this was wild. Wait, Gabriel said it had been thousands of years since God had allowed an angel to get close to a human. What did that mean? How close was he going to get. Had Kyle been right all along? But this was crazy, I mean…wasn't it?

"Don't even go there." Gabriel said and looked at me. "Now, can we get back to Nathan?"

"I'm not sure what you've just told me, and I am totally confused. First to get close to a human, what does that mean?

"It is not the right time for that discussion."

"Not the right time?" I stood up and looked down at him. I needed to know more.

He stood up and looked down at me. "I mean not now; in time, yes, but not now. Now it's time to learn about Nathan."

My life had gone from making some sense to now feeling like I was wondering through a large forest with no sun or moon to guide me. I closed my eyes and took a deep breath. I understood, yet I didn't. Why me? Why now? All kinds of questions were flying through my mind. My heart was racing as if I was running at full speed, and then a sudden, calmness overcame me. I heard a voice, but not Michael's. It was like a whisper in the wind, yet it was clear.

"*I know your deeds. See, I have placed before you an open door that no one can shut. I know that you have little* ***strength****, yet you have kept My Word and have not denied My Name.*"

I knew this verse; it was in Revelations. I saw the cliff in my head, saw Michael push me off, and then I saw when I walked off. I felt a sense of purpose, a new sense of urgency. After everything that had already happened to me, I should know that I was chosen for a purpose, and I should have great confidence in it, but until that very moment, I don't think I had. I think I finally understood Mom's unswayable faith, her unyielding love for people and for God. She understood that she had been chosen and had accomplished more than any mortal human could have. Somewhere in my future, I would too and I knew it. Now, I really knew it. I had been chosen by God for some great purpose, a purpose bigger than me. As the indescribable calmness spread throughout me, I also felt Michael and his mighty arms and wings wrapped tightly around me. I knew when I opened my eyes he wouldn't be there, but I felt him nonetheless. I think it was his way of letting me know that he was still near and still watching me.

"So," I sat back down and looked up at Gabriel, "what were you saying about Nathan?"

He smiled. "He needs a little help heading in the right direction, a little nudge, if you will."

"What do I need to do?" I asked.

By 6:00 that evening, I was laying back in my bed thinking about all Gabriel had told me, mainly about Michael, but I had listened and kept my focus while we talked about Nathan. But now that I was alone, my mind couldn't help but wonder to Michael again. This "getting close to a human" still had me confused. Did he mean as close friends, or was there more to it? I closed my eyes and could see Michael's beautiful turquoise eyes, his long hair, and his massive chest. He was so big, and I was just a small human. My heart began to race as I remembered being held tightly against him.

I awoke almost completely drenched in sweat, my heart still racing. I glanced at the clock; it was going on 8:00am. It took me a few minutes to catch my breath, and then I headed for the shower. I had no idea what had happened to leave me in such a state, but it was not the first time I'd experienced it. It had happened before. I dried off and got dressed.

## CHAPTER 16

# BAD NEWS

Mom and David were in the living room when I headed to the kitchen.

"I thought you were going to sleep all day," she said as I opened the fridge.

"I had a lesson with Gabriel at four this morning."

"Four? Good grief! You weren't kidding about dream lessons. So, what kind of lesson is at four in the morning?" she asked.

"One about the future and what has to be done," I told her.

"Okay, I have to ask." Mom got up and came to sit on a bar stool. "What does Gabriel look like?"

I laughed. "Pretty normal. He has brown hair and dark blue eyes."

"Did you ask him about Mary?" she asked.

Mary? I had to think a minute. "No, Mom, I didn't ask him about telling Mary she was pregnant."

"Really, I think that is the first thing I would have asked him." She smiled. "How was your lesson?" She then asked.

"Eye opening." I pulled the milk from the fridge and got out the cereal.

"How so?" she asked.

"It seems I'm supposed to give people a nudge in the right direction. Influence, I guess."

"How is that eye opening? We already knew you were supposed to help people."

"Well, I guess it's just that I dream about these people long before I am to meet them, and it's just weird."

"I guess that would be strange. Are all your lessons going to be at four in the morning?"

"I sure hope not, but he didn't say. So, what are we doing today?" I asked her.

"I thought we might go birthday shopping."

"Sounds great." I needed something to occupy my mind and keep me busy. Mom was quite the expert shopper.

"I thought we might get you some clothes. You seem to be outgrowing everything I just bought you."

I didn't like clothes shopping, but I did need jeans before fall, and my shorts were climbing up, too, which meant I was probably getting taller. I almost laughed, I wasn't really tall at all compared to Michael.

"What's that smile for?" Mom asked.

"Oh nothing. I'm just glad to be getting taller."

"Since when?" She looked at me.

"I've decided I want to be as tall as Uncle Daniel, maybe taller."

"What's brought on this sudden change?"

"I don't know, maybe the fact that when you're taller than everyone, they seem to listen more. I have a lot to say and I need people to listen."

"That's true in a sense. People who are taller seem to demand a certain presence when they're in a room, so maybe this is a good thing and will help you in your missions." Mom left the kitchen and returned with a tape measure. "Let's see how tall you have gotten. I tell your Dad you have grown a foot all the time, and he just laughs at me." I walked over and stood against the wall. Mom put her finger to the wall then I moved. "Put your finger here," she told me as she got the tape measure and ran it up the wall. "Six foot-two inches," she announced. "You're just an inch shorter than your Dad!"

"How tall is Uncle Daniel?" I asked.

"I believe he's six foot-four, but I'm not sure."

"I hope I reach seven foot then."

"At that height, you would definitely demand attention when you walked into a room!"

"I wonder if Kyle has gotten any taller this summer."

"Your Dad says he's grown, but I don't know how much. He says he has filled out a lot, too, has a few muscles."

"I'll believe it when I see it." We both laughed.

I was now even more excited to go see Kyle. Six-two? I was now taller than just about everyone I knew. A few months ago, and I would have been bummed, but now I was thrilled. It's crazy what a difference a few months can make in your whole outlook. David made a noise and got my attention. He was standing at my feet with his arms lifted.

"Hey, cutie, do I look extremely tall to you?" I asked him as I picked him up. He just grinned and laughed.

"Let's get going. I hear there are some good deals over at the mall today," Mom said as she…?

"Let me finish and brush my teeth

"I'll go get David ready." She went down the hall.

I finished my cereal, cleaned my bowl and spoon and put them away then went to the bathroom. My hair was longer, too, I noticed in the mirror as I brushed my teeth. I hadn't had it cut since spring, but I still liked the way it looked. I put a small amount of make-up on, and put in some silver hoops, then slid on my flip flops.

Mom and David were waiting by the door.

We spent all day going from store to store and from one mall to the next. I had a whole new wardrobe by the end of the day. David had several new outfits and so did Mom. We had a great time, I had to admit. I found that having no one to impress, but always wanting to look my best, made me a little pickier about the clothes I chose. Mom had made several comments throughout the day about the things I had chosen, and about how grown up I had become.

It was going on 7:00 pm when we got home. I used the elevator to take our haul up to the house. David had been as good as gold all day, but had crashed on the way home, so Mom put him to bed. I sat everything on the couch then slowly started going through each bag and putting them into piles.

"Tomorrow, we can wash them all and get them put away. We'll go through your closet and take your other clothes to one of the shelters," Mom told me as she opened one of the bags and started pulling out clothes.

"Sounds good to me. I'm beat."

"Me, too. I think we did well." She looked at our clothe piles.

"I had a good time, Mom."

"Me, too, sweetie; it was a good day. I even think David had a good time watching us." She laughed.

He had laughed and thought I was playing peek -a- boo every time I changed in a dressing room, which I did a lot. It was so funny. He would laugh and cover his eyes every time I came out.

"I think he did, too."

"I'm going to take a long hot bath, and then head to bed. I will see you in the morning, sleep tight." Mom gave me a hug and headed for her room.

"Night, Mom. Thanks for the clothes."

"You're welcome," I heard her say from down the hallway.

I was tired, but not nearly sleepy, so I decided to play on my laptop a while before I went to bed. I had a few email notices about games I played and a couple of emails from Turtle. The first one was from a few weeks ago. Her aunt Ginny wasn't doing well at all. Seems like she had taken a turn for the worse and now Turtle's Mom and brother had came to help her. I was sure sad to hear about her Aunt Ginny; she was really a nice woman. The second email from Turtle was marked yesterday. They had taken Ginny to the hospital on Saturday, and she had died yesterday around noon. I pulled my cell phone from my pocket and searched through my contacts. I had Ginny's number, and hit send to call it.

"Hello," a sad voice answered.

"May I please speak to White Turtle?" I asked.

"Just a moment," the voice said.

"Hello."

"Turtle, I am so sorry about your Aunt. I just now sat down at my computer."

"Kara?" Turtle said.

"Yes, it's me. Is there anything I can do?" I asked.

"I don't know. It is just crazy here right now. The funeral is Tuesday, and by then there will be family in from everywhere. We have more people than beds, and there are more people coming. Fox and I seem to be on kid duty and are watching everybody's kids."

I could hear the sorrow and stress in my friend's voice. "How is your Mom?" I asked.

"Not good, not good at all. And with Aunt Ginny gone, I don't know how Uncle Ross is going to handle the twins, and that's all Mom can think about. Uncle Ross, well, he has just about lost it. The twins are not old enough to understand and that's even harder on him."

I wondered if I could help her and Red Fox with the kids. I walked down the hall to Mom's room, and then through it to Mom's bathroom door.

"Can you hold on a second?"

"Sure."

I hit mute on my phone, then tapped on the bathroom door.

"Mom."

"It's unlocked," I heard her say, so I cracked the door and stuck my head in. All that I could see was her head above the tub.

"I just got an email from White Turtle. Her Aunt Ginny died yesterday, and they are burying her Tuesday."

"And you want to go help, right?"

"Yes."

"That's fine, but you need to be back by Thursday morning because our flight leaves that afternoon."

"Thanks, Mom."

"Give them my condolences."

"I will." I closed the door and took the phone off mute.

"You think you could find room for one more? I would love to come help you and Red Fox. Mom said she didn't mind, and to tell you she was sorry for your loss."

"Oh, that would be so great!" Turtle had a little bit of lift in her voice.

"I'll call you in the morning with the details," I told her. "Turtle?" the line got quiet.

"Kara?" I heard Red Fox. "Mom was calling for Turt, so she had to go. She said you're coming to help us."

"Yes, you think that will be okay?"

"It would be great; Turt really needs a friend right now. I think this is affecting her more than she's letting on," he brother told me. "So, how are you getting here?"

"I'll go online and take the first flight to Kentucky that I can find. But I'll need an address for the taxi."

"Don't worry about a cab. I'll come get you myself," he told me. "Just let me know what time your flight will arrive."

"What time does everyone get up? I don't want to call too early in the morning."

"How about I call you when I wake up?" he asked.

"If I don't answer, call Mom and she'll give you the details in case I'm already on the way."

"Okay, then. I'll talk to you tomorrow."

"Bye."

I got off the phone and back on my laptop, looking for flights.

"Have you found a flight yet?" Mom had gotten out of her bath and come to help me get my travel arrangement taken care of.

"No, I just got on the site."

"There's one." Mom pointed over my shoulder. "It leaves at 7:00 in the morning. Is that too early?"

"No, I don't think so. The quicker I get there, the more I can help Turtle and Fox."

"Did you ever find out exactly what was wrong with Ginny?"

"No, but I'm sure I will while I am there. Okay, I have my seat reserved, now to get my clothes washed and packed."

Mom and I went to the living room and started going through the new outfits. Soon we had a load in the washer and were packing the rest of my stuff.

"How are you getting from the airport to Ginny's?" she asked

"Fox is picking me up. He's supposed to call. I should call him back now then I don't have to worry about him calling in the morning. I was thinking I wouldn't find a flight that easy."

"Yes, you'd better."

I grabbed my cell phone and called Fox with the details on my flight.

"He will be there waiting when I land." I told mom, as I laid my phone down.

"Good," Mom said. "As soon as your clothes get out of the dryer, you better hit the hay."

"I will. Do you want to take me in the morning, or should I catch a taxi?"

"I'll take you."

"Are you sure? I don't care to get a cab."

"No, I'll take you. Just wake me in plenty of time to get David fed and ready to go."

"Alright, I will."

"Night, sweetie. Love you."

"Love you, too, Mom, Thanks for letting me go."

"You're welcome."

Mom went to bed and I waited for my clothes. While I waited I went through my closet putting my old things in bags to go to the shelter so Mom wouldn't have to while I was gone. Most everything went but a couple skirts.

Finally, the dryer buzzed and I carefully folded everything and packed it in my bag. I had left my ticket open-ended so I could return at any time. I planned on coming home Wednesday, but I would just have to wait and see how it all went. I was in bed by 10:00, but wasn't the least bit sleepy. I was plenty tired, but my eyes just didn't want to close.

*"Kyle?"*

*"Yes," h*e answered right away.

*"I'm heading to Kentucky. Turtle and Fox's Aunt Ginny died yesterday."*

*"Really, what was wrong with her?"*

*"I don't know."*

*"How long you staying?"*

*"Until Wednesday or Thursday."*

*"What about your training?"*

*"I am done with Michael, and Gabriel is here, but his training is a little different and I can do it anywhere."*

*"When did you finish with Michael?"*

*"Day before yesterday."*

*"Gabriel? I thought James was next?"*

*"Something came up, and James couldn't make it I guess."*

*"Something come up? Okay, spill it. What happened?"*

*"I don't know. I am not in the Heavenly realm."*

*"But you're not telling all you know. What happened, Kara?"*

*"Who said anything happened?"*

*"Kara, you're not fooling me. I hear the change in your voice. Something happened. What was it?"* I really didn't know myself, so how was I suppose to tell him? *"Kara."*

*"Not now, Kyle. Maybe next week or when I see you, but not now."*

*"I will hold you to it, so be ready. I want to know what's going on.'*

*"I'll tell you what I know when I see you, promise."*

*"Are you okay?"*

*"Yeah, I'm fine. But just like our lives have been really strange this summer, this one is the strangest and will floor you. It did me, anyway."*

*"That bad, huh?"*

*"Yes and no, just a little incomprehensible."*

*"Are you sure you won't tell me now."*

*"No, this is an in-person thing. I have to see you reaction to this news."*

*"Okay, then. Give Turtle and Fox my love."*

*"I will, see in a week or so."*

I had to keep my mind clear of Mom and my plans because Kyle didn't know. I closed my eyes and thought of Michael. I could see him in my mind, but it was like seeing two people: I could see him human, but also angelic. My mind had a movie effect going. Like the human was him, and the shadow was his Angel form. Kyle was going to flip when he found out who the Angel in our linage was.

CHAPTER 17

# UNEXPECTED JOURNEY

My alarm screaming woke me. It was 4:30. We needed to be at the airport an hour early for security, and Mom needed to get David up and moving. I hoped traffic would be nonexistent this early so we could make good time getting to the airport. I woke Mom and then we got David up and fed him breakfast. We were on our way to the airport by 5:15. I was on the plane by 6:30 and in the air by 7:15. I played games on my phone and listened to some music until we landed at 10:30. Fox was waiting when I exited the ramp.

"Kara!" he yelled "Meet you at baggage claim," He said, pointing in that direction.

"Okay," I yelled back.

Thirty minutes later, we were in his Uncle's truck and on the road.

"Man, you have gotten tall!" Fox told me.

"Yeah, I'm just an inch shorter than Dad now. Fox, what was wrong with Ginny? Turtle never really said."

"She had brain cancer."

"Oh, my goodness."

"Do you remember the car wreck her and Uncle Ross had a few years back?"

"Yes."

"Well, if you remember, she had some brain damage, but nothing bad. Evidently, it caused some scar tissue to form and then it turned to cancer."

"When did they find out it had turned to cancer?"

"This spring. She started having trouble remembering things and they did some tests and found it."

"Could they not do anything?"

"No, it was too far down in her brain. If they would have tried, they said they would have done more harm than the cancer was doing, and she would most likely die on the operating table. She got better for a while. They gave her all kinds of drugs and chemo, but then she started going downhill fast."

"I'am so sorry, Fox"

"I think it was good it didn't take long. It would have been horrible to see her suffer for a long time."

"I wish Turtle had told me, but she never said a word."

"You know Turt. She tries to be brave and stand tall. I think it really got to her. She has been here since they found out it was cancer. She called Mom and me to come help when Aunt Ginny's health really started going downhill. I don't think she has shed a tear yet."

"Poor Turtle. Why didn't you call me?"

"I guess I should have, but I really didn't think of it."

It sort of made me angry that I didn't know. Maybe Dad and Kyle could have healed her.

"I want to warn you, Turt looks rough. She's lost a lot of weight. She and Mom both have. I think they were both stressed to the max."

"They're not the only ones who have lost weight. You look like you've lost a few pounds yourself."

"I have, but only a few. I bet they've both lost at least twenty pounds, and neither one had it to lose."

Turtle came running out of the house when we pulled up. Oh my gosh, she was tiny, I think a strong wind could have blown her away.

"Kara, you're a giant! When did you get so tall?"

"Oh, I don't know," I joked with her. "I just woke one day and my feet were hanging off my bed." I wasn't about to say anything about her weight. "How are you?" I asked as we walked to the house. Fox had my duffle bag and followed us.

"Okay I guess. I wish your visit would have been in better times, but I'm just glad to see you."

"Me, too, Turtle, me too."

She had been right about the wall-to-wall people. The house was packed and there were three campers in the driveway. Kids were everywhere, from little bitty to my age, and a couple were a year or two older. I think every teenager there was assigned two or three little ones. Indian families are huge, and Ross had a big family, so it was a crazy scene.

I let Mom know I was there and a gave her a brief rundown of what happened to Ginny. Then I told her it was total chaos and I would talk to her as soon as I could. I was assigned three kids: Squirrel, who was three, Devin, who was five; and Breanna who was six. Turtle had three she was watching, too. Fox was watching the twins, and their cousin Troy was taking care of one. Troy was older and the little boy Zack he was watching was a menace and had to be within arm's reach at all times. The four us gathered our herd of kids and went to the housing area's playground. Man, I sure felt sorry for Troy; Zack was like a wild hyena. Lunch was hot dogs and chips in the back yard, and by 7:00, I was worn out, but it wasn't until 9:00 before parents started coming and getting their kids. Most of the teenagers were tossed in the back yard in tents. I shared a tent with Turtle, Fox, and Troy. I don't think any of us said a word when we laid down. We were all so beat. But that night, as usual, my training continued.

"Can you give me a hand?" Nathan asked me.

"Sure, no problem." I sat my bag down and helped him carry an old water heater to the dumpster.

"Nathan, can ask you a question?"

"Sure, Kara, what is it?"

"How did you end up homeless?"

Nathan smiled at me. "I wondered when you would get around to asking me that."

"You don't have to tell me if you don't want to."

"It's okay. I think it would do me good to tell it, like therapy sort of."

"Let me show you into my office so you can lie down on my couch." I smiled back at him.

"Ha ha." he said. "You won't catch me laying down on the job. I guess it started when I started drinking, socially at first. Who would have thought a drink with the guys after work could have led me to this point?"

"Kara." Someone was shaking my arm.

I opened my eyes to find Troy inches from my face.

"Turtle left the tent twenty minutes ago and hasn't come back."

"Thanks." I carefully got up and left the tent.

I looked around the yard and then quietly went in and looked around. I couldn't find her anywhere. I went back to the tent, but she still wasn't there.

Troy came out. "You find her?"

"No, not yet."

"What's up?" Fox stuck his head out.

"We can't find Turtle. She got up about thirty minutes ago," Troy told him.

"Great." Fox crawled out of the tent.

I closed my eyes and focused everything I could on Turtle. Voices went through my head as I looked for her.

"*They know I'm here so you better let me go.*" I heard Turtle plain and clear, but where was she?

"Turtle's in trouble. Spread out and look for her." I turned and headed for the playground.

"Wait, how do you know?" Fox asked.

"I just do. Now go look anywhere she might go to be alone. I'm going to the playground."

I took off at a dead run.

I could hear Turtle's muffled scream in my head and saw five guys on the playground as I came around the last house. Shock filtered through the anger as I noticed one was purple. Really? How could Turtle's mate be in this bunch? I could feel every one of them as I ran towards them. I heard one of them swear, and then saw him draw back his hand. I caught it before he could hit Turtle, who I could now see in their midst. The young guy turned to look at me.

"Well, well," He said. "Looks like more fun. Get her."

Two of them held Turtle and three of them came toward me. I smiled at them. "Are you sure you want to tangle with me, boys?" I used a little intimidation on them. After all, I was taller than any of them.

"Oh, a feisty one." One of them smiled.

"You have no idea," I told him.

The four of us circled. I used the time to search each one of them for weapons. Only one of them carried a knife. One of the three had long hair. He was the one that came at me first, and he was the first to kiss the ground. The second and third came at me at the same time; both hit the ground hard. Only one got back up.

He pulled his knife and smiled, "Come on, girly."

I heard Fox let out a war cry as I saw him come around the corner. Great, someone else to protect, I thought, but the cry took the guy's attention for a second and it was enough time for me to disarm him and get him to the ground. The other two let go of Turtle and fled as Troy, too, came around the corner. The two that were down managed to get up and flee just as Fox got to the playground, but I still had the one on the ground.

Turtle had sunk to the ground when the two let her go. I let the guy I was holding go and went to check on her. Fox was on him before he had a chance to even move.

"Turtle?" I knelt beside her. "Are you okay?"

The tears were flowing freely down her cheeks and she was shaking visibly, which was bad enough, but the fact that she was as purple as the guy Fox held made me sick.

"Is she okay?" Troy dropped to the ground beside us.

Fox was furious and started beating the crap out of the guy on the ground.

"Fox." I stood up. "Stop it!" I caught his fist before he had a chance to hit him again.

"Why should I?" he shouted in anger. I looked down at the guy. Why this guy? His nose was already bleeding and his eye was starting to swell.

"Give me a reason why I shouldn't let him beat you to a pulp?" I asked him.

"We weren't going to hurt her. We were just having some fun."

"And maybe beating the crap out of you would be fun for her brother, here, too."

He looked at Fox, whose fist I still held.

"They didn't hurt me," Turtle had managed to say through her tears.

"But they were going to," Fox said through gritted teeth.

I let go of Fox's fist and knelt down in front of the guy. "I will make you a deal." I looked him square in the eye, but I watched his purple aura, it had a tinge of red.

"What kind of deal?" He looked up at me.

"I'll let you walk away, but only if you promise never to get involved in this kind of activity again."

I focused hard and looked at the guy. I had to bring peace if this was who Turtle was meant for.

*Who does this witch think she is? I will do what I want, when I want.*

"I think I'm the one who is going to change you," I answered his thought.

He looked at me. *Did she just answer my thoughts?*

*"Yes, I did."*

*"How are you doing that?"*I saw the red flicker in his aura.

*"It doesn't matter how. What matters is your word. Give me your word that you will straighten up and never do this again."*

*"Or what?"*

*"Or I will find you and you will wish I hadn't."*

Fox was staring at me. "What are you doing?"

I looked at Fox, "Turn your back to us." I looked over my shoulder. "All of you."

"What?" Fox looked at me like I was nuts.

I pulled the knife I had taken from my back pocket. "I need a few minutes to convince our friend here to never touch another person."

Fox smiled. "It's about time. He turned around." And walked towards Troy and Turtle.

I glance over my shoulder as all three of them turned their backs. The guy on the ground came to his feet and started to run. But he wasn't go anywhere. I held him in place with a though.

"What have you done to me?" You could hear the panic in his voice. He couldn't even budge.

"*How do you like it,"* I asked in his head, "*to be held against your will?"*

"Let me go!" he yelled at me.

"*Not so fun now, is it?"* I stepped close to him and leaned down to look him in the eyes.

"No."

"Promise me no more and mean it." I watched his aura carefully, the red was almost gone.

"I promise, now let me go."

"Not till you truly mean it." I could still see a twinge of red.

"I already promised you I wouldn't."

"But you still don't mean it in your heart." I lifted him in the air until I did not have to lean over anymore.

"How are you doing this? What are you?"

"Promise me and mean it, or I will find you and you will pay. I mean if you ever lift a finger against another helpless, defenseless person again, you will pay dearly."

"I promise, I promise, please let me go." His voice had a plea for help and he had fear in his eyes. His aura was now purple with no red. I set his feet back on the ground and glanced over my shoulder. I was glad to see that all three of my friends' backs were still to us. I turned back and let him go. He turned and I thought he was going to run, but he turned back.

"Who are you?" he asked me.

"A friend, if you want one." I stuck my hand out.

He looked at it and at me. Slowly and cautiously, he put his hand in mine. I smiled at him and he smiled back, although I could still see fear in his eyes.

"I'm Kara." I felt Fox come up beside me.

"I'm Hector." He looked over my shoulder. "I'm truly sorry. What can I do to make up for what I did?"

Fox just glared at him.

"I'm okay." Turtle said.

"You're going to leave it at that?" Fox asked, still mad.

"Yes, and you are too." I let go of Hector's hand and faced Fox. Hector didn't move. I put my hand on Fox's chest. "Calm down."

"Calm down?" He sort of pushed against my hand, but of course it didn't budge.

Hector walked toward Turtle and Troy. I took hold of Fox with both hands and held him in his place, or at least make it look that way.

"Don't go near her," Fox yelled at him.

Troy stepped in front of Turtle and Hector stopped. "I'm sorry."

Turtle peaked around Troy, and then stepped around him to face Hector.

Hector stuck out his hand to her. "My name is Hector Ramones."

"White Turtle." She took his outstretched hand.

I let Fox go and he turned and stalked off. I followed him.

"How could you just let him go, then get all buddy-buddy with him?" He suddenly turned and pinned me to the side of a fence we were walking by.

"Because if you can change an enemy into a friend, you will have a friend for life. He will never forget what you did for him, and because he will stand by you no matter what happens. But if you just make an enemy mad, then you will become angry and make enemies yourself."

Fox backed up from me. "What makes you so sure he is changed? I bet tomorrow he will be hurting someone else's sister, and you will the one to blame for it."

"Fox." I stepped close to him. "Let it go."

"What if it was Kyle? Would you have let it go so easily?"

"You know that I would have."

He looked up at me. "I will never understand the faith you have."

"That's it, Fox. It takes Faith."

Troy, Turtle, and Hector came around the corner. "Are we interrupting something?" Troy teased, since I was standing about two inches from Fox and he was looking up at me.

Fox turned and looked at Hector. "You better pray you never hurt another person because if you do, Kara will not stop me again."

Hector looked at me, then at Fox. "I promise you I won't."

Fox held out his hand to me. "Knife."

"No, this is mine. I was the one. It will fall on me if he breaks his promise."

Fox looked at me then stepped aside. If this was the only way for Fox to believe it, then so be it.

"Are you willing to swear on your life with your blood that you will never hurt another soul?"

Hector looked at me as I pulled the knife from my pocket. "What are you talking about?"

"If you are serious about you promises, then prove it by making a vow with me."

"A vow?" he questioned.

Fox took the knife from me and I held out my palm and he sliced it. "She is willing to sacrifice for you, Hector." He looked at him. "Are you willing to protect her soul?"

Hector looked at me, then at Turtle, then held out his palm to Fox. Fox sliced it and put our palms together. "If you ever break this vow, she will pay for it same as you." He looked Hector in the eye. "In other words, if you harm another soul, the pain you inflect on them will be passed on to her, and if you kill, she will die."

I could see the question in his eyes before he thought it. "*Is this for real?*" He looked at me.

Turtle walked up and put her hand on our hands. "Thank you." She looked at Hector.

I didn't need to say anything. I could see how Turtle's thank you had affected him. His purple glowed brightly.

My hand was throbbing by the time we walked back to the back yard. Turtle went in to get some alcohol and bandages for our hands.

"What's going on here?" Hector asked.

"My Aunt died." Fox told him.

"Is that why Turtle has been here all summer?"

"Yes." Fox looked at Hector, but held what we all knew he wanted to say.

"You have a huge family."

"Cheyenne families are huge," Troy told him.

Fox smiled at him "Yeah, we do have big families."

"You're not Indian?" Hector asked Troy.

"Do I look Indian? Do I have a weird animal name?" He looked at Fox. "No offence, cousin."

"Nonc taken." Fox laughed.

"Kara is not an animal name...is it?" Hector looked at me.

"I'm not family, just friend, but I am Indian," I told him.

Turtle returned and cleaned Hector's hand as Fox cleaned and wrapped mine. The sun was starting to rise when Hector left. We were all tired, so we and crawled back in the tent.

"Should we even attempt to go back to sleep," Turtle said as we lay down on our mats.

"Turtle," we heard her mom come out the back door.

Turtle and I crawled back out and went to help fix breakfast. It wasn't thirty minutes before any else one was up. I pushed the spatula through the skillet of eggs, but as I did I dozed off a couple of times. Fox came up behind and grabbed my sides. Eggs flew everywhere, but at least he helped me clean them up. By noon, we had our entire group back at the playground. All four of us set slumped on the bench, watching. Troy was even letting Zack get a little crazy, he was so tired.

"Want some help?" I heard Hector from behind us.

We all leaned up and looked back. Hector and four girls stood there.

"Love some," Turtle answered him.

"These are my sisters: Mary, Hannah, Cassandra, and Julia."

Fox and Troy both came to their feet. Hectors sisters were all pretty. Mary looked to be about nineteen, but that was just a guess. Troy was all smiles as he introduced himself to her and her sisters.

"I'm Troy." He stuck out his hand.

"And that is White Turtle, Kara, and Fox," Hector introduced the rest of us.

"Gracias, Hector." I smiled at him.

"Su bienvenida." He nodded his head.

The afternoon went a lot better than the morning, thanks to Hector and his sisters. All five of them pitched in as if they were family. Turtle's Uncle Ross was the only one who noticed Hector and his sisters. He knew both sides of the family and knew they weren't from either. But other than that, they went undetected.

The next two days went by like the last two had, busy. I thought for that many people in one place, they were doing good getting along. There had only been one heated argument that I knew of. The tribe had wanted Ginny taken back to be buried on tribal land in Montana, but Ross wouldn't hear of it. Ross had won since he was her husband and Ginny had moved away with him, but there was still tension about it. Since she was now being buried here, even more family had arrived, and the yard was now a campground. I was glad that Hector and his sisters had showed up every day to help. Thank God they were burying her tomorrow.

The service started at dawn. I was glad each family took control of their own kids for the funeral. I stood in the back since I was not really part of the family. Fox had told me to stand with them, but it felt a little awkward, so I silently moved to the back.

Time slowly passed as people talked and ceremonies were held. Where she was being buried was very nice. It was at the edge of a quiet little cemetery on the outskirts of the city. I noticed a car pass by once then I noticed five figures at the other edge of the cemetery. I thought they might be Hector and his sisters, but, these shapes were all male. I couldn't see who they were because the sun was at their backs. They never got closer, but just stood there.

I looked around and no one else seemed to notice them. I looked back to them and focused. I wanted to know who they were.

*"I can't believe I'm doing this,"* one was thinking

*"How did I let him talk me into this? Look how many of them there are,"* was on another's mind.

"*He's crazy,"* yet another thought.

*"Crap, I think there are more than was at the house. I hope the guys can hold it together."* That had to be Hector.

*"I can't do this. If she told, we're dead."*

It had to be the other four from the playground. How in the world Hector had convinced them to come was beyond me. I would have been like the one thinking I was dead, especially after seeing this mass of family and friends.

*"The one to your left is about to bolt."*

I saw Hector reach over and grab his arm.

"No one knows, but the four that were there anything about the playground. Just stay calm. All you have to do is tell White Turtle you're sorry, then you can go." Hector told him.

Finally at noon, the casket was lowered into the ground and people started leaving. Fox and Turtle found me as I stood still, watching Hector and his friends.

"What are you doing back here? You were supposed to stand with us," Turtle told me.

"There is someone here to talk to you. I pointed towards the five figures.

"Is that who I think it is?" Fox looked at me.

"Yes, everyone of them, including Hector."

"Who is that?" Troy came up behind Fox.

"The guys from the playground," I told him.

"Oh, crap," he said.

"Shall we go talk to them?" I looked at Turtle and stuck out my arm.

She put her arm through mine. "Yes, let's do."

"It's not like they would try anything." Fox laughed. "There's a whole tribe out here."

We all laughed and walked towards them.

Hector greeted me first with his outstretched bandaged hand. "Kara." He smiled.

"Hector."

I looked at each of the four that stood there. Blue covered each one with no red in sight.

Hector turned to Turtle and stuck out his hand. She took it and stood there hand in hand. "My friends would like to tell you something, if you would let them."

She only nodded as the first one came and stood in front of her.

"My name is Hose', I am sorry if I hurt you." I recognized him as one of the two who held her to the pole.

Turtle looked at him. Then let go of Hector's hand and gave Hose' a hug.

"Thank you," she said and gave him a big smile.

Turtle had broken the ice and the rest of the apologies came easier. Soon everyone was talking and the tension had left.

"Red Fox, you guys come on, we're leaving," his Mom yelled.

"So you're Red Fox, not just Fox?" Hector smiled at Fox.

"See you back at the house." Fox looked at him and then at the other guys.

"See you there." Hector nodded.

## CHAPTER 18

# PASSING THE TEST

When we got to the house, the entire front yard was full of tables and chairs. At the front, there was a huge table with nothing but food. There was also a bunch of new people. I recognized some as neighbors. But in their midst were four young Mexican girls, each smiling ear to ear. Hector and his friends were not far behind us, and they each helped serve and clean up.

By nightfall, over half of the family had left. Thankfully, it was who ones that had the most kids and there wasn't many left. The ones that were, were with their parents, and we had the backyard all to ourselves.

"So, you got some guy waiting in Chicago for you?" Marco, one of Hector's friends asked. He had taken a liking to me.

"No, not really." I smiled.

"Who would want her? She's a giant." Fox dropped down on the ground beside me. "Seriously, you don't?"

"Well, I was sort of seeing someone, but with all the crazy training I've been going through lately, I just really didn't have time, so I sort of called it quits on him."

"Training?" Fox asked. "What kind of training?"

"Well, not long after David was born, me and Kyle started self-defense training."

"Who's Kyle?" Marco asked.

"My brother."

"Her twin brother." Fox added.

"You have a twin?"

"They don't look anything alike." Fox added.

"Yeah." I laughed. "He's short."

"Who's short?" Hector and Turtle sat down.

"Her twin brother."

"You have a twin? How cool," Hector said.

"How is Kyle?" Turtle asked. "It's been strange him not being with you."

"He's been helping restore a house all summer, so I haven't seen him since May," I told her.

"Oh, wow, how did you mange without him?"

"That's what I was wondering. The two used to be inseparable." Fox looked at her.

"All right, so I have missed the big duffus," I admitted to them.

"Wait, he's been gone since May? But what about this training you were starting to tell us about?" Fox said.

"Oh, yes, Dad put us in self-defense classes for a little while before they left for summer. And while they've been gone, I got to take martial arts classes while Dad has been teaching Kyle how to hunt."

"Well, that explains how you got the drop on us," Marco said.

"What belt are you?" Hector asked.

"My teacher, Ms. Cho, didn't use the belt system, but she did say if she did I would most definitely be a black belt with a few degrees added on."

"I wish I knew Kung Fu or something," Turtle said. "Then I could take care of myself." She looked at Hector.

We talked a little more, then finally the guys left and everyone turned in. I lay beside Turtle, listening to her breathe. Soon she was sound asleep, along with everyone else. But, of course, like always my mind wandered off. I thought of the last dream and lesson from Gabriel, which of course made me think of Michael. Finally, I just got out the tent and sat in one of the lounge chairs and looked at the night sky.

"Why are you so troubled?" I heard a familiar voice from behind me.

"Michael!" I jumped up so fast my chair toppled over. When I turned to look at him, something felt different. He looked the same, but the feeling I got from him was not. There was no comforting, no peace. I almost felt anger. I took a step closer, but put my guard up.

"What are you doing here?" I asked him.

"I thought you would be glad to see me?" He stepped closer to me.

"Who are you?" I stepped back away from him.

"So, I can't fool you. You are quite perceptive in your gifts," he said. His eyes and hair stayed the same, but his appearance changed slightly. The biggest change was to his aura. The grey-white had a red outline, and it was bright like …like the demon from my dreams.

He smiled at me. "Yes, you are quite perceptive, but I expected nothing less from you."

"This battle is ours, not hers," came another voice from behind me. This time it was Michael. He pulled me back and stepped between me and whoever this was.

"So, it is true." His stature began to grow in front of us. Michael also started changing. I soon found myself behind Michael's legs, peeking around to see what was going on.

"Leave her out of this. This is about you and has nothing to do with her."

"Oh, but it does, or you would not be watching over her."

Michael drew his sword. "I was given the task by the Maker, and I would never go against Him. I am not like you."

"Oh, but you could be." He drew a sword that was identical to Michael's.

I looked at the two of them. They looked a lot alike. This had to be Lucifer himself.

"Oh, so perceptive." He smiled towards me.

"Why don't you join me, brother. The two of us would be unstoppable, even for Him."

Michael just shook his mighty head. "You have no power over me, brother, no influence here. Go back to the depths from whence you came." Michael swung his sword and Lucifer disappeared.

Michael put his sword up and turned and stepped toward me. As he did, he returned to his human form. He held open his arms and I flew into them.

"You did good here this week." He pulled me back and looked at me.

"I don't know about that."

"Oh, but you did, just like the dream about the castle. A second chance can sometimes make all the difference in the world to in people's lives."

"Why was Lucifer pretending to be you?" I wasn't worried about if I had done good here or not. I wanted to know was why he had appeared as Michael.

Michael pulled two the lawn chairs over and sat down in one. I sat down in the other.

"Putting you in my care was like raising a red flag to a bull. He wants to know why you are so special. Just from seeing you, he knows who you are, and now he is really curious as to why you were put in my care. He knows as well as I that the Maker does nothing without meaning."

"But why was he masquerading as you?"

"This was just the first of many tests I am sure he will try to pull on you."

"I know I am not supposed to be scared, but I suddenly am." We were talking about Lucifer testing me. How could I not be scared?

"You have nothing to fear."

"You keep telling me that, but I am only human, and if I have nothing to fear, then why this?" I touched my necklace. "Why must you watch over me?"

"You're right; you have a choice here. You can either stand and fight, or give up."

"You know I will fight. I am a warrior. It's in my blood."

"You're right and that is why. The evil you must face will be stronger than most mortals can bear."

"Great."

"Have you not learned anything? Do I need to throw you from a cliff again?"

"Maybe you should."

Michael stood up and pulled me face to face with him. "You are stronger than you give yourself credit for. You knew something wasn't right, and you put your guard up. You used your feeling to judge, not just your eyes. You acted, instead of reacted. You were wise in all that you did. You're ready for whatever he may throw at you."

"I don't know about that. What about next time? Will it be a person I know or a stranger? And then what will I do? How will I know what to do?"

"Stop it." He stepped back from me. "You are strong and you can handle anything."

"How can I handle anything? I haven't even been trained by everyone that was suppose to train me. What about James? You said James was supposed to train me. What was he supposed to teach me?"

"Don't worry about that. You have all you need."

"I wish I had as much confidence in me as you have."

"Don't doubt yourself. You are a strong young woman who can—no, *will*--make a big difference in many people's lives."

Michael had hold of both of my arms and was looking directly into my eyes. I saw that same swirl of intensity that could be both fearsome and calming. "I know you better than you know yourself." He smiled.

"Oh, that's not good."

He laughed, "Why not?"

"Because you can see things I can't, so maybe you know of some hidden talent I have yet to discover. But from my point of view, I am just a mere puny human."

He laughed again. "Kara, you are the strongest, most talented and well trained human there is. You will succeed at everything you ever try. You will be envied by many, and loved by everyone. And the fact that you are totally sold out to the Maker will make your life hard, but the most rewarding, too."

I just stood there and looked at him. What could I say to that? He had more confidence in me than I had. But that is not what amazed me the most about it. It was the fact that I knew who he was. He was no mere mortal man telling me this; he was Michael, the mighty archangel, the Warrior of heaven. If he had this much confidence in me, then there had to be something to it. And besides, if I ever needed him, he promised to be there.

"Exactly," he said.

"So if it was a test, why you?"

"Because you trust me and he thought he could get close and find out what was going on."

This sort of made sense, but yet again, it didn't. Why would he try to act like Michael, knowing Michael was watching? Wouldn't it be silly to think he wouldn't show himself?

"My watching over you is a little different then what you think. I am not constantly watching you. I am what you would call tuned into you. The only time I really stop and watch you is when you become uneasy. Like when you knew it wasn't me, you became leery and put up your guard. That is what got my attention."

"So, if I hadn't known it wasn't you ..."

"Yes, he could have got as close to you as he liked."

I suddenly didn't feel as protected as I once had. "But I couldn't see the difference, not even in his aura until he changed it."

"He could not hide his true nature from you, and that is a big advantage for you. Now you know what to watch for."

"I can't let my guard down for a second, can I"?

"You can't shut your senses off; they are always on guard. But you do need to pay attention to what's going on around you. I think you have been doing a great job of that." Michael suddenly smiled.

"What?" I asked him.

"He hasn't checked on his daughters in a while, and I don't think realizes there have been boys born. But as soon as you are with them, he will, and he will think he has won a battle"

"He'll think he beat the curse, won't he?"

"Yes." He looked at me.

"I think I am starting to see the bigger picture. This is just like before, when he thought he had won. Isn't it?"

"I figure as much, but it has not been revealed to me. I have to go." He stepped back and smiled at me. "See you in Montana." Then he was gone.

I looked up at the stars. I felt about half-scared now that Michael was gone. *"Kyle."* I really wished he was here.

*"What?"*

*"I need you."*

"*You alone?"* he asked.

"*Yes."*

"What's wrong?" He was now standing in front of mc. I stood up, and he put his arms around me. "What's wrong, Kara?" He stroked the back of my hair.

"I meet Lucifer tonight."

"You did what?" He pulled me back and looked up at me.

"I meet Lucifer."

"Lucifer! Why in the world would Lucifer be here?" he asked.

"You know that thing I needed to tell you in person to see your reaction? Well, it turns out Lucifer is the angel in our linage."

"Whoa!"

"I came out here earlier because I couldn't sleep and Michael showed up. But it wasn't Michael; it was Lucifer pretending to be Michael."

"I don't like being unable to read your thoughts or feelings. I would have been here instantly if I had felt you scared." He held me back and looked me over like Mom always did when we were little and fell down. "You're okay, aren't you? What happened?"

"Yes, I'm fine, just a little shook up over it."

"Just a little shook up?" I could feel his fear. "How did you know it wasn't Michael?" he asked.

"It felt wrong."

"Felt wrong?"

"Yes, Michael makes me feel all calm and peaceful; I didn't feel that at all when Lucifer showed up. He may have looked like him, but he did not feel like him at all."

"So what did you do?"

"I didn't do anything. Michael showed up, and he left."

"What did he look like?" Kyle asked.

"A lot like Michael, but the feeling was so different that it outweighed what he look like."

He pulled me back close to him and wrapped his arms around me tightly. I wished I could calm him the way Michael calmed me. I hadn't even thought about it upsetting him when I called out to him. I had been selfish and wanted my brother.

"We are going to have to put a block on your head so you'll stop growing." Kyle changed the subject, but I could still fear his worry.

I laughed, "I am not the only one that has grown this summer." He wasn't much shorter than me and he had filled out a bunch. Now he wasn't much smaller than Dad through the chest, and his hair was now long enough to hang just over his shoulder and was all neat and tidy looking. "You're going to have all the girls chasing you."

He grinned. "Oh, yeah?" We both laughed, and it felt so good.

"Are you going to be okay?"

"Yes, I'm sorry, I just needed…"

"Yeah, I know, I miss you, too."

I smiled at him. "You better get back before you're missed."

"Yeah, Dad and I were hunting. I better get back before he realizes I am gone." He grinned.

"Thanks for coming." I hugged him once again.

"Love you, too, sis. See you next week," he said, then vanished.

Once again I found myself alone. I sat back down in the chair and stared up at the stars.

"Kara…wake up." I looked up to find Fox standing over me. "What are you doing out here? You didn't sleep out here, did you?"

I was still sitting in the chair. Well, I was now slumped down in it.

"I guess I did. The last thing I remember was coming out here and looking at the stars." I told him. I stood up and stretched. Man, I was stiff. Chairs were for sitting, not sleeping.

"What time does your flight leave?" Turtle asked from behind me.

"Not until 3:00." I had gotten online yesterday after the funeral. I needed to get on home and wash my clothes and rest a day before heading out again. "So, what are we doing until then?" I smiled.

"Mom said I could use the van today so we can all take you to the airport. So, maybe we should go do something fun before then."

"Fun." I said sarcastically. "I thought that's what we were having with all those little kids." We all laughed.

"Uncle Ross told me of a place when we first got here that was over on the East side that has golf, laser tag and all kinds of things. I think it's by a movie theater, too, if I remember correctly," Fox told us.

"Sounds like fun if they can do without us." I smiled.

"They better," Turtle said, "we have done nothing but babysit since you got here."

"I'll go talk to Mom and get directions from Uncle Ross." Fox left us standing there.

"I better get my stuff packed and loaded, and then we won't have to come back and get it." I headed for the tent.

"Good idea," Turtle said as she followed me. "I'll help you."

Hector and his buddies showed up and we followed us over to Walter's Golf and Game center. Show Place East was right beside it, but we decided against a movie and spent our time playing miniature golf and laser tag. We had a great time, and I sure hated to go, but I had things to do and things to get ready for.

"Here." Turtle handed me a small wrapped box as we got out at the airport. "Happy Birthday."

"It's your Birthday?" Hector asked.

"Not till Monday." I smiled.

"Open it." Fox said.

I opened the small box. In it was a beautiful silver and turquoise ring.

"I hope it fits." Fox smiled. "We didn't know what size you wore."

I fit nicely on my index finger. "It fits perfectly." I gave each of them a hug.

"Thanks for coming," Turtle said.

"You couldn't have kept me away," I told her.

Hector handed me a piece of paper. "Sorry I don't have you a birthday present, but I do want you to have my number and my e-mail address." He smiled.

I took the paper and gave him a hug. "Meeting you was painful." I looked at my hand. I hadn't noticed it had almost healed overnight. Must have been Kyle's effect on it.

"I'll agree with that," he said. He looked at his own hand then back at me. "I promise to keep my word." He smiled.

"You better." I looked at him. "*I would hate to have to hunt you down.*" I added in his head.

"How can you do that?" he asked.

"Do what?" I looked at him then winked.

I said bye to everyone as we walked through the terminal. Turtle and Fox walked me to the gate.

"I going to miss you," Turtle hugged me tight.

"Me, too," I told her.

Fox put his arms around me. "Thanks for coming. I have missed you." He leaned back and smiled.

I smiled at back. "I've missed you guys, too."

The flight back was quiet and relaxing. I lay my chair back and closed my eyes. It seemed like it was only seconds when the pilot announced over the speaker to fasten up that, we would be landing soon.

Mom and David were waiting at the airport when I arrived. I think he had grown during the four days I was gone. He pointed and was saying 'Sissy' when I walked up.

"Is it possible for him to have grown since I left?" I asked Mom as I picked him up.

"I think he's growing like the weeds in a garden. One day they're small and the next day, they're at your knees."

I was quite amazed at David and the words he was now saying. He was no ordinary four- month-old.

"How was White Turtle?" Mom asked as we drove home.

"She's okay. I think spending most of the summer there as Ginny got worse had really taken its toll. She was thin as a rail, and I mean really thin. I bet she has lost twenty pounds."

"Oh, my, goodness," Mom said. "She didn't' have any to lose."

"I know. She looked about sick herself."

"I imagine she did. How about Rabbit; how was she doing? I can't even understand how losing a sister would be."

"I think she was handling it okay. She had to be there for the twins. They didn't quite understand, but I think everyone was making an effort to not just completely lose it in front of them. Turtle and them are staying another week or so then. Hector's sister Mary offered to help their Uncle Ross with the boys after they leave."

"Hector, who's Hector?" Mom asked.

"He's just a neighbor friend who happens to be Mexican, so he has lots of sisters who offered to help out. Mary is nineteen and is the oldest girl in her family. There are six girls and three boys."

"Wow, that's a lot of kids."

"Yes it is. They all seem to be pretty nice, or the ones I meet were. I meet three of the sisters. They are barely a year apart."

I spent all evening washing and repacking my clothes. David was running all over the house going and getting stuff, trying to help me pack my bag. He brought me coasters from the living room, pans from the kitchen, and toilet paper from the bathroom. I finally just opened another bag and let him pack them all in. It was so cute. By ten, I was packed and ready. I was excited about going. Mom laughed when she saw me getting pans out of one of my bags after she had put David to bed.

"What are you doing with those?" she asked.

"David helped me pack." I told her. We both laughed.

"I saw Kyle last night," I told Mom, "And he is almost as tall as me now."

"Really?"

"He has even filled out. He's almost as big as Dad."

"It's about time he put some meat on those bones," she told me. "He was way too thin"

"Are you ready for the big shocker, though?"

"What?" Mom's eyes got big with anticipation.

"His hair has grown out and was pulled back and neat."

Mom just rolled with laughter; well, we both did.

# EPILOGUE

7 years later...

A sudden shiver ran up my spine. Kyle looked at me. I had reacted to it physically.

"What is it?" he asked.

"I don't know." I looked around as every hair stood up on the back of my neck. I didn't see anything, yet the feeling kept getting stronger until I was physically shaking.

Michael, what's happening to me? I asked in my head, hoping he would answer.

I found myself suddenly standing and doing a 180 so I was looking directly behind me. A large black car was pulling into the parking lot behind us. The windows were so black that I couldn't see anyone in them. I found myself walking towards the now parked car.

"Where are you going?" Kyle was beside me.

"Stay with David." I never took my eyes from the car.

"With all the training we've had, you expect me to go stay with David? We're a team."

"This is something I don't think you can help with. The car is glowing red," I told him.

"Exactly why we don't need to separate."

"Kyle, where are you going?" We could hear David running up behind us.

Kyle turned picked up David and walked back towards the playground. "*I will be right here if you need me.*" We both knew how important David was. Kyle and I had trained to fight together, but if this was a demon, Kyle would have no power where I did.

I stopped in front of the now parked car. I watched as the driver side door opened. A tall slender man got out and walked toward me. His glowing figure reminded me of the movie Ghost Rider, although he wasn't in flames. But his aura was red and pulsing.

He stopped a foot from me. "So you're the one all the fuss is about," the man said as he looked me up and down. "You know that little thing won't protect you?" He reached up at touched the charm on my necklace. "Not from me."

He didn't touch my skin, but the feeling I got when his finger tips were so close to my skin made my stomach turn.

"Who said it would," I found a sudden strength in the fact that he was trying to intimidate me.

"A feisty little thing, aren't we?" He smiled as he looked over my shoulder towards the playground.

"Something you want?" I asked him.

"He shall never reach the age of eight." He looked at me.

"Well, well, is someone scared of a little boy?"

He stepped closer to me. "The battle starts now!"

"Bring it!" I told him.

"Oh, I will. Hope you're ready, little girl," he said, and then turned and walked back to the car. "When you least expect it." He smiled and got in the car and drove away.

CPSIA information can be obtained at www.ICGtesting.com
Printed in the USA
LVOW12s0332120914

403668LV00001B/2/P